The Doctor's Nanny

The Caregivers, Volume 1

Rose Fresquez

Published by Rose Fresquez, 2020.

THE DOCTOR'S NANNY

First edition. November 1, 2020.

Written by Rose Fresquez.

To Joel, Isaiah, Caleb, Abigail and Micah. I love you so much and I'm so blessed to laugh and cry with you every day. Thanks for being my inspiration.

To Kari Murphy and your family, thank you for reflecting Christ through your actions. Thank you for all the times you've generously given your time to help us during hard times. There's so many of those times, but one time in particular, my whole family had the flu, and you risked you life, and drove through the blizzard to bring us soup and Sprite. You're an inspiration to this story.

ACKNOWLEDGEMENTS

I want to thank the Lord, my Savior. Without you, Father, there's no point in trying to do anything at all. It's my prayer that I can honor you with my words. I thank you for connecting me with an amazing group of people who helped support me in accomplishing this novel.

To my husband Joel, who works so hard to provide for our family, so that I can stay home and take care of the kids. I'm so blessed that we get to journey through life together.

To my children Isaiah, Caleb, Abigail and Micah, you fill my heart with joy. Thanks for the giggles, laughter and encouragement.

Unending thanks to my editor, Deirdre Lockhart. Your insights and wisdom have helped shape this story.

To my insider team, thanks for always suggesting the coolest ideas.

To Nicole Cook, Deb, Katherine, Elizabeth and Trudy, you ladies are so amazing for the time you invested to brainstorm, beta read and critique my manuscript. Thank you from the bottom of my heart.

CHAPTER 1

The call that would change Ryan Harper's destiny arrived on a snowy Friday afternoon. It wasn't uncommon for him to work a seventy-hour workweek, but for the first time in two months, Ryan wasn't scheduled to work that weekend.

What made this weekend special was that, as often as people died in his Operating Room, he hadn't lost a single patient that day, nor had he handed down bad news to anyone. Not being a villain in someone's story for a day was worth celebrating. And served to confirm tonight was the best day to propose to Katie.

He pressed a Bluetooth button in his Mercedes to answer the phone before voicemail snagged the call. "Bree, what's up?"

His twin dragged out a long breath. "Glad you answered."

Snow flurries floated in the air as he navigated rush-hour traffic on the one-way streets of Downtown Denver—something he'd learned to expect. December snow was inevitable. "Isn't today your anniversary?"

"The big fifteen." As her excitement pulsed through the speakers, he could picture her brown hair bouncing with her nod. "About that, any chance you can be my last-minute hero?"

He chuckled at the term she used whenever she needed him to watch her kids. Although she rarely asked him to do such a task unless it was an emergency. "Okay, I'm listening."

"My babysitter came down with the flu and—"

"You need me to be your hero tonight." He finished the sentence for her. "Katie and I..." No. He didn't need to explain his plans for the evening or give Bree a guilt trip for her request.

"If you and Katie had dinner plans, bring her with you. Josh can watch and play with his siblings while you two have your date in the dining room. I just need an adult to oversee things."

Happy screams rang in the background. He suppressed the urge to honk at the car that cut him off.

Asking Katie to marry him would have to wait for another day. However, a date night with four kids running around the house could be the idea to ease Katie into the thought that kids could be fun. "What time do you need me?"

"Six."

He looked at his dashboard. "That's in forty-five minutes."

"Sorry for the short notice."

Another car cut in front of him, so close he almost instinctively swerved out of his lane. He held back a curse and honked.

Call forgotten, he glanced through the rearview mirror before switching lanes.

A siren wailed in the distance. Horns honked as cars moved aside to create a path. Traffic required his full attention. He raked a hand through his hair as he tried to catch a breath.

"Ryan, you're still there?"

"I have to focus. See you soon."

With his house across town from Bree's, he should head straight to her rental in Englewood. He pulled over to call Katie first.

Almost forty-five minutes later, he parked on the tight street. Streetlights illuminated the development where ranch homes huddled a few yards apart. He sat there, fingers still clenched on the steering wheel as every bit of him wanted to move the car rather than risk parking at the curb, but Bree's minivan blocked the driveway.

Trekking the few steps to the front door, Ryan dusted off the snow from his hair. The dark sky floated with thick white flurries, and the forecast promised more snow to come. Cold air seeped through his cardigan as he rang the doorbell.

"Ryan—you should have a coat on." His brother-in-law swung the door open and, scowling, stepped aside to let him in the house. "What are you thinking standing out there?"

"Hi, Mom—I mean, Gavin."

After closing the door with his foot, Ryan stomped the snow off his shoes on the doormat. Warm air blasted him, and his tense muscles relaxed. He rubbed some life back into his hands, then shook Gavin's hand, the man's mahogany skin a contrast to Ryan and Bree's fair complexions.

"You look pretty sharp." His gaze swept over Gavin's dark suit. "Happy anniversary."

Gavin adjusted his collar and tie. "Thanks, man. We appreciate your help to—"

"Uncle Ryan!" Two torpedoes tore past their dad and flung their arms around Ryan. His nine-year-old nephew, Pete, tugged on his hand while eleven-year-old Josh gave him a couple of shoulder punches.

"Uncle Ryan!" With a squeal, his niece lunged into him.

As he crouched to wrap his arms around the eight-year-old, Zoe's thick curls tickled his chin, and his heart felt light. He hugged her closer and breathed in the strawberry scent of her. He shouldn't be here as Bree's hero. He should have planned to come. Two weeks was too long to go without seeing them.

Zoe wiggled back, her big brown eyes fixed on him, her head cocked to one side. "Are you staying the night with us, Uncle Ryan?"

"Not tonight."

"Can we build a robot while you're here?" Pete tugged at his hand again.

"Hah. A robot will take the entire night." Josh folded his arms across his chest. "How about we wrestle or play Monopoly?"

"Pretty please, can you stay the night?" Zoe clung to his other hand. "I have lots of crafts we can make together—oooh! I also have some new songs."

"Hey!" Gavin's deep voice boomed in the living room. "Let your uncle have a seat before you hound him." He gestured to the kids. "Come help me choose the movie you will watch with him tonight."

They followed him to another room, each one voicing the movie of their choice.

"Ryan!" Bree called out from the kitchen. When he approached, she held a plastic bowl in her hand, scooping a sloshy liquid and lifting it to Carter, her seven-month-old.

Yellow food splashed from Carter's mouth as he babbled upon seeing Ryan.

Ryan smiled and ruffled Carter's unruly curls, his palm resting by a tiny ear, the baby's brown skin so soft beneath Ryan's awkward hand. "Who's my buddy?" Ryan made a funny face, and Carter giggled. Wiggling in his high chair, he swung his arms in the air and kicked his feet in delight.

Bree lifted another spoonful to the baby's mouth. "Thanks again for coming to the rescue."

Ryan tore his gaze from Carter to Bree. Her blue eyes mirrored his own. "Anytime."

"Let me guess"—she wiped the yellow stuff splattered on the bib—"Katie is not coming, is she?"

No need to convince Bree that Katie didn't care for kids. She'd always come up with an excuse whenever Gavin and Bree invited them for dinner.

She had, however, been understanding of tonight's change of plans and supported him to help his sister. She just hadn't been keen on having a date while they played Legos and shared pizza or mac and cheese.

He couldn't blame her. He loved his girlfriend, despite their minor differences.

He thrust his hands in his jeans pockets as he conjured up a simple response. "Katie needed to get home.... Didn't want to drive in the snow." Completely true, though not the reason she'd canceled.

Bree arched a brow. "You're sure you don't want kids someday?"

Katie didn't want kids, and with his work schedule, he'd come to terms with that. He got to play with his niece and nephews whenever possible, tonight being another opportunity. "I think your four kids are enough for the two of us."

"When are you putting that ring on her finger anyway?"

They'd dated for five years. He bought the ring four months ago. He'd been too busy to think of taking his relationship to the next level.

Now that he'd missed popping the big question tonight, he had no idea when he'd get around to it. "Pretty soon I think."

He barely had time to see his sister and parents, let alone get married. *Maybe I shouldn't rush things.*

Leaning against the counter, he crossed his arms, ready to change the subject. "So, what do I need to do?"

"Carter will need a bath before bedtime. Pizza—the kids' anniversary treat—will be delivered in thirty minutes." Bree gestured her chin to the refrigerator and a printed list of instructions. No doubt Gavin's work. While Gavin was organized and calm, Bree was the complete opposite, yet they made a great team.

Ryan ambled to the fridge and, rubbing the back of his neck, stared at the long list. Four hours. He could do this.

"Don't worry. Josh will help," Bree said, perhaps reading his mind. "He knows the routine, and I already told him to be your helper."

She took off Carter's bib and tossed it in the sink, then used a moist wipe to clean his gummy face.

Once Bree set Carter on the linoleum floor, the baby crawled toward Ryan and tugged at his pants. Ryan crouched and scooped him up in his arms while his sister carried the high chair to another room.

Sticky fingers patted Ryan's face, and he tried not to think of how long he had to wait before taking a shower.

He instead breathed in Carter's baby scent, savoring his warmth, shifting the wiggly baby to his hip. His hair was gooey when Ryan tugged at it. "You fed your hair too, huh?"

Carter flapped his arms and smiled, warming Ryan's heart.

Several minutes later, the kids said goodbye to their parents. Ryan peered through the screen door, giant snowflakes danced to the ground. He shook off the uneasy feeling. "The weather doesn't look too good out there. You sure you don't want to go another day?"

"If you think that's your easy way out"—Bree embraced him—"then no siree."

They kissed their kids good night one more time, and Gavin put his hand to the small of Bree's back before they walked out of the door.

Between wrestling with the boys, attempting to build Pete's robot, adding glitter glue to Zoe's crafts, and listening to her songs, Ryan felt drained. He gave Carter a bath—correction, Carter gave Ryan a bath. He splashed water all over Ryan, and he'd ended up borrowing some of Gavin's clothes. Three hours acting as a parent was no picnic.

With the kids in bed, he dropped on the couch, too exhausted to do anything. In another hour or so, their parents would be home.

He ignored the unsettled feeling that had taken residence in his heart ever since Bree and Gavin left.

An instinct he and his sister experienced whenever the other was in danger.

Brushing off the thought, he shook his head and unlaced his shoes. His body settled in, exhaustion all but taking over. After yanking one shoe off, he kicked it off his foot and worked on the other. Overcome by the long day and soothed by the warmth and silence, he felt his body become heavy. He let the day wash through him, out of him. He lay on the couch and gave in to the pull of sleep.

Later, not sure how much later, his phone jolted him awake. Groggy, he stretched his hand for it on the coffee table.

"Ryan Harper?" The calm deep voice came from the other end of the line.

"Yes, this is he." His stomach lurched, the feeling odd.

"Your sister..." Everything was a blur as the man spoke. "You should come to Swedish Hospital right away."

This wasn't a request for him to come to the hospital to treat a patient. This was the ominous call that went out when there was a family emergency.

His heart thundered in his ears, and his hands trembled as he let the words register. With the help of his other hand, he forced the phone to his ear. "Is Bree okay...?"

Silence followed. Then the man told him to hurry. It wasn't Gavin's voice. Something terrible had happened to Bree or Gavin—or worse to both. Otherwise, this stranger wouldn't be calling.

His world turned dark, and a knowledge—horrible, real, yet surreal—fogged his vision. Things were never going to be the same. He let the phone slide out of his hands to thunk on the floor. The cloud of darkness engulfed him. His body numb, he wondered for the first time how a body felt while surgeons opened the heart and poked and prodded it.

CHAPTER 2

Ryan tossed a heavy soaked diaper in the dispenser next to the changing table in Carter's room. He was becoming an expert at changing diapers in under two minutes.

The gray wall was still the color it had been before he'd designated it for the baby. Opposite the changing table, a mobile hanging with giraffes and lions dangled above a mahogany convertible crib.

He smiled at Carter, who lay on his back, rubbing a tiny fist over his drowsy eyes. Ryan pulled the animal-print onesie down and closed the snaps. He then slid the squirt's chubby feet through the wool jumpsuit.

An infant, already an orphan. A knot formed in his throat at the thought of Carter never experiencing his father's or mother's love. He'd regressed when his parents died. Not only had he stopped sleeping through the night, but he'd also become fussy and restless.

The pediatrician said it was normal behavior even for kids his age not to sleep through the night, but Carter's siblings said he'd been sleeping through the night two months prior to their parents' deadly accident.

Though tired himself, Ryan exhaled a long breath as his chest constricted, mostly for Carter. There was no need to wake up an infant if they wanted to sleep in. The baby should be at home and not dragged to a daycare center in the wee morning hours.

Carter finally smiled, exposing two upcoming front teeth and melting Ryan's heart. "It's going to be another big day, buddy." He scooped up the yawning baby, pressed a kiss to his cheek before settling him on his shoulder. He breathed in the clean baby smell as he trotted downstairs to the kitchen and strapped him in the high chair.

While he fed Carter a squeezable oatmeal packet, his nine-year-old nephew sat in the breakfast nook, staring at his bowl of Wheaties. The same thing he'd done for the last ten minutes or so. Perhaps he wasn't fond of almond milk. Or was it the cereal?

"Pete, just finish your cereal and get dressed."

Pete picked up the spoon and moved it through the cereal. No doubt, he wasn't going to eat it, despite holding back any protestations.

Josh was pacing back and forth, fully dressed in his uniform with a navy backpack strapped to his back ready to go.

Zoe ambled in, pulling her thick curls back in a ponytail as she hummed. "Guess what song I'm singing, Uncle?"

She always had something brewing in her mind. Her cheerfulness continually numbed his sorrows. Bree's bubbly personality radiated through Zoe.

Ryan looked down at her, the pendant light showcasing her tangled mess of hair. "Why don't you finish fixing your hair or something?"

"I'm all done."

Just like his nanny, Ryan hadn't figured out a solution to his niece's hair. Poor thing had to keep it in a ponytail every day.

"Are you going to guess my song?"

Zoe's cheerful face was hopeful, in anticipation of his response. He didn't have time to listen to any songs, let alone guess one. "I don't know, sweetie."

The last three months had been all but a blur for him and the kids. With his sister and brother-in-law's sudden deaths, the kids had become orphans, and he was their legal guardian. So help him Lord, because he had no idea what he was doing.

During the first two months, Ryan's mom had taken off work and flown in from Virginia so she could help him transition to his new role.

After Mom's departure, he'd hired a nanny who had everything under control—until she got called to Puerto Rico for a family emergency. He had no idea when she'd be back with her dad in the final stages of cancer.

Today was his third day in charge of the kids by himself, and he already felt drained. Lately, he'd been waking up an hour earlier so he could do his cardio workout and have breakfast before he woke up the kids. He needed those two things to get him through the long hours standing in the Operating Room. Even the extra hour wasn't enough for him to sweep the house, clean the bathrooms, and load breakfast dishes in the dishwasher.

The house cleaner couldn't have chosen a worse time to move out of the state so she could follow her boyfriend. It was high time he taught the kids to help around the house.

"Pete, forget the cereal and get dressed." He'd kept the irritation from his voice but somehow didn't make it firm enough. The boy didn't move, just sat there yawning as if he wasn't ready to face the day.

Ryan set the empty oatmeal packet on the island. With one hand, he adjusted the collar on his blue button-up shirt as he shoved the bottle in Carter's mouth with his other hand. Carter yanked his curls displaying his enjoyment of his drink, leaving some curls clinging to his forehead.

Zoe continued singing as she gathered her backpack from the hook by the front entrance.

"Josh"—Ryan motioned to the white porcelain bowl on the marble counter where he kept his car keys—"can you start the car?"

All he had to do was press the key fob from the kitchen and the engine would fire up.

"Zoe, can you get Carter's diaper bag?"

"Okay." She sprang closer, resting her forearms on the island. "First, listen to this other song I just made up."

Ryan tossed the empty oatmeal packet in the trash as he listened to her song, and then, thanking her for sharing it before the song ended, he reminded her to bring the diaper bag from Carter's room. He'd temporarily enrolled Carter into a drop-in daycare until the nanny returned.

He glanced at his watch—six forty. Still enough time to drop off Carter at daycare and get the kids to school before work.

Using a wet wipe, he wiped the sticky oatmeal off Carter's mouth and cheeks. He then took off the plastic bib and stuck it on the dishwasher's top rack.

Getting to the car turned out to be another chore altogether. While Ryan carried Carter to the infant car seat, the squirt burped, and warm liquid gushed from his mouth to Ryan's shirt, seeping through to his skin.

"Great." He had to take another shower. Otherwise, he'd smell like baby spit all day. "Sorry, guys."

Josh agreed to change Carter's clothes while Ryan ran back upstairs to shower and change.

He was exhausted before his day even started. No doubt, he was going to be late for work.

That's how the rest of the day had gone, running behind for each procedure and patient meeting. By the time he managed to sit and stare at the clock, it was almost two thirty. The kids needed to be picked up in thirty minutes, and he had two more patients to go.

He ran a hand through his hair and grabbed his cell phone while tipping a photo of Bree and Gavin and the kids toward the light. A knot formed in his throat. They all looked so happy. Pushing the photo back into place, he scrolled for Katie's name. Surely, Katie, who was a nutritionist at the same hospital and was off by two, wouldn't mind helping him out this one time.

"Hey," she answered on the second ring.

"Can you please help me pick up the kids from school?" No need for preamble. Katie, like him, preferred straight to the point.

She was silent for so long he thought she'd hung up. "Hello?"

She let out a long sigh. "I guess I'll just cancel tomorrow's reservations at this point."

"It's not that I don't want to go out. It's just been..."

"Crazy, I get it, but our relationship doesn't seem a priority anymore." It wasn't the time to discuss their relationship, but at her mercy, he listened to her rant. "You know I'm not cut out for kids."

No point arguing that again. But with no other alternative... "This one time, please. I'll make it up to you."

"Just this one time." Her voice drawled in that slow hesitant way when he knew she was still doubting something. "You better call that number I gave you for a temporary nanny. I don't want to fill that role."

It wasn't that he'd asked her to help with the kids before, but she probably saw it coming. "I will, as soon as possible." He needed sanity too.

Four hours later, Ryan punched the hospital elevator button.

He loosened his shoulders. He was finally heading home. He adjusted the strap of his computer bag slung over his shoulder just as the door opened and a young couple holding hands stepped out.

"Harper, wait," a feminine voice called as he pushed the button to the basement garage.

Jia tugged at her suit skirt as she walked toward him, and he slid a hand between the closing doors, triggering the sensors to reopen it.

"I was coming to find you." She patted her short dark hair as she breathed heavily.

With the kids having a school counselor, he sought out the hospital counselor—a perk from working here. "What did I do wrong?" he teased, even though he didn't expect her to respond. She was straightforward, which Ryan liked, although some misinterpreted that as rude.

Jia pulled out folded papers from her handbag. "These are your tickets to *Disney on Ice*."

She'd recommended a family activity with the kids as part of a bonding opportunity.

He shivered, cold just thinking of it. "Does it have to be *Disney on Ice*?"

"That's what kids will like, not golfing."

He doubted he'd enjoy a Disney show, but it wasn't about him anymore. He unfolded the printout papers. "How much do I owe you?"

"My gift to you." She adjusted her glasses. "If your girlfriend changes her mind, let me know, and I can get another ticket. She might not sit with you, but—"

"She won't change her mind." Katie had been adamant about not wanting to go when Jia had texted him about the outing. She hadn't mentioned what outing surprise she had in mind.

The elevator beeped. He stepped aside so Jia could exit first, then followed her into the lit employee garage. "Thanks again."

"Anytime." She dug in her purse. "I have that number for you, in case your girlfriend's nanny doesn't work out."

Accepting the business card, he rubbed his thumb over the number written on the back in ink. Two contacts for a nanny was a good place to start.

After mild traffic from Sixth Avenue to I-70, his headlights flashed across his two-story modern rustic home in Genesee, thirty minutes later.

When he stepped inside the house, Zoe had her feet braced up on the wall and head dangling over the cushions upside down. The two boys were sitting on the couch, game consoles in hand and eyes riveted to the TV, while the Minecraft theme song played in the background.

"Hey, guys!"

"Uncle, you're home." Zoe thudded her feet to the floor and darted to him, throwing her arms around him. The day's tension melted with her genuine welcome.

The boys mumbled their hellos before their gazes returned to the game.

After returning Zoe's hug, he crossed the tiled floor to the adjoining kitchen and set his keys in the ceramic bowl. He then set his bag on the long counter against the wall he designated his office.

"Did you get your homework done?" he asked when he ambled back to the living room.

Zoe winced, staring at him without responding. He asked the boys, his voice louder over the TV music. "Did you get homework done?"

They stared at him, their silence the answer he needed. "You have to turn off the TV."

Wow. Now, he sounded like a dad. *You're a dad now.* "Bedtime is in an hour." If there was one thing he kept a steady routine for the kids, it was their bedtime. Good sleep was vital to anyone's health.

Once the three kids left the room, he frowned. Where were Katie and Carter?

Soft footsteps whispered against the hardwood stairs, and Katie emerged. Her blond hair, slightly tousled, offered a backdrop to Carter resting on her shoulder.

Ryan smiled at her. She could get used to the kids. "You look natural—you know, with the baby."

He bent to kiss her forehead, but his smile fell flat when she faced him and her hazel eyes flashed with fiery golden flecks. His teasing words died in his throat when Carter let out shuddered gasps as if he'd been crying.

"H–how did everything go?" he whispered, careful not to wake up the baby.

She eased the baby from her shoulder and set him in Ryan's arms. "Josh changed his diaper, and I fed him."

"Thank you."

"You need to hire a new nanny."

"I know."

"I can't do this again."

Did she mean watching the kids, or was she breaking up with him? He didn't ask, afraid of her answer.

His nephews and niece were polite to strangers. "Did the kids do okay?"

Keys jingled in her hand when she dug them from her handbag on the counter before she walked toward the door.

"Katie." He followed her, keeping his tone hushed as he bounced the now wiggly Carter in his arms.

She didn't respond but opened and slid through the door without another glance at him.

Ryan closed his eyes, resting his cheek against the top of Carter's curly head as he breathed in the sweet baby scent he found soothing. He tried to focus on something other than the door that just closed between them. Yes, he knew they'd have to figure out the next steps to their relationship since the kids were in the picture, but he didn't expect things to end this soon.

She's probably as tired as I am. He breathed deep and snuggled Carter onto his shoulder. After all, taking care of four kids when you're not their parent wasn't a picnic.

Setting his personal life aside, Ryan climbed the stairs and strode to Carter's bedroom. He bounced him a few more minutes until his breathing steadied. Kissing his forehead, he bent to nestle him in the crib. He took out the stuffed teddy bear and Carter's soft blanket, just to prevent any suffocation.

Tiptoeing out of the room, he closed the door behind him. Then he walked to his room and flopped his body on the bed, gazing at the ceiling.

War raged in his heart as his mind replayed Katie's departure. Lately, she seemed needier, which was another stress to his already full plate.

Perhaps he should let her go. Hmm... Why was his heart somewhat light at the possibility of ending their relationship?

Ryan sat up, shaking his tired mind of the illusion. He'd find a nanny for the kids so he could take Katie out the next time he was off early. *That's a temporary solution.*

A ball bouncing downstairs reminded him of his new role. He straightened as the realization hit. Whether Katie was in his life or not, the four kids were his priority, and for them, he'd set his dreams aside.

CHAPTER 3

There was no explanation as to why Destiny Brown was always late, other than some psychological reason she had yet to discover. She fell prey to the temptation to do *one more thing* before leaving, and today was no different. Not only had she slept in but she'd also decided that morning was a great time to paint Jia's door before the *Disney on Ice* show.

Up until two weeks ago, Destiny had been the manager of a local shoe store. When the developers bought the building to demolish it and rebuild apartments, she and her colleagues lost their jobs.

She was thankful for her neighbor Jia, who offered her one of the extra rooms in her house. Although Jia made it clear that Destiny didn't need to pay rent, she intended to do so by the end of the month—if she got a job by then.

Stress never stopped her need to dance along to an upbeat song. Mercy Me's "Best News Ever" played on the radio as she squeezed her yellow VW Bug in between a Ram truck and a suburban in the Denver Coliseum's overflowing lot.

She flipped down the visor and glanced at her face in the mirror. As usual, a few annoying curls refused to stay in place, dancing against her forehead. Destiny's hair was between golden and brown. A combination of her mom's African-American tight curls and her dad's red hair.

She shoved them back and tucked them behind her ear, forcing stubborn curls to comply, though she knew that, once she started walking, they'd be right back on her forehead.

She could only hope thirty minutes wouldn't be too late to interrupt a show. She hadn't expected a detour due to an accident on the

19

Interstate. She trekked the concrete sidewalk along the arena. The warm air was a soothing welcome as soon as she stepped inside.

After digging in her purse, she retrieved her ticket and handed it to the red-vested man at the entrance. Despite her tight budget, she felt herself being carried by the scent of popcorn to one of the vendors assembled in the hall.

Do I really have cash to spend on snacks? Jia had bought her the ticket, her way of cheering Destiny up from a long week of unsuccessful job hunting. Jia had also secured her an interview for a nanny job on Monday, but Destiny doubted she'd get hired with no babysitting experience. She was almost tempted to pursue a new career, but at twenty-nine, she couldn't entertain the idea of going back to school. Several people did it, but not her. Not when she'd barely graduated from high school. Studying and learning had never come easy for her.

She wasn't going to worry about careers and interviews. Right now, she was a little girl reliving her memories—and having fun.

"One large kettle corn and a blueberry slushie please."

Destiny swallowed at the total and handed the man her Visa card.

He, in turn, handed her the bag and drink, which she may have bought just to collect the special-edition Rapunzel cup.

Her heels clicked against the cement floor as she walked toward the auditorium's entrance. She paused to check her ticket—section 216. She strained to study the numbers above the entrances. *There we are.* She slid open the black curtain and entered the arena.

The dim lights made it hard for her to locate her row, and her hands were too full to think about reaching for her phone. What good was a flashlight app if she couldn't use it at a time like this?

With the audience enraptured by the music as Donald Duck and Goofy sang the Mickey Mouse theme song, she crouched past several rows until she found row 8. Her shoulders sloped. Her seat was in the middle of a full row.

The man at the edge was slumped into his chair. His eyelids had shut, and his chin sank on his chest.

"Excuse me," she whispered, half-afraid to wake him.

He startled and stilled, then raked his hair.

"Can I get past to my seat, please?"

He whispered to the three kids next to him. They all folded their feet to the side, leaving enough room for Destiny to squeeze through.

"Sorry for the inconvenience."

"It's okay," said the smallest child, a girl about eight years old.

The girl held the seat of the folding chair in place for Destiny.

"Thanks." Destiny flopped into the chair and tucked her handbag to the side of the seat before ripping open the popcorn bag on her lap.

Cheers and clapping erupted as a new song and characters appeared on stage. Destiny glanced up just as a girl dressed in a blue flowy gown started singing "Let it Go."

She barely heard the girl next to her humming. Weren't all kids into *Frozen* music these days? She sensed the girl watching her. Maybe she wanted some popcorn. Destiny shifted in her seat and held the popcorn bag out to her. "Would you like some?"

The girl turned away, peering over the two boys, and spoke in a hushed tone to the man at the end of the row.

Her dad, Destiny assumed, waved his hand. "We're good thanks."

The two boys ogled the bag before shifting back to the stage.

"But I want some." The little girl leaned her head over her brothers and spoke over the music, but her dad put a finger to his mouth.

"Shh."

A song from *Tangled*, Destiny's favorite Disney movie played. She propped the popcorn in front of the kids. Small fingers crept into the bag for handfuls, some spilling to the floor.

The other boy, eleven or twelve, stared at their dad, then back to the bag, before stretching out his hand. Destiny tucked the bag on the girl's lap so her siblings could have easy access.

Reaching for her slushie, Destiny handed it to the girl. "You can share it with your brothers."

The little girl's face lit up as she assessed the cup. "Rapunzel!"

Aha, another Rapunzel fan. Destiny might have to buy another slushie after all.

The popcorn was polished off by intermission.

Destiny squinted when the bright lights turned back on. As voices hummed and jabbering people moved out of their seats, she twisted to the kids beside her. Now visible in the light, they huddled together as if they were the only three people in the world, their little voices rising in excited pitch, their family resemblance obvious in the skin slightly darker than hers.

The older boy met her curious gaze over the younger kids' heads, and something in it pierced her heart—sadness. She'd been about his age, the last time she came to the concert with her dad. Unlike the boy's haunting expression, Destiny had been thrilled to be at the concert with her dad beside her.

Unable to look into those eyes, she lowered her gaze to the little girl, her frizzy hair just the way Destiny's used to look before she'd figured out the right conditioner. The girl's mom was probably still experimenting with different hair shampoos and conditioners.

Tapping the girl's shoulder, Destiny introduced herself. "I'm Destiny, by the way. What's your name?"

"Zoe." The girl smiled so wide a smile it seemed to sing louder than the characters on the stage had. "Thanks for sharing your popcorn."

How polite. "Glad to share it."

The boys were talking to their dad, and Destiny didn't feel like interrupting. The bathroom and water fountain break would have to wait.

After a few seconds, the boys stood and spun toward her, then spoke in unison. "Thank you."

"You're welcome."

She rose and asked the boys their names and shared hers, and the man gestured his chin to the empty bag she'd folded in her hand. "I owe you a bag of those."

When he pulled out his wallet, she held up her hand to stop him. "Please, they saved me from gobbling up an entire bag." She smiled. "Trust me, I tend to get carried away with popcorn."

His blue eyes twinkled. "Don't we all." Then he stretched out his hand. "I'm Ryan, by the way."

His wavy brown hair was the kind that seemed fun to ruffle. She shook his firm hand. "Destiny."

"I need to go to the bathroom." Zoe wiggled in her place and positioned herself before her dad.

The man's face wrinkled like she'd just asked him to step on the stage and sing along to a Disney song.

"I don't want you to go alone...." He turned, likely scouting for an exit, and scratched at the scruff on his chiseled jaw. "Um...uh."

People coming in and out of the stadium clearly showed the way to the exits. But, by his frazzled expression, he didn't have a solution to Zoe's problem.

Destiny sucked in her bottom lip. She could offer to help, but would he trust a stranger to go with his daughter? The lip slipped free. "I can take her."

He tugged at his shirt collar underneath a dark sweater, doubt squinching up his forehead.

She retrieved her ID from her purse and handed it to him. "You can hold onto this."

He lifted his hand. "No, I can..."

She shoved it in his hand, and he studied it. Then his shoulders loosened, and all the breath seemed to rush from his lungs. "That'll be great if you don't mind."

"We'll be back." Zoe quickstepped as though dancing to some unheard song as she followed Destiny, shuffling through people in the wide aisle.

While they waited in the long line, Zoe chatted about her dance lessons, then cocked her head to one side, big eyes blinking. "Your *real* name is Destiny?"

At Destiny's nod, she giggled. "I've never heard such a name! It's like a word—I *luuuuv* it."

What a sweetheart. "It's not common, right?" Destiny chuckled. "I love Zoe too. Does your dad bring you here every year?"

"Our dad and mom died." All the light dimmed as her little face fell. "Uncle takes care of us."

Destiny's elation vanished as she peered into downcast brown eyes. She placed a hand to her heart. "I'm so sorry, honey."

Having lost her parents at an early age, Destiny could relate. "Your uncle must be amazing for bringing you guys here." Even if it didn't seem like he wanted to be here, Destiny admired him for showing up.

"He's very nice."

When it was their turn, Zoe asked if Destiny could go in the same stall with her. But that didn't seem wise. So Destiny hunkered before the girl and forced an upbeat tone. "I'm not going to leave you here, honey. I'll stand outside your door so you can see my shoes from underneath. When it's my turn, you can do the same for me."

The girl eyed her as if debating whether she could trust her not to abandon her in a crowd, then gave a nod that sent her untamed ponytail bouncing. "Okay."

After the bathroom, Destiny found herself back at one of the vendor booths with Zoe. Forgetting her tight budget, she retrieved her credit card for another bag of popcorn and slushies for all three kids. "What flavors do your brothers want?"

Zoe spoke to the teenager behind the stand, telling him the flavors and characters of the cups they wanted for their slushies.

This is a good deed. Still, a shiver of worry coursed down her spine. *Please, God, let me get this job come Monday.* She would pay back the credit card if she got hired.

"Will your uncle like one?"

"He doesn't like sweets."

"Let's get him water then."

Seven bucks for water was a rip-off, but again, this was a special occasion—and a good deed.

When they returned to their seats, Zoe presented her brothers with their drinks. "Coke flavor for you and a berry for you, Pete."

"Oh! Thanks!" Josh said, and Pete whispered his thanks.

Destiny handed Ryan the water. "This is for you."

He looked up at her. "I'm good, thanks." He then patted the pockets of his gray pants and pulled out her ID.

She wasn't about to drink seven-dollar water, and she couldn't take it back for a refund. "I already had a drink." At the water fountain. "At least take this for the road or something."

He arched his eyebrow, probably wondering why she wouldn't take no for an answer. He reluctantly took the bottle. "Thanks."

As the lights dimmed, she slid back in her chair. Watching the second half of the show as she peeked at the kids gobbling the popcorn. Through the corner of her eye, she saw Ryan sip his water. Good. Her seven dollars were not thrown down the drain.

Forty minutes or so later, the show ended, and they waited until the crowd dispersed before they got out of their seats.

"Gotta go potty again." Zoe spoke to Ryan.

His blue eyes as pleasant as a sunny day, he offered a sheepish smile. "Do you mind helping me out?"

"I don't mind at all." Destiny reached for her ID, but he dismissed her with a wave.

"It's not necessary. We'll need to go to the men's restroom as well."

Josh nodded.

With plans to meet back in the hallway, Ryan and the boys left for the men's room.

As usual, the women's restroom had a longer line.

The crowd was thinning when they returned to the hallway and she spotted Ryan. His lean frame had no extra ounce of fat. She couldn't contain her smile as the boys ran around him as if in a game of tag.

"Thank you so much." He broke away from their antics, even as Josh grabbed his younger brother.

"My pleasure."

As they strode toward the door, Zoe talked about her upcoming recital.

Destiny snuggled her yellow cardigan closer to her body to shield herself from the breeze. Several people passed them on the concrete sidewalk.

"Uncle, can Destiny join us for lunch?" Zoe clutched Destiny's arm.

"Uh..." He gripped the back of his neck. "We have to get home to Carter."

Carter was probably their dog.

As Zoe gave all the reasons to accommodate Destiny's hanging out, Ryan's brows creased as he seemed to search for a response that would end Zoe's request.

Destiny intervened. "Maybe next time." Not that they were going to run into each other unless Zoe wanted to.

"Can you come to my recital then?" Pleading brown eyes blinked up at Destiny, then at her uncle. "Can she?"

"Honey..." Ryan thrust his hands in his pockets, then peered at the boys who were putting each other in headlocks a few feet ahead. "She probably has other things to do than—"

"Tell me when and where.... I'd love to come." If by any chance she got hired on Monday, she'd ask her boss upon hire for that particular time or day off.

Ryan scrambled for his phone and moved a finger over the screen. "April twenty-ninth."

She fingered her phone and entered the date and recital venue on her calendar. She then added a reminder for two days ahead, just in case.

They walked the remaining distance to the parking lot, Zoe skipping and singing something about Destiny being at her recital. The boys shuffled along, poking at each other while Destiny fell in step beside Ryan.

"You don't have to come if you have other things to do," he said.

She gave him a sideways glance. "How many times do I get invited to kids' hip-hop? I'm counting on it."

"Well." He stilled. "See you in a few?"

It would've been necessary to exchange phone numbers in case she got lost, but it would seem odd to ask for his number. She turned to the kids instead.

"It was great to meet you guys."

"See you at the recital. " Zoe threw her arms around Destiny for an embrace.

Her heart soared at the genuine warmth radiating from the amazing girl. She rarely hung out with kids to know how they acted, but this one made her feel like nannying might not be so bad. That is, if all kids were like her and her siblings.

"See you too." She waved to the boys and Ryan, then parted from them.

As she started her car and switched on K-LOVE, Destiny struggled to push the kids' faces out of her mind. Something about them tugged at her heart, something she couldn't fully discern.

There was Ryan, his eyes heavy with exhaustion. He had to have a wife who helped him with the kids. He had a big heart taking in his nephews and niece instead of sending them off to foster care.

Putting the questions aside, she bounced to the music and smiled when she thought of Zoe's invitation. She was now looking forward to the recital, not just because she loved dancing, but to see Zoe and her siblings again.

CHAPTER 4

Ryan's coffee maker clock showed ten when he lifted the carafe to pour himself a cup. He savored the fresh aroma as he tilted the cup. He was going to need extra caffeine if the interviews kept going this way. What an unproductive morning!

With the first two interviews not meeting the requirements, doubt was starting to creep in. Not only was the next candidate fifteen minutes late, but she'd never emailed her resume.

He set the cup on the island and dragged a hand through his hair as he tried to remember her name. He'd called her the night of his argument with Katie when she watched the kids. Had he even texted her his email address like he'd said he would?

Coffee forgotten, he walked over to the counter he used as his office. Retrieving the phone from the stack of files, he deposited himself on the swivel chair and scrolled through the texts.

"Where's her number?" He exhaled, holding back his frustration when he didn't see any texts from unfamiliar numbers.

No wonder he didn't get her resume.

He massaged his temples and retrieved his coffee from the island. In case the next interview didn't work out, he could hire one of the nannies he'd interviewed.

His mind replayed why he didn't hire any on the spot. One of them was overqualified and perfect for the job, except she wanted the weekends off. With Ryan's unpredictable schedule, he needed someone flexible for whenever he got called in.

The second interviewee, although qualified, had not only left him light-headed from her strong perfume but also looked too uptight to be a nanny.

Even if he were desperate, the kids needed someone with a friendly face—someone they'd feel comfortable with. They were his kids, they missed their parents, and he would get them a decent nanny.

He contemplated pouring himself another cup. His stomach growled a reminder that he'd skipped breakfast in an attempt to do his cardio workout and clean the house before the first interview.

With not enough time to blend a smoothie, he stood and swung open the white cabinet—the food pantry.

"Wheaties," he mumbled. "That would have to wait until after the interview."

He snagged an energy bar, ripped it open, and crunched the wrapper in his hand before tossing it in the trash can.

When he polished it off and the doorbell hadn't rung, he grabbed his phone to check for any missed calls or text messages. None. "Maybe she decided to cancel."

He paced, several questions roaming through his mind faster than his pacing through his kitchen. With the day off, he'd hoped to hire a nanny. He raked his hand in his hair. "What kind of person shows up late for an interview and doesn't bother to call?"

The doorbell cut off his rant, and he crossed the tile in three long strides, ready to reprimand the candidate. This was so unprofessional.

Huh? His breath whooshed out, taking all the sharp words with it.

The morning sun glinted gold over her brown hair as it danced above her shoulders. While Zoe's hair was frizzy dark curls, this woman's curls were vibrant and glossy.

"Ryan?" She blinked.

He couldn't remember her name, but those eyes he hadn't forgotten. They weren't quite green or blue but rather an interesting combination of the two. Blue-green eyes rimmed with kindness and calming energy.

"Hi," he finally spoke, the tension easing from his shoulders. What was her name?

How could he forget? She'd rescued him by escorting Zoe to the bathroom, twice.

She smiled, her white teeth flashing against a shade of brown skin—an alluring amber. A slightly lighter tone than the kids' but not by far.

"I–I hope I'm not at the wrong house." She fumbled for her phone, probably to check an address, bringing him back to the present. "You're not, by chance, hiring a nanny? I promise I'm not stalking you." She peered, both ways, then back at him. "Maybe I'm lost. I was—"

"As a matter of fact"—he rubbed the back of his neck—"I'm hiring... a nanny, I mean."

"Dr. Harper?"

"That would be me." No need for formalities. "Call me Ryan."

He couldn't even remember his own name these days, let alone a stranger's. Her name was a noun, a word of some sort. "Ahem." He cleared his throat after a lengthy silence.

As if reading his mind, she extended her hand. "Destiny Brown."

That was it. "Yes. Sorry, I..."

She dismissed him with a wave. "It's okay. You have too much going on to memorize a bunch of names."

Had he shown his inadequacy to keep up with the kids when they met? Cringing, he opened the door wider and stepped aside. "Come on in."

He caught a whiff of her hair when she brushed past. A hint of coconut and something tantalizing. He closed the door and turned to the hallway.

"I'm so sorry. I took the wrong turn and couldn't call." Her voice rose over the click of her heels on the tile as she offered all sorts of reasons why she was late. "I don't want to talk on the phone when I'm driving."

"Don't worry about it."

She paused, perusing the space, though there wasn't much to see. He hadn't hung a single photo since he moved in two years ago. With her back to him, she angled toward the lone picture on the counter next to his laptop. A picture of Bree, Gavin, and the kids.

He fumbled with the two papers on the island as he set them on the permanent stain from Zoe's artwork. He had to do something to keep his eyes from wandering to her.

She spun around, clasping her hands together. "I'm sorry about...your sister and brother-in-law."

He didn't have to inquire how she knew about his sister, not if Zoe had spoken to her. Unless Jia, his counselor had disclosed Ryan's family to her. It was nice of her to be concerned about a stranger though.

"Thanks."

The sunlight streamed through the floor-to-ceiling windows, sending enough natural light in the house. "I love the place." She gestured toward the mountain scenery through the sunroom, then at the clean surfaces. "The kids must be good at cleaning up their toys too."

He'd picked up Zoe's scattered artwork and darts this morning, but no need to scare her. "Yes...sometimes."

Without permission from his brain, his eyes scanned her while she stood mesmerized by the scenery.

Trim and fit, with a floral dress resting just past the knee. Her agility would come in handy when chasing after the kids. The mismatched earrings were worth a double take. One ear had a dangling feather earring and the other an oversized hoop.

She caught him staring. Or was he smiling? Heat burning the back of his neck, he swallowed, then gestured her to the barstools around the island. "Feel free to have a seat."

She smoothed down her dress. "I hope this is the right attire for the job."

What did he know about fashion? "You're great. Fine, I mean."

"It's been a while since I had an interview so..." As she wiggled into her seat, her gaze wandered to the brewing coffee pot. She sniffed. "I just love the smell of coffee."

She was either nervous or bubbly—hard to tell. She didn't need extra caffeine added to her already high energy, but he asked out of politeness.

"Would you like some?" Surely, there was still enough for two cups. "I made extra."

The stool scraped the tile as she pushed it back and rose, beaming. "You sure?"

He stood so he could help her, but she lifted her hand to stop him. "Tell me where the cups are, and I'll help myself."

Carefree, he liked that. "Cups are on the right." He pointed to the cupboard. He then gestured to the stainless refrigerator. "I don't have cream, but you can use almond milk." That was the only dairy-style liquid he had.

She scrunched her face. "Almond milk doesn't sound appealing to add to coffee. I'll try it black." Then she tested a sip, and her shoulders relaxed, both hands folding around the cup. "Mmmm...This is the best coffee I've ever had. Do you grind it?"

He made coffee regularly, but there was no special skill to it. "It's just Caribou Coffee. Glad you like it."

When she set her cup on the island, her eyes settled on Zoe's remnants of paint. He'd tried to wipe it off, but the stubborn stain wouldn't barge.

"Nice artwork."

"Thanks to Zoe, I need serious stain remover."

She pulled a plastic bottle from her purse and splashed some pink liquid over the markings. She wiped it with a tissue. "Nothing nail polish remover can't fix."

He scrunched his nose at the stench, but by the time she finished wiping, not a single remnant of pink and purple marred the white marble.

Huh. "Thanks."

Destiny started talking a mile a minute. "Like I said, it's been a while since I had an interview." She talked about the shoe store where she'd been the manager. "My boss had owned the shop pretty much her whole adult life, and she had to retire when... until..."

He only half-listened as she rattled on about unemployment insurance being her last resort. She seemed to enjoy talking. She and Zoe would get along well. Come to think of it, they already got along well.

"I never went to college, but again, I always felt content selling shoes because I love shoes... you know?" She reached for her coffee and lifted the cup to her mouth. But she was *still* talking. "Don't get me wrong, I love dancing the most, and my friend lets me teach at her studio sometimes. But there's no decent pay in that unless it's a full-time studio...."

Without knowing it, she was answering most of the questions he'd intended to ask.

"I didn't get your resume—"

She waved a hand. "I was glad when you didn't send me your email address. I dread writing resumes.... Face to face is far better."

True enough, but she hadn't talked about the most important thing—experience. "Have you ever nannied?"

She shrugged, toyed with her cup, then grinned. "Only a couple of times—*if* pet sitting counts."

He stifled a chuckle, almost wanting to remind her kids were not pets, but with such honesty and kindness in her eyes... "Why do you want to be a nanny?"

She bit her lower lip and looked at the counter by his laptop. "If you'd asked me a month ago if this was a job in my future, I'd have laughed. Not until last week when Jia told me and you called, did I entertain the idea."

She sipped her coffee, lowered the cup, and traced a finger around its rim. "Honestly, this is the first decent job that has presented itself since I lost mine. There aren't too many options out there for someone like me."

She underestimated herself. Surely, there were jobs she could do. But telling her so wasn't his place.

"Can I have your ID, please?" He seemed to see through her warm eyes. She was honest, and Zoe fell in love with her right away. He still needed the ID to make a copy for his records, run a criminal background check—hey, he couldn't be too careful with the kids—and add her to his insurance. Actually, Jia already confirmed this candidate's criminal background check. *Disney on Ice*, Destiny sitting with them, was all Jia's doing.... The ticket that could've been Katie's, she must've given it to Destiny.

Destiny reached for her handbag and unzipped a few side pockets. She frowned, zipping and unzipping more pockets in the bag. "Got it here somewhere."

She turned her purse upside down, scattering all the contents on the granite.

Tampons, a credit card, loose change, pens, and scrunched receipts tumbled onto the counter.

She was a bit of a disaster. Late. Unprepared for the interview. No resume or experience. He'd be crazy to consider her.

He shook his head and put his hands up. "You know what, it's fine. You can bring it later." It felt so right to hire her.

"Sorry I had to switch out my purses.... Got it!" She brandished the card from the pile as if finding some kind of rare treasure that would be in his thoughts. His eyes locked on her wide smile on the ID. Despite her innocence, she looked as if she had a wild streak.

"You don't have a six-passenger car, by any chance, do you?"

A silly question. Why would she have an SUV? Her yellow Volkswagen seemed enough to suit her vibrant personality.

"No."

If he made a mistake of hiring her, he'd blame Jia for recommending her. "I will have you start tomorrow. Will that be okay?"

Her eyes widened, her hands slammed into the counter as if grasping to balance herself. She swallowed, licked her lips, then whispered, "Does that mean I'm hired?"

Why not? He liked her. More importantly, the kids liked her. Wasting no time, he told her how much he'd be paying her.

Her mouth opened before she closed it and opened it again. "That's a lot of money."

It wasn't. Not when he was asking a live-in nanny to give the kids around-the-clock attention if necessary.

"I'm not even qualified."

"You will realize I'm underpaying you once the kids start taking up all your attention."

"That's what I'm here for." Her eyes sparkled. Her priceless smile reminded him of Zoe's. "I can't believe it!"

"I'll go make a copy of your ID." He left for upstairs. A small desk tucked in his walk-in closet had a printer he rarely used. He scanned her ID, then brought it back to her. "Let me give you a tour."

She followed him upstairs, starting in Carter's bedroom.

"Where's the baby?"

"At the daycare." He needed to be free to conduct the interviews.

Ryan's room was at the opposite end of the hall. No need for her to tour it.

She led the way back downstairs. Her slender body swayed with each step. The high-heeled sandals added a few inches of height, making her legs a mile long. She'd talked about dancing. He could see it through her movement.

At the bottom of the stairs across from the kitchen, he opened the guest room door.

"Is this your bedroom?"

"It's yours." Valeria, his other nanny, always went home as soon as Ryan got home. She'd only stayed on days when Ryan worked a night shift, about once every two months.

"I love the queen bed." Destiny plunked on the bed and touched the padding as if to test it out. Her eyes danced up and down the wide window. "Beige is such a warm color. What a neat room."

"Unfortunately, there's no bathroom. You'll be using the one across the hall."

"It won't be a problem." Still sitting on the bed, she gave one last bounce, then hopped to her feet. "I've never had a bedroom with a bathroom in it."

Ryan led her downstairs to the kids' bedrooms, kicking a Nerf gun to the side. "Be careful not to trip over the toys."

"Thanks for the heads-up." She bent and picked up a tub of Legos, carrying it to a shelf.

"These are the kids' rooms." He pointed at the doors.

Once back upstairs, she wandered to the sunroom and hugged her arms around herself. "I love this view...."

Unlike her other raving "I love" lines, this time, the words seemed to trip over hesitation. He stopped beside her. A few feet from the patio, jagged rocks and boulders framed a breathtaking mountain view. "It's why I bought the house."

"No offense, but don't kids play outside? If I were a kid, I'd want to climb those rocks."

The fall would be petrifying. "That's why they will never play in the backyard."

She placed a hand to her chest, almost gasping her next words. "Good. I can't stand heights."

Did she think he'd let the kids climb those rocks?

Wanting to utilize his day, he asked, "Do you have time to go car shopping?"

Her eyes widened and lips parted. "Now?"

"If you have plans, no worries." He waved a hand. "You're going to be driving the car, so I figured you should be the one to test drive."

Valeria had a minivan, so he simply paid her money for gas and mileage. "Today is the only day I have off this week."

"I've always wanted to go car shopping." She tipped up her chin, then gave such an enthusiastic nod her curls bounced off her shoulders. "Let's do it." She gathered up her purse, from the counter while he grabbed his wallet and keys. Then he led her through the back hall into the garage.

He'd found a nanny. Whether she knew what she was doing or not, she was excited about the job and loved his kids. And they liked her. How could anything go wrong?

WITH THE CAR ENGINE roaring to life, Destiny moved her hands around the soft leather steering wheel. She breathed in the new-car smell before pressing the buttons to move the leather seat.

Ryan sat in the passenger seat, focused on the windshield as if studying the new cars in the overflowing lot. He was a man of few words, wasn't he?

Hands comfortably at ten and two, she wiggled back in the seat a little, making sure her feet reached the pedals just right. All while he did...nothing. Huh. "Don't you want to check the seats and see how they work?"

He gave her a sideways glance. "It's your car. As long as you're comfortable, we're good. We still have a thirty-day-return policy."

"I've never driven a new car before." She adjusted the mirrors, flipped open the visor, and tucked a loose curl behind her ear before opening the console. This was so exciting—how could he just sit there kinda dead-like? "Have you?"

Okay, a silly question to ask a doctor. He probably wouldn't even answer. She flexed her ankles against the pedals while Mr. Silent sat there.

"Yes...yes, I have."

Okay... She wasn't going to ask what that meant. Sounded like a lot more than just a casual yes, though. After another hour test driving three other cars, Ryan left the decision up to her.

She chose the Highlander over a minivan or suburban. It wasn't too big a car to park, yet it had seven seats, perfect for this family.

"I still think it's so expensive." She'd never imagined buying anything other than a used car. She was thrifty that way.

"I need something reliable if you're going to be driving the kids in it."

Her stomach growled, and his eyes bore into hers.

Heat tingling up her neck, she winced. "Sorry, I slept in and didn't have time for breakfast."

"You must be starving. We still have an hour before I get the kids." He motioned across the street where a Chick-fil-A sign flashed words in red. "We can eat over there. The kids' school is only two miles from here. Maybe you can come with me to pick them up."

Seeing the school would help her know where to drive come morning. Even though she'd met the kids before, she was nervous to meet them as their nanny. Would they like her?

She exhaled a long breath—breathing techniques something she knew from her Zumba. "It will be nice to see the kids again."

Soon, they sat by the window. Destiny bit into her chicken sandwich and sipped the lemonade to wash down the crusty meat while Ryan munched the market salad. Greenstuff mixed with berries, apples, and chicken.

How did anybody choose greens over a sandwich?

"Do all doctors eat healthy?" Seemed it was up to her to get a conversation going.

He shrugged. "I don't think so."

"Do you enjoy salad, or do you just eat it because it's good for you?"

A ghost of a smile floated across his lips. "At first, I ate it because it was good for me, but now, I enjoy it."

Interesting. "I'll only eat salad if a doctor recommends it as a prescription." She did not have the urge to stick her tongue out at him. Did not. Not her boss. Not a grown man when she was a grown woman. So she sipped her lemonade in a straw and set the disposable cup on the table. "But I don't have to worry about that since I never go to the doctor's anyway."

Ryan was quiet so long Destiny squirmed in her booth, nervous for yapping too much.

"Did you have a bad experience with a doctor visit?" He set the fork over his salad and leaned forward. "When was the last time you had a well care check up?"

That sudden belly flop had nothing to do with his closeness. It couldn't. "I rarely get sick, and I've never been able to afford insurance." The small store she worked at couldn't afford benefits for their employees.

"Adding you to my insurance." He straightened in his seat and picked up his fork, forking the leaves and lifting them to his mouth.

Her and her big mouth. Did he think she'd been hinting? Seriously? Every bit of her stiffened as she planted both hands on the table. That was going too far. "I can't ask you to pay for my insurance when you're already overpaying me."

"If you get injured at my house, I'd be paying a lot more. You're already covered for three months or whatever period you're working for me—I worked it out with my agent while you were looking over the cars."

Wow. She couldn't argue, except to be grateful for his generosity. "Thank you. I'm going to give this job my very best."

He rescued a strawberry from the remaining lettuce, slid it onto his fork, and saluted her with it, eyes twinkling. "That's all I need. Zoe will be thrilled to see you. She's been talking about you since the show."

Destiny tinkered with her hair, curling it with her finger. At least, one of the kids would remember her. "Has she really?"

"Oh yeah." He picked up his empty bowl and added Destiny's sandwich wrappers into the bowl. The chair scraped the tile when he stood. "Ready to go meet the kids?"

She grabbed her empty cup, hoping to refill it on the way out. "As I'll ever be."

CHAPTER 5

With eyes steady on the winding road, Destiny gripped the steering wheel. Her other hand dug into her purse to retrieve a packet of gum. She handed it to Josh in the passenger seat. "Here, guys. Sorry I didn't wake up early to make breakfast."

"Gum...thanks!" Josh plucked the packet from her hand.

"I love gum!" Zoe exclaimed when her brother passed it back.

Gum wrappers scrunching from behind followed Pete's thank you.

The kids' wide smiles flashed through the rearview mirror. *It's just gum.*

"ATA!" Carter screeched, impatiently kicking his feet, his hands outstretching determined to snatch the gum packet from his sister.

"Sorry, bud." Destiny shifted her eyes back on the road. "You're too little for such pleasantries."

She'd woken up at six, way earlier than she'd ever started her day. Ryan was leaving with a laptop bag slung to his shoulder and a protein shake in hand.

"Good luck on your first day!" He'd saluted with the shake. "Made some coffee for you."

And he was gone, vanishing through the back hallway to the garage. She was going to need coffee. She'd also need to start waking up a lot earlier. Little had she known that feeding Carter, getting his diaper changed, and dressing him would take forty-five minutes.

She'd then spent ten minutes fixing Zoe's hair, which had left her no time to make breakfast or lunch. The kids said Ryan had been letting them eat school lunches for the last week.

She would go shopping for groceries so she could fix tomorrow's lunch.

Her racing heart relaxed when she turned to I-70, to the steady flow of traffic. She needed a proper intro to her day. Prayer had been a big factor with her dad, in the car when he dropped her at school. "Is it okay if I pray with you guys this morning?"

"Sure." Josh shrugged.

"We used to pray with our parents before bed." Zoe's animated voice came strangely soft.

Pete was silent.

Destiny prayed, mentioning each kid's name. "And, Lord, we pray for Ryan's surgery he has to perform this morning."

"Amen," all three kids chimed.

Twenty minutes later, she arrived at the school car-line and slowed behind an Acadia, following it to the drop-off zone. Kids stormed into the wide-open double doors, likely a gymnasium.

"Have a great day," Destiny said as the kids stepped out, following the other students in uniform, as they darted for the entrance.

"Bye," Zoe sang out, and the boys waved.

Destiny inhaled, taking her first breath of the day, and remembered to turn on the radio. K-LOVE.

"Here's some music, little guy." She glanced through the rearview mirror. Carter huddled against one side of his car seat, content sucking his thumb.

What was she going to do with the baby for an entire day, except for feeding him and putting him down for a nap? How do they put babies to sleep, anyway? In movies, they rocked them to sleep. That's what she'd do.

At home, she set Carter down on the polished kitchen tile and tucked a shaker in his chubby hand. As he shoved it in his mouth before rattling it, she opened the stainless steel fridge, in search of dinner ideas. The compartmentalized groceries implied a man who liked things orderly. Whew, she'd never organized a fridge in her life. But if she could keep the shoe store in perfect order, she could do this.

Dairy shelf—almond milk, eggs, three cheese sticks.

Vegetable bin—premixed salad package, half a bag of pinkie-sized carrots, two bell peppers.

Freezer—individually wrapped meats.

At least, he ate meat. With the almond milk and his salad yesterday...she'd been afraid to ask! As cool air hit her cheeks, she exhaled a bit of relief and pulled out one package. New York Strip Steak.

She'd never cooked steaks before. Ryan had left her some cash, and he'd ordered her an employee credit card, which would be arriving tomorrow.

After rummaging through the baby-proof cabinets—and accidentally breaking one of the plastic locks—Destiny found a slow cooker. A perfect solution. She washed her hands and tossed the frozen steaks in the pot.

Snapping on the lid with a sense of satisfaction, she gave a firm nod. Done. Then she wiped down the counter. The carafe with dark liquid reminded her of the coffee Ryan made.

She'd never drank coffee without cream in it until yesterday. She poured herself a cup, which she slid in the microwave to warm up, then savored the first sip. He sure knew his way around coffee. "Hmm."

Carter's cooing sounds were refreshing. He crawled over and tugged at her denims.

She peered down at him. "Are you ready to be picked up, little guy?"

She scooped him up, hoisted him on her hip, and trekked up the stairs to his bedroom where she snagged the basket half-full of blocks from his dresser. She carried it down and clattered them on the rug.

Carter picked one block, turned it in his hand, and lifted it to his mouth.

"Everything tastes good for you, doesn't it?"

Attempting to entertain him, she sat on the rug and stacked the blocks. "The tower is falling." She knocked the blocks over.

He giggled, exposing his two pearly teeth, and his deep laugh warmed her. Such a small act made him happy.

Hoping to hear the hearty laugh again, she repeated the activity of stacking the blocks, but this time, she added car sound effects. "Vroom! Here comes the bulldozer." She tumbled the blocks over.

The little guy's entire body shook as he let out a deep laugh.

She did it three more times until he stopped laughing and was more interested in gnawing on the blocks.

Carter grunted, pulling at his puffy hair. When she handed him another block, he chucked it back on the floor.

"Maybe you're hungry."

She swooped him into her arms, leaving the blocks on the floor in the hope to come back and play after feeding him.

Once he was fed, she wiped Carter's chin and hands and kissed his soft head. She set him back on the floor to wipe his seat.

A distinct odor permeated the kitchen. She sniffed and glanced down at Carter, his forehead somewhat purple. Diaper change. Her real job was just starting.

She'd watched Ryan demonstrate how to change a diaper last night, and it seemed pretty easy.

Carter rubbed his eyes when she hoisted him on her hip. "I guess we only change your diaper in your room."

She turned, tripping over the barstool. Carter slipped out of her hands and landed with his head hitting the tile. She blinked, her heart racing as she crouched for the wide-eyed and unmoving baby.

She could feel his heart beating against her chest, but... *Why are you not crying? That's alarming.* She walked back and forth, bouncing Carter up and down. "What do I do?"

Would this be the time to call 9-1-1? Was he traumatized by the fall, bleeding internally? All the questions didn't give her immediate answers.

"Carter..." Destiny ruffled his soft curls and bounced him, up and down. "You okay?"

Not that he could respond.

She hoisted him to her hip and grabbed her cell phone from the counter. With a shaky hand, she dialed Ryan. Her heart pounded as she prayed he'd answer, prayed Carter was okay.

Briiingg.

Please pick up.

Briiinggg.

He answered on the third ring. "Everything okay?" The breathless words reverberated through her speakers.

She couldn't contain her breathing too.

"Hello...?" He spoke more urgently.

"Um, sort of... I just..." She choked down a horrified sob and relayed what happened. "I'm so sorry."

"Is he breathing?"

She glanced back at Carter when he started yanking the phone from her hand. Relief flooded through her, and she let out a slow exhale. "Thank you, Jesus!"

"What?"

"He's grabbing the phone from my hand and wants to put it in his mouth...." She started laughing, even as tears slid down her cheeks. He was so adorable. He had his mouth open like a baby bird waiting for food to be tossed in.

Ryan let out a long sigh, probably just as relieved. "You can't—You need to be careful. He's very wiggly at this stage." How calm he sounded! "I forgot to tell you all the safe codes for babies."

He emphasized the safety measures and mentioned a few signs to monitor for concussion. "Try to keep him awake as long as you can."

So much for giving the job her best. It wasn't even halfway through the day, and she was failing. "Okay."

When she hung up, she headed upstairs to change Carter's diaper. He was sucking his thumb and rubbing at his eyes.

"No sleeping for you, little guy."

She tried to tickle him, played her Zumba playlist, and danced in front of him, in an attempt to keep him alert. But keeping him happy and awake? Even harder than pleasing her most picky shoe-store customers.

After almost two hours, she gave up. She held him in her arms and sat on the couch as she watched him suck his thumb and close his eyes. She kept her eyes on him to make sure that his breathing remained steady as his chest rose and fell. It was relaxing to sit and savor his baby scent. Could she pull off three months of this? She tucked his sweet head in the crook of her neck and closed her eyes, every bit of her going soft inside. Oh yes, she could. That's if she made it through week one without being fired.

When Carter woke, she fed him yogurt and sang to him, played blocks, and read him a book with baby animals. Soon, she had to get his siblings from school.

"I'M STARVING." ZOE'S words rang from the backseat as Destiny drove away from the pickup car line.

She needed some groceries to add to their dinner and lunch. "We'll pick up a snack at the store."

While at King Soopers, she made the mistake of asking what the kids wanted to eat. Since they couldn't agree, she let each of them get a snack of their choice. By the time they left the store, each kid except Carter had a sixteen-ounce soda in hand, donuts, cookies, and chips.

Note to self: Never take kids shopping, because you spoil them and forget everything on your list. She'd have to go shopping after Ryan came home—that is if the good doctor didn't fire her for dropping his baby and poisoning his family with sugar.

She snapped a picture of the kids as they ate their snacks and texted it to Ryan. What better way to let him know Carter was fine and she hadn't messed things up again. She typed after sending the pictures.

Destiny: So far so good.

Her phone chimed an incoming text.

Ryan: Coke and Dr. Pepper this late?

Caffeine! Oh boy, she'd messed up—again.

Destiny: Sorry.

She then added a tearful emoji.

"Guys, I need your help." She spoke to the three kids as they gulped down the last of their soda at the breakfast nook. "I've never babysat before. What things do you like to do?"

"Movie nights," Zoe said. "Every Friday we used to eat pizza and watch a movie with Dad and Mom."

"Board games," Josh added.

"Science experiments," Pete said. Then he pushed away from the nook, headed toward the back porch. "I'm going to check on the bunny."

Hmm, she hadn't met his pet yet.

Josh left for his room to get his homework done, and Zoe was chirping about her day at school when a scream shot through the floor-to-ceiling window.

"Help!"

She jumped to her feet. "Pete! Zoe, can you keep an eye on Carter for me?"

The little guy was crawling through the living room.

"Is Pete okay?" Worry edged Zoe's furrowed brows.

"He should be." That was her only hope when she yanked open the porch door. The jagged rocks came to mind. She jerked and darted forward.

A yelp escaped from Pete.

He was barely hanging on as he grasped onto a sharp boulder. The hundred-foot drop below him sent her heart plummeting.

Destiny crouched and extended her hand for him to hang onto. "I got you," she promised, breathless. "Take my hand."

His hand slipped out of hers, and he landed on a lower rock.

Not good. Destiny started breaking out in sweat as panic thudded her heart. She flung her feet over and gripped the rocks to go after Pete. Pain shot through her shoulder where a rock sliced her T-shirt.

But she had a strong grip on Pete's hand as their feet landed on a semi-flat boulder. They'd be fine as long as she didn't look down.

His panicked sobs echoed in her ears.

"Are you okay?"

His lips quivered as tears streamed down his cheeks.

"Climb on my back." She gripped the ledge while he crawled on her back.

When she lifted one leg to start the climb, her foot lost balance. Pete's tight hand around her neck cut into her windpipe as they tumbled backward from one rock to another. She kept her eyes closed, and all she could hear was the pounding of their hearts.

Thank goodness, they landed on another flat boulder. A desolate pine tree stood amid the rocks. She reached for it, gasping when she looked down at the drop.

"Heights are fun, right?" Yeah right. She shivered. "They're not too bad. It's like a tree house."

"It's not like a tree house." Pete's words came in gasps, his heart thundering against her back.

"We're climbing this tree, to get to the top of that rock." She gestured to the rock near its higher branches.

She'd climbed a few trees in her wild days. Who knew that the skill would come in handy someday?

With Pete on her back, she lifted one foot on one branch then another until she was on top of the rock leading into the backyard. Thank goodness, she'd worn tennis shoes that afternoon, instead of flip-flops. *Thank You, Lord!*

Zoe was singing and entertaining Carter when they entered the house.

Destiny set Pete down.

"What happened?" Zoe jerked at the sound of Pete's soft sobs.

Shaking tremendously, Destiny led Pete to the couch and wrapped an arm around his back. "We had a tumble over the rocks."

The girl's eyes widened as she gawked at the minor bruises on Pete's face. She rose and took his hand, then touched a slight bruise on his elbow before she assessed Destiny.

"Your shoulder's bleeding." The concern pinching up that little face tugged at Destiny's heart.

Destiny tapped a hand to her throbbing shoulder. The rock had ripped her shirt. "It's not too bad." She almost got two kids killed in one day. She could handle any beating to her body, as long as the kids were safe.

"You have a bruise on your face too." Zoe pointed out before she left the living room and returned with a first aid kit.

"Thank you, sweetheart."

Destiny wiped Pete's face with a washcloth and encouraged him to shower. Zoe was by Destiny's side offering to help patch her up.

"Let me shower first, okay?" Destiny rested a hand on Zoe's shoulder. "Thank you for your help today. You were a hero yourself looking after Carter like that."

An hour after she'd cleaned up and reminded the kids to do their homework, the garage door opening announced Ryan's arrival.

Destiny dashed for the kitchen to check on her forgotten dinner. That was the beauty of Crock-Pots. Toss in your food and forget it until dinnertime.

She frowned when she took off the cold lid. No steam and the meat remained as red as when she'd put it in the pot that morning. It was thawed if that was her mission.

What a day.

She could hear the kids' happy greetings to their uncle.

"You guys are full of energy."

Thanks to me, loading them with caffeine.

"How did it go?" he asked when he dropped his keys in the bowl on the counter. Carter crawled toward him, and Ryan scooped him up. He kissed his forehead and peered into his eyes and his face as if checking for bruises. He then shifted his gaze back to her.

She winced and gestured to the pot. "I ruined dinner, forgot to turn on the pot." While at it, she might confess *some* things had gone wrong. "I might have gone over the budget a little." Not that he'd given her a spending limit, but she'd spent twenty-dollars on junk snacks.

He arched a brow, his mouth lifting into a soft smile. "Next time don't feed them that much sugar or caffeine."

Or take them shopping with her. "Will do."

He set Carter down and slid out his phone from his dress pants. "I'll order through Uber Eats."

"Can we have pizza?" Zoe asked. "I'm not hungry, but I'll eat pizza."

Ryan glanced over at Destiny. "Is there anything you would like to eat?"

She wasn't picky. "The kids like pizza. I'll go with that."

Excited cheers rang from the boys as Josh chased Pete shooting Nerf darts at him.

At least Pete wasn't dwelling on the near-death incident. Destiny had learned that Pete had it in mind to adopt one of the wild rabbits roaming their property.

When Ryan hung up the phone, Destiny reached for a receipt and handed it to him. "Here are my expenses for today."

He barely glanced at it. "You don't have to show me receipts every time you shop."

While he went to his room, the kids continued chasing each other and squealing. No wonder Ryan didn't want her to give them caffeine.

The pizza and salad arrived just as he returned. He looked relaxed in his athletic shorts and a navy T-shirt showcasing his broad shoulders.

Tempted to reach out and brush away the damp hair clinging to his forehead, she clasped her hands behind her back. Her heart skipped when he caught her checking him out.

She averted her gaze to Carter's pureed carrots. Lifting another spoonful, she spilled it over his nose instead of his mouth. Oops! "Sorry..." She wiped him just as Ryan and the kids took their seats at the island.

Destiny composed herself and prayed for their meal. By the time she remembered to ask Ryan's permission to pray, his deep voice rang with the kids in a collective amen.

The kids spoke over each other when he asked about their school day. As she scooped more puree, Destiny felt like disappearing. Maybe, if she ran and hid, he wouldn't have to ask how her afternoon went.

Carter wiggled in his high chair, more interested in his siblings' pizza than baby food. He outstretched his hand out, babbling nonsensical words. "Ata...ata."

"Destiny got hurt," Zoe blurted. "She was saving Pete from falling on the rocks in the backyard."

Ryan's fork clanked on his salad plate.

Destiny ducked her head. *Why* had she let Zoe mark her forehead and cheeks with telltale Band-Aids?

Ryan pushed back his chair and walked around to Pete's side. He frowned at his bandaged forehead. "Are you...?"

"I'm okay." Pete scratched at the Mickey Mouse Band-Aid. "I was trying to get the bunny, but he ran away from me."

If she had superhero powers, the vanishing one would be her favorite.

Zoe stood behind Destiny's back, and her little fingers touched her skin. Through the corner of her eyes, she saw her hand motioning Ryan over. "Her Band-Aid is already full of blood."

She'd put on a sleeveless top, so Zoe could easily apply the bandages. Had she known Ryan was going to place his hand on her, a cardigan might have been necessary.

"Did you spread on an antibiotic ointment before the bandage?"

"Oh!" Zoe's precious little face fell, and her lips wobbled. "I forgot that."

It wasn't necessary. "I'm okay though, but I'll get it for Pete." Destiny edged her chair sideways, finally breathing when Ryan took his hands off her back.

"I told you guys to never go back there." Ryan eyed Pete, then ran a hand over his face. Fear edged in his furrowed brows. "You could've been hurt."

Pete's expression crumpled.

"I'm sorry I wasn't helpful."

Poor Josh. She hadn't noticed him—the big brother, sitting there shaking his head, hunching his shoulders. He already took so much on those shoulders. He didn't need to feel he'd failed in any responsibility. She'd have to talk to him later, let him know what a wonderful big brother he was.

Uncomfortable with the conversation that almost ended their lives, if God hadn't intervened, she switched it.

"How did the surgery go?" Last night, he'd talked about the epileptic patient he had scheduled for surgery when she'd asked why he had to leave so early.

A glimmer of surprise hit his blue eyes, one brow rising above it. Surely, that wasn't awe. Perhaps respect? She nearly snorted. Wouldn't be if he knew more about her afternoon.

"It was good. Thanks for asking. I'll follow up tomorrow morning, to make sure he displays no adverse reactions or side effects from the procedure."

Carter babbled in the high chair, now fully fed. As soon as she took the first bite of her pizza, both boys ogled her food.

How could they be hungry after the late snacks and pizza they'd already eaten?

"Are you going to eat that slice?" Josh asked.

"Oh no." Ryan waggled his finger between the boys. "That's Destiny's dinner."

She reached for the butter knife on the island and sliced one of the pieces in two. She gave them to the boys while Zoe made sound effects for Carter.

After the kids went to bed, Ryan summoned her to the island to discuss their safety.

Her whole body shook until she couldn't contain the violent sobs when he asked how Pete had gone to the backyard. She buried her hands in her face as the tragic events replayed in her mind.

"I don't blame...you if you want to fire me." She sniffled, swiping at her tears. Losing her job was far better than losing a child.

Ryan's hand tapped her shoulder. "I'm not going to fire you. I just want to make sure you keep an eye on the kids all the time."

Bad enough she'd failed at her one duty, now she'd *sobbed* in front of her boss. She wasn't a nanny—she was a *ninny*. After a few minutes, she blew out a breath. She might have managed to tell him a thing or two about the tumble over the rocks, but she had to assure him she intended to do her best. "I will watch some videos about parenting or something like that."

The next day, during Carter's nap, she looked on Pinterest and read parenting and food blogs for recipes. She also sought out activities for kids from infant to age twelve.

Her research paid off when the rest of her week was much easier with meal preparations and entertaining Carter. She took him to the library and to a playground in Denver. She wasn't familiar with things in the mountains yet. Genesee was beautiful, but she hadn't spotted any playgrounds yet.

She still needed to figure out a morning routine so Josh could get to school ten minutes before the bell rang. That was Josh's plea every day of the week.

By Friday, she was exhausted and anticipating her weekend off, with nothing else to do but sleep in. She'd have a better handle on things come next week.

CHAPTER 6

Ryan's long workdays felt lighter with Destiny's presence at home. How nice not having to rush and pick up the kids from daycare or panic about what they would eat.

He could hear the kids' happy screams as he stepped out of his Mercedes in the garage and walked into the back hallway.

It was almost ten, way past their bedtime. But if he was learning anything about Destiny, it was her inconsistency in routine—and it was driving him crazy. Tonight he'd endure the ruckus as long as it didn't end up with him getting reeled into dancing.

Three days ago, he'd come home while they were having a dance party. Disney and superhero movie-theme songs blasted through the Alexa device. Destiny and the kids pleaded with him to dance too.

He'd felt silly at first, but the kids' genuine smiles made it worth it.

He almost chuckled at the recollection of dancing to a Spider-Man theme song.

The smell of popcorn permeated the kitchen. A toy clattered underneath his feet as he almost tripped, startled when it burst into a loud ABC tune.

Right, Destiny wasn't his house cleaner—cushions, socks, and papers littered the living room floor, and darts covered most of the kitchen.

Playing with the kids was her priority. He wasn't complaining—well, *he* wasn't. His blood pressure, however, kicked up a notch.

She had her hands full. Besides taking care of the kids and cooking their meals, she also sent Ryan videos and pictures of the kids—mostly videos and pictures of Carter. He was grateful she did

56

because it helped him stay up-to-date with the kids' day-to-day activities.

Even if she were the house cleaner, he couldn't possibly bring himself to scold her. He still cringed over reprimanding her that first day. The fear she'd expressed through her tears... A shiver coursed through him, but it couldn't compare to the terror that night. Although he'd never raised kids, he'd been a kid once and knew their curiosity could lead them into danger.

He stilled as he remembered the panic he'd experienced that day...Carter falling on the tiled floor. Then Pete. His stomach churned whenever he thought about what might have happened if Destiny had called 9-1-1 instead of going after Pete on that cliff. It might have been too late for the EMTs to rescue him.

Though he'd asked Destiny about the details, the breakout of goose bumps on her forearms and her shiver had been enough for him to accept her brief response. "Let's just say, I'm not fond of heights," she'd said.

Yet she'd risked her life to go after Pete. Either she was brave, or she took her job seriously. That alone qualified her for the best nanny.

After setting his keys and laptop bag on the counter, he climbed the stairs two steps at a time to his room. A warm shower refreshed him. He changed into athletic shorts and his Colorado University T-shirt.

Laughter echoed from downstairs, leaving him torn between being past the kids' bedtime and going to say good night. A rich loud laugh rang up the stairs—not a kid's laugh. Destiny's.

The kids' voices and giggles burst over each other.

What were they laughing about? He wasn't the funniest guy, but he could whip up a few jokes to make someone smile. Except, he hadn't made the kids laugh about anything lately.

Curiosity forced his feet downstairs.

Laughter faded when he approached the boys' bedroom door. Then he winced and suppressed a groan when he stepped on something sharp. He stooped to pick it up. A Lego, of course.

He leaned against the closed door and listened to Zoe's voice. "A boy at school called me a nerd."

"How did you feel?" Destiny asked, her voice gentle.

"I got upset and cried a little."

"I think it's okay to be upset." Her thoughtfulness warmed him. "What you do when you're upset is very important."

"But you are a nerd!" Josh teased.

"Am not!"

"I love nerds," Destiny spoke up. "When someone calls you a nerd, you should take it as a compliment. Your uncle is a nerd, and look how many lives he saves every day."

Ryan sucked in a sharp breath. Whatever made her say that?

"You think it's a good thing?" The lilt was back in Zoe's curious voice, the sadness vanquished.

"It means you're smart, and there's nothing wrong with that."

Ryan closed his eyes, missing his twin more than he had in all these too-busy months.

"How about you, Pete?" Destiny asked. "What was the high and the low of your day?"

Pete generally had few words, so Ryan stilled, more curious about his response.

"The teacher let me use mechanical pencils today."

"Why?"

"Because I turned in all my homework on time this week."

He'd better buy more mechanical pencils.

"I have a question though," Josh interrupted. "If God loves us, why did He take our parents away?"

Great question, one Ryan had wanted to ask God if he ever talked to Him in the near future. Even if prayer wasn't part of his lifestyle, he'd always believed in God until Gavin and Bree's death. *That* planted seeds of doubt.

"It's hard to understand why God does what He does"—Destiny's response pulled Ryan from his thoughts—"but the one thing we can be certain of is His love for us. You know what I mean?"

"No." A hard edge blunted Josh's voice.

"Kind of like, He loves us and has big plans for us, plans we can't see right now, but someday, we will look back and say, wow, now I see why God did that."

Another brief silence passed beyond the door as the kids seemed to soak in her words.

"I ask God the same question when I miss my parents the most," Destiny said. "I say 'Why, God?' I feel better when I cry and pray."

The kids asked about Destiny's parents.

"My mom died as soon as I was born, and I was twelve when my dad died."

She'd lost both her parents? Just like his kids. Unease settled in his stomach. She appeared so put together and jolly—how could he have suspected she'd experienced such tragic loss?

She was perfect for the kids. She could relate to them. Even better than he ever would.

The room fell silent, and the kids seemed content with her answers.

She told them to talk to her whenever they wanted to talk about anything. Then she led them in prayer.

With his emotions getting the best of him, he didn't hear what she prayed for except for her mention of his name.

When she finished, Zoe echoed a prayer, "Thank You, God, for Destiny and for Uncle and my brothers."

Josh thanked God for their shelter.

Pete was praying too? "We're grateful for Uncle taking care of us...."

He had no idea his niece and nephews could pray. He scrubbed a hand over his burning eyes. Man, he knew so little about these kids.

Tears stung the back of his throat. His chest hurt. Letting out a slow sigh, he turned to leave. He needed to clear the lump in his throat.

"Uncle Ryan?" Zoe's voice rang behind the door.

Great! That stupid lump in his throat. He'd been caught eavesdropping.

He cleared his throat, put on his best face, and approached the door in one stride, swinging it open.

"Oh...hi." Destiny's eyes brightened beneath the recessed lighting.

"Hey." He gave a curt nod and perched himself on Josh's bed across from Pete's.

Zoe dropped Destiny's hand and sprang to her feet to hug him.

"Hi, sweetheart." Ryan breathed in her new scent of conditioner—coconut with a hint of vanilla. Same luscious scent as Destiny's.

"Good night, guys." Destiny stood, and the kids bid her good night before she strode out of the room.

Josh eyed him. "You came home early."

"It's not early. You guys stayed up late."

"We watched *Aladdin* today." When was the last time Pete sounded so lighthearted?

"Destiny said we can have movie nights every Friday." Zoe, sitting on the edge of Pete's bed, bounced, clapping her hands. "We ate popcorn too. Maybe you can watch the movie with us next week."

He had no idea what his work schedule for next Friday night looked like, but the kids' cheerfulness made him want to clear it and spend time with them. "Maybe."

The kids chatted about their week—the pillow fights and board games they played before watching a movie.

"Destiny saved you some pizza," Josh said.

Ryan hadn't had dinner, but eating pizza that late wasn't an option. "That was nice of her."

After he'd said good night, Zoe wanted Destiny to tuck her in, but Ryan convinced her he'd try to do as good a job as Destiny. The night light in her room made it easy for him to see his way out without tripping over her Barbie dolls on the floor.

CHAPTER 7

Destiny was stacking dishes in the dishwasher when he returned upstairs. Her slender back was to him. He smiled when he spotted her feet in the neon-green cozy socks.

Not wanting to startle her, he addressed the mess. "Pillow fights, huh?"

She spun around, tucking a wayward curl behind her ear. It bounced behind a smile just as wobbly. "Uh, yeah..."

Life Is Good arched in red crayon-type print over her yellow nightshirt.

With toys still littering the floor, he crouched and picked up a handful of darts, tossing them in the basket.

"I can clean that up in a little bit." She spoke behind him, her reflection before him on the living room window. She rubbed her arms, shifting from foot to foot—sometimes she reminded him of Zoe—full of energy and zeal and far more vulnerable than even he suspected.

He picked up the cushions and set them back on the couch. "You should have the kids clean up their mess before they go to bed." He avoided looking at her—in reality or reflection—and hoped he wasn't being too bossy.

Somehow, his peripheral vision betrayed him as she put her hand on her forehead and lifted it in a salute. "Yes, sir."

Sarcasm, huh? His mouth quirked as he sensed her humor.

"I'm sorry." She stifled a laugh, one hand coming up to her mouth to cover a grin she couldn't seem to contain. "I didn't mean to make light of your comment, but I just lied. I need to summon up the courage to ask them to work."

She wasn't scared of playing with them, yet she was afraid to remind them to clean up after themselves.

"It might make your life easier if you put them to work."

With a shrug, she leaned against the counter. "We'll see. Would you like some dinner? I know it's late, but I can microwave you some pizza."

Loose strands of hair danced on her forehead. Beneath them, her eyes were as weary as his felt.

He raised his hand. "I'm good, thanks though. You need to get some rest too."

She turned back to the dishwasher, snapping it shut before wiping her dripping hands with a kitchen towel. "I'm going to make the kids' lunches—much easier to do it tonight than in the morning."

She opened the refrigerator and pulled out lunch meats, setting them on the island.

She wasn't a morning person. He'd learned that over the last two weeks. No wonder she was making lunch now. Except tomorrow, they'd be home, and he'd be at work.

"Any reason you're making Saturday lunches tonight?"

"I signed up the kids for a family walk through the nature center. If I make lunch in the morning, we'll be late."

Josh had complained about being late in the last two weeks. "I can help." Ryan washed his hands and stepped beside her. He couldn't risk her wearing herself out and quitting. "It will go faster if we work together."

She lay bread slices on the cutting board. Their hands brushed when they reached for the butter knife at the same time.

"Excuse me," they said simultaneously. He pulled his hand back, and so did she.

"You pay me a lot of money so you don't have to come home and work again."

"Do we need mustard or mayo?" He ignored her protests.

"Both."

He swung open the refrigerator, which was better stocked, but less organized than before she'd shown up. He had to dig things out of the way to find the condiments. And they weren't on their shelf in the door. He eyed the bag of oranges in their place, his finger twitching to move it to the drawer. But he'd volunteered to help, not chastise her. So he shut the fridge door, vowing not to think about the mess inside it. "Just tell me what to do," he said instead.

"Josh doesn't like mustard on his sandwich. Pete likes both mayonnaise and mustard. Zoe will only eat peanut butter and jelly."

"I'll make the peanut butter and jelly first." That he could do. He'd made several during his college years.

Her tantalizing scent was distracting, though, vanilla and spring. They worked in silence until he brought up something from her conversation with the kids.

"You like nerds, huh?"

A smile curved the corners of her mouth as she spread mayonnaise over the bread. "I guess, since I'm not a nerd myself"—she shrugged—"I figured if I use you as an example, the kids would be more receptive."

Okay, so *maybe* he'd been a nerd, though he never got teased about it. He'd made it to the football team in high school, which boosted his popularity.

"Let's make your lunch while we're at it." Destiny pointed a mustard-filled knife at him, barely missing his CU shirt. "I know you like salads and stuff—you eat anything besides that?"

He ate at the hospital. But many days he was too busy to make it to the cafeteria, and he ended up starving.

"Great idea." He frowned at the bread bag with its primary-colored spots. If he was going to eat bread... "You don't by chance have whole wheat, do you?"

She wrinkled her face. "I can buy you some next time." She handed him two slices of white bread, which he smeared with avocado, lunch meat, and raw spinach.

"I noticed two percent milk is stocked up, rather than almond." He tucked the lunch meat back into its proper place in the refrigerator.

"The kids didn't like it. I didn't want to have it go to waste."

"They'd learn to eat healthy, don't you think?"

"Life's too short to eat things you don't like all the time."

He grinned, amused by her unusual responses. "Oh really?"

"It's good to break healthy habits from time to time. Did your parents always make you eat healthy things as a child?"

Mom always sent Twinkies in their lunch boxes. He laughed. "No."

She was right. He'd set his regiment, and having a nutritionist girlfriend only emphasized his healthy eating habits.

He'd needed a reminder of what it was like to be a child. "Thanks for taking care of the kids."

Her stiff shoulders loosened, a tendril of hair wisping across her neck as she peered up at him. "Thanks for not firing me on my first day."

Accidents did happen, even to the most qualified nannies. "How is it going so far?" He slid the last sandwich in a Ziploc bag. He'd tried telling her to use the containers, but she said it piled up more dishes for her.

A brief silence settled between them before she responded. "It's challenging. But it's also rewarding to know the kids and their unique personalities." She smiled as she relayed their personal interests.

That mustard butter knife came dangerously close again as she gestured. "Pete's something else. He's into projects, you know? He's like a scientist, always ready to test out the next chemical. He also loves animals and cars. Zoe with her crafts and drawing—she brightens my world. Josh"—she relinquished the knife, his white shirt safe as she put a hand to her chin as if thinking—"he can be so serious. I worry about him, taking too much on his shoulders. He likes to read and play board games. He says he's out of books. Do you have any suggestions for him?"

Ryan had never been into fiction reading. "He might not like the books I liked at his age."

"You never know."

"I'll have to think about it first." In other words, he'd ask a surgeon who had preteens what his kids enjoyed reading.

His feet hurt from standing all day, so he pulled out a stool to sit as Destiny talked about Carter's adventures.

"I looked everywhere for him, turns out, he'd crawled into the lower cupboard." Her laugh was contagious. "He laughed at me when I found him."

Ryan chuckled—who could help it while she was laughing? "He was playing peekaboo with you. I appreciate the pictures you send."

"I think, one of these days, he's going to make the first steps. Every time he pulls up and I get the camera app ready to record him, he plops to the floor."

"I hope he knows how much we need that video"—he caught the *we* in his sentence—"I meant...I."

"I know."

The stool scraped the tile when she slid one out and sat across from him. "I've been meaning to ask." Those blue-green eyes bored into his. "When you were little, did you always tell your friends, 'I want to be a surgeon when I grow up'? I mean, I don't think anyone just wakes up and decides to take up your career."

She rested her hand on her chin, waiting for his response.

Something twisted through his whole body. Stiffening against the pain, he tried to keep the hurt out of his voice. "We were about twelve when my twin sister had a complex brain procedure, a tumor." His parents had been terrified. They hadn't said it, but he'd seen it. They assumed she wasn't going to make it. "When she survived, I knew what I wanted to do."

Bree had lived several years after the tumor. She'd been a survivor with a fierce will to live. It wasn't fair that he was alive and she died leaving her kids orphaned. Ryan dragged a hand through his hair.

A warm hand tugged at his other one and squeezed it. Just a brief touch, meant to comfort, yet it shot a bolt of electricity through his whole body.

"I'm so sorry for the loss of your sister and brother-in-law."

"Guess that's life...." She'd experienced loss too. He opened his mouth to ask about her parents, but she silenced him with her next question.

"What did you do for fun before the kids came along? You know"—her mischievous smile bunched up her cheeks, twinkled in her eyes—"whenever you were not working."

"Biking, golfing with friends, going out with my girlfriend, Katie." Rarely did he go out with Katie—he'd been busy during the first years of his residency. "Just as I was getting a grip on my schedule, the kids came along. Man, did that put a dent on our relationship."

"Go out with Katie next Saturday—that's if you're not working." Such a firm nod bounced her curls, dipped her chin. "Take her on a date. I'll watch the kids."

He pressed his lips tight, unsure how much to tell her, but she leaned forward, eyes intent, her whole posture promising she wouldn't be dissuaded. He found himself saying more than he normally would. "She never wanted kids. Our relationship—not sure it will survive." He rubbed his eyes, the throbbing tension behind them relaxing a bit. He was now a parent, and nothing would ever change that.

"I'm sorry—about your girlfriend and the changes the kids add to your relationship."

Her face expressed genuine concern, but he shouldn't have told her about his personal life. "I didn't mean to pour all that on you."

"It's okay." A half-smile, nowhere near the usual wattage of her smile, quirked her lips. "You're doing a great job with the kids. That's an admirable quality in itself. Yet you still have it together."

A mirthless laugh ruptured from his throat. If only she knew! He was far from holding anything together. "Glad I have someone else fooled then."

"Don't underestimate yourself." She slapped the countertop. "If Katie doesn't go out with you, I still want you to go do something you enjoy, whichever way you choose."

A day off without work or taking kids places would be wonderful. Who could resist such a temptation? However, it would be the second Saturday in a row he'd had her work.

"It's your day off. I...have lots of things to do around the house. Laundry." Talk about a legit excuse. His hamper was overflowing.

"I'll get your laundry done and anything else you need taken care of."

He'd never let anybody do his laundry, except his mom. But this one time? He might take her up on it—if he didn't have underwear in the pile. "Don't worry about laundry."

"My gift to you. I might never give up my Saturday again, so you better jump on this chance."

A smile eased the tension from his face at her teasing tone. "I will go then."

"Oh." She tapped her chin, and animation lit her face. "Zoe's concert. It's another opportunity to invite Katie. If she sees the kids more often, it'll help her ease into the parenting role."

Ryan rubbed his forehead, the tension back behind his eyes. He was ready to move on without making further plans involving Katie. But Destiny sat there, waiting for his response.

"I thought the same thing when I had her watch the kids." His throat tightened, the words emerging nearly inaudibly.

"How badly do you like this Katie?" Destiny arched a brow. The girl was persistent. "If you feel she's the one, you have to give it your best shot."

The one? Was she? *How badly do I want Katie?* He was always busy, and Katie understood his odd hours. She put up with last-minute date cancellations whenever his surgeries went longer than expected. But how badly did he want her? He'd never asked himself that. Why not?

He'd always thought she was the one he would marry. But, unless she changed her mind about accepting kids in her life, their relationship was over.

Unease swirled through his gut. Five years together—and nothing to show for it.

"Why are you helping me?" Rarely did anyone sacrifice their time for someone else. Only Jia, but she was paid to.

"You deserve to be happy." Destiny plopped her chin in her hand. "You take care of others, but it's important to take care of yourself too. Ever heard the saying, 'happy uncle, happy kids'?"

She totally made that up. He grinned. "Never heard of it."

"You have now."

Ryan chuckled, stifling a yawn. Unsure of his next topic of discussion, he stood. "How else can I help?"

Her chair raked the tile when she hopped to her feet. "You better go to bed."

"You too... Good night."

"Good night, Ryan."

He stopped short of turning. "Have I already told you you're doing a great job with the kids too?"

She smiled. "If you set a nanny cam, you might have to change your statement."

He could only imagine the chaos she had going on. That would be quite the show. He gripped his neck and winked. "I might do that."

Destiny Brown *was* fascinating. He took the stairs one at a time, content he'd made the right decision hiring her.

CHAPTER 8

The wind swished past Ryan, his friend, Lucas, was behind him as they biked through fresh loams of aspens and pines the next weekend. The smell of damp leaves and fresh pine was refreshing. Accomplishment surged through him as he made his final climb to the top.

Panting from exertion, he leaned against a ponderosa. He eased off his backpack and helmet and shook his hair free.

The sun had peeked through the clouds. Rain clouds that had been forming on the horizon earlier had disappeared, and the howling wind seemed to be dying down.

That meant an entire day of biking ahead. He lifted a fist pump in the air as Lucas ascended the final climb. With the back of his hand, Ryan wiped the perspiration from his forehead. "Looks like the weather is clearing up."

"I'm starving," Lucas grumbled, yanking off his helmet and leaving his blond hair disheveled. "Please tell me you have more than energy bars in your backpack."

Ryan's growling stomach indicated it was close to lunchtime. "You didn't eat breakfast, did you?"

Lucas wiped a palm across his glistening forehead. "If *you* didn't want us hitting the trails so early, *I* might have had time to eat something."

They'd eaten their energy bars when they hit a different trail. But, for once, they had more than snacks for their ride. Thanks to Destiny. "I have lunch. Don't worry."

"Seriously? Way to go!" Lucas reached out a hand for a fist bump. "I can't believe you had a mind to pack lunch."

If he told Lucas who made lunch, he'd be hounded with all sorts of questions.

Like a brother, Lucas found no greater joy than getting under his skin. And like a brother, he'd always be a faithful friend. Ryan peered down the expansive valley. "Looks like we've earned ourselves a cool slope down."

"Man." Lucas strapped his helmet to his handlebars. "Makes the climb worth it."

Besides connecting with nature and escaping the city, the best things about mountain biking were the cardio and riding down a steep slope.

When they sat on rocks, Ryan handed Lucas a Ziploc bag with whole wheat bread enfolding a slab of turkey and an exotic mix of low-calorie ingredients.

Lucas eyed the sandwich, then the lunch box with a bright green ice pack. "You don't eat bread, let alone make a sandwich... *two* sandwiches."

There'd be no dancing around it since he'd never packed snacks for Lucas before. "Destiny made it." Ryan retrieved the drinks and tossed one to Lucas.

Lucas dropped his bagged sandwich in an attempt to catch the can. "An Izze too?"

That's what it was? Ryan picked up the can and studied the ingredients. Ninety calories wasn't too bad after the ones they'd burned off this morning. He popped it open, ignoring Lucas's baffled look, and sipped the orange-flavored juice. Not bad. Water was his drink of choice, but apparently, Destiny was changing things.

Lucas shook his head and chomped into his sandwich. "Are those cookies I see?"

She'd packed four sugar cookies, but the juice would do for Ryan. "They're all yours."

"I love this nanny already." Lucas spoke over a mouthful. "What's she like?"

Ryan tilted the can to his lips, choosing his response as he thought of her killer smile, her attentiveness when he was talking.... "She's nice."

"A little specific here." Lucas's brow lifted. "I mean is she attractive?"

Attractive? Hmm. To call her hair brown would be an injustice. It was the color of honey with a sheen of silk, shimmering shades of gold depending on the light—a perfect backdrop for her flawless complexion. Her eyes alone could drive a man out of his mind if he gave them too much thought. But he wasn't one to go after his nanny. "She has warm eyes." That was as far as he could sum it up. He stared at a chipmunk scampering around them, probably just as curious about those sandwiches as he was.

"Is she hot? Do you like her?"

Ryan blinked at Lucas's bold questions, which shouldn't be surprising, but one alarmed him.

"I'm with Katie."

With a snort, Lucas popped his Izze, then used it to gesture at him. "She's good with the kids?"

She was excellent, but he'd downplay it. His gut tightened over Lucas's enthusiasm. "If you mean doing whatever the kids want, yes. Keeping a routine, nope."

His friend guzzled his drink, then wiped a drip from his chin. "Who cares about routine if the kids are happy?"

Lucas and Ryan had been best friends since high school and parted ways for college—until they reunited working at the same hospital.

"Maybe stop chasing Katie and switch gears."

Hah! Easy for Lucas to say. "She's my *nanny*. Plus, Katie and I are—"

"A work in progress, I know." Lucas took a slow sip of the Izze. "Reality check here. She doesn't like kids, and you're now a parent."

"Maybe she'll change her mind?" He doubted so, but Destiny's advice about trying harder rang true.

"About her shoes, not her lifestyle." The sneer didn't suit Lucas's usual puppy-dog expression. "Seriously, man. Maybe I've forgotten. What exactly do you like about Katie?"

In his first week at Olive Medical, he'd done rounds with her. She'd been so thorough with each patient's dietary plan that Ryan had been struck by her beauty and drawn to her intelligence and organization. Now and then, he wondered if those were strong reasons to spend the rest of your life with someone.

He scratched his jaw, with a day's worth of growth, sensing Lucas's microscopic gaze. "I'm in middle school, and Dad's giving me a pep talk here?"

"Don't tell me it's still the same boring things like"—he made air quotes—" 'we have a lot in common and organization,' blah..."

Lucas had always respected Katie and Ryan's relationship. But he'd been furious when Katie suggested Ryan's parents be the kids' legal guardians. "It's just taking her a little while to warm up to the idea."

"Why are you not spending your free time with Katie now?"

He shrugged. "She had plans with friends, and I didn't want to let my day go to waste." She'd been available for the afternoon, but he hadn't felt like hanging out with her. He'd told her they'd try for another day.

"Good luck. If you're not interested in your nanny, can you put in a word for me?"

"Not your type."

"Attractive is exactly my type."

"She doesn't... I mean, I..." Lucas's past heartbreak made it hard for him to take relationships seriously. Ryan bit into his sandwich and chewed the delightfully strange combination of strawberries, cream cheese—he'd seen the low-fat container in the fridge—pecans, turkey, and wheat bread. Who knew bread could taste so good? That girl was a rare treasure. He saluted with the sandwich. "You'd mess things up, and I'd lose my nanny. Not happening."

"You like her, don't you?"

"Of course, she's my kids' nanny."

"You know, exactly what I mean. It has nothing to do with her being your kids' nanny or making sandwiches taste interesting."

"I'm with Katie." Ryan took another bite of his sandwich, ready to put the conversation behind him.

"Last I checked you still have the kids. Seems you and Katie aren't gonna make it."

"Either way," Ryan mumbled over a mouthful. "Destiny's too young." He'd seen her ID.

"Good grief, Harper, it's even better that she's young." Lucas wagged a finger, getting under Ryan's skin. "Counting on you to set me up."

Ryan grunted. "Welcome to the twenty-first century. We don't set up arranged marriages anymore."

He then devoured the sandwich, more upset at himself than Lucas. The brewing anger had nothing to do with his friend's realistic taunts, but everything to do with Lucas's interest in Destiny.

DESTINY SPENT MOST of her Tuesday morning figuring out her evening strategy. Pick up the kids from school, feed them, and turn around within an hour to get them to the concert.

Her mind spiraled as she glanced through the big glass window in the Greek restaurant.

Ten to twelve people occupied the tables throughout the naturally lit room. Not busy, which was another reason she was sitting across the table from the restaurant owner.

"This little guy is so adorable." Timon's dark hair danced over his shoulders when he shook his head. "His hair reminds me of yours back in the day, before you pumped it up with fancy shampoos." He smiled at Carter and poured more Cheerios onto the high chair tray.

Carter's chubby fingers picked up a piece and found their way in his mouth. His other hand tugged at his hair, not because they were talking about it, but because he played with it when he was happy. Warmth flooded her chest, sluiced through her veins, and relaxed her muscles. "Yes, he is cute."

Timon leaned forward and rested his hand near hers on the linen tablecloth. His smile tightened at the edges. "Tell me more about this family."

Her brows shot up. "Don't the pictures I send give you enough details? The kids are sweet"—she shrugged over the ups and downs—"but they're kids."

Having spent time in the same foster home, Timon always acted like the big brother she never had. At some point, she'd been the only girl out of the six kids in the home, and he'd made sure all the other boys didn't tamper with her.

Once, they'd tried to date, but both felt strange about their relationship being romantic. So Destiny fixed him up with a friend who'd been swooning over him.

"What about this man? Their uncle, what's he like?"

"Good grief"—she swatted at him—"are you a detective or something?"

If Ryan was single, she'd be in line with the other girls who found him attractive. "He's a decent man...good looking, but if you're worried about us being anything, he has a girlfriend."

Timon's forehead unwrinkled, and he ruffled Carter's hair. "Good. Would hate for you to repeat the same mistake."

"How can I when you won't let me forget it?"

"I'm not ready to serve jail time."

The night she'd broken up with her ex, six months ago, she'd been so downcast as she made her way to the car.

In an attempt to browse through the channels for the most upbeat song she could find, she'd ended on some channel—a preacher's broadcast as it turned out. The man's enthusiastic voice compelled her to listen. "The world will not offer you satisfaction," he'd warned. She'd listened to the rest of his words as he referenced readings from the Bible. "Come to me, all you who are weary, and I will give you rest."

The weight of restlessness crashed down on her chest. She sobbed as memories of her dad came to mind. When he'd prayed with her in the mornings and took her to church. How she longed to have that childhood peace once more. At the end, the preacher gave out a phone number if anyone needed prayer, and Destiny called. That was the beginning of her new life—with God at the center of it.

That night when Timon called her and she told him about her boyfriend's wife, he'd gone to the guy's house and punched him for being a liar. Hence Timon ending up in jail.

"Between yours and my paycheck, I think we can bail you out." Destiny laughed. "Just don't go punching people again."

"You'd better run a background check next time you date a guy."

Destiny rolled her eyes.

He smirked, then saved her by changing the subject. "Still doing the dance studio?"

"I can't right now with my long hours, but I still help out on Saturdays if Jenny has clients."

"Ma...ma." Carter bubbled and yanked the plastic bib off his chest, clapping it in his hands before shoving it in his mouth.

"He just called you his mom."

Her laughter joined his burbling. "That's his second word. He's been calling everyone dada, and now he will be calling everyone mama."

Timon pushed back his chair. "I better get your baby fed." He tousled Carter's curls and tickled his pudgy chin, then laid his hand on her shoulder. "Has anybody told you these kids look like you? If I didn't know you, I'd mistake you for Carter's mom."

It would be sweet to have kids someday, especially if they were as fun as Ryan's kids.

"One mom at the library said the same thing." When she'd taken Carter to story time.

When they got their food, she bowed to pray. Then she dug a plastic spoon into the mashed potatoes and blew on it to make sure they weren't hot before feeding him.

Carter almost frowned as if deciding whether he liked the taste or not. She fed him another bite when he opened his mouth. "You like it, don't you?"

After they finished, Timon reappeared with to-go boxes stacked in a bag. "Take these for the kids and for your boss too. That way you don't have to cook tonight."

"You're the best!" Squealing, she embraced him, then drew back and wagged a finger. "But I still need to pay for all this."

"Nonsense." He tapped his temple as he always had when indicating thinking. "If your boss likes the food and the baklava, he'll spread the word to his rich doctor friends."

The pastry with honey-like syrup may not fly with Ryan. "He's a salad guy. If you packed him a salad, then you'd have a customer for life."

"That will change once he eats my food."

How many times had Timon cooked for the foster kids when their foster parents had "better" things to do? He'd earned his confi-

dence early from grateful kids who'd long grown sick of peanut butter and jelly for dinner. "We'll let you know."

After leaving the restaurant, she stopped at King Soopers and
bought a single red rose for Zoe. Her dad always got her flowers
whenever she had a recital, and it always made her feel special.

She had no idea what she was doing, but she wanted those kids
to have a wonderful childhood. She wasn't their mom or trying to be,
but seeing them happy made her happy.

CHAPTER 9

Ryan drove the one-way streets of Golden, circling the block for parking. After he'd driven around three times, a Sorento pulled out, and he snagged the vacated spot. Perfect location in front of the building for Zoe's performance.

He opened the passenger door for Katie. Taking her hand in his, he led her toward the building.

She'd agreed to come when he asked her during their dinner date two nights ago. Thanks to Destiny's selflessness, he'd had someone to watch the kids so he could go.

He stood a bit taller. Tonight might be the turning point. Now that Destiny was available, he and Katie could go out once a month.

"Where do we start?" Katie flung back her blond hair when they walked through the tall double doors into a massive lobby.

He slid his phone from his dress pants pockets. "Let me text Destiny."

He typed: We're here, in front of the fountain.

Minutes later, Destiny emerged, hoisting Carter on her hip. She lit up, the way she did with anyone. Hard to tell if she was smiling at him or Katie. He smiled back anyway.

"Hi!" She reached her free hand out to Katie and introduced herself.

"Nice to meet you." Katie's tight-lipped smile vanished before he was sure she'd given it. Her penciled eyebrows lifted as she scanned Destiny from her vibrant curls to her radiant eyes and knee-length floral sundress.

Her posture relaxed, Destiny nodded toward Katie's feet. "I like your shoes."

"Thanks."

Carter cooed, waving his hands for Ryan. He squirmed, almost falling out of Destiny's hold.

"Hey, buddy." Ryan ruffled those irresistible curls before reaching for him. His heart quickened when his hand grazed Destiny oddly. "Sorry."

He shifted his hands, his face heating when there wasn't a better way to pick up the baby. Carter's other hand gripped Destiny's hair, and she bent, yelping. Ryan bent awkwardly to offer help, and her lips were almost buried in his neck.

A string of her wild curls tangled around one of his shirt buttons. *Oh, man, this was his nanny—live-in nanny, no less!—and he shouldn't have any reaction toward her.* He held his breath, ignoring the tantalizing scent wafting from her hair as he grasped Carter's hand and wriggled chubby fingers from her curls. He gripped the button, twisted it to yank it off—much better than having a heart attack, if his racing heart was any indication.

Neither lady paid attention to the button that clinked to the ground, and he didn't plan on searching for it. Even if he tried, he wouldn't find it with feet scuffling past them.

Destiny straightened and fluffed her hair. "Whew!" She cleared her throat. Her cheeks gave a slightly rosy color, but he didn't stare too long, afraid of what Katie might see—if she hadn't already noticed his heated face.

Katie frowned at Destiny, then Ryan, her cool gaze taking the heat from his skin.

He buried his face in Carter's neck, savoring the baby scent. Much safer than looking at the two women.

Then Destiny motioned for them to follow as she started walking. Her voice wavered when she chatted, a nervous habit. "I wasn't late today, and I got great seats."

Carter threw his arms in the air for Destiny before they entered the auditorium. He fussed and wiggled in Ryan's hold until Destiny scooped him up.

They sat in the third row from the front, which sat seven people. The boys sat at the end near the wall, and Ryan slid next to them with Katie on his other side. Destiny, bouncing Carter close to the aisle, hadn't taken her seat.

The boys high-fived him and waved at Katie. People murmured as they waited for the program to start.

"That's your nanny?" Katie whispered while Destiny slid into a chair by the aisle, leaving two empty seats between her and Katie. "You didn't mention how pretty she is."

Unsure of a response, Ryan kept his focus on the stage's red curtains. A woman with a tight bun was rearranging preschool-aged girls in puffy dresses.

Without his permission, his head spun in Destiny's direction. With Carter on her lap, she bent to the squirt's ear and whispered something that sent him clapping. Ryan didn't have to study her eyes to know the green dress brought out their green hue.

An elbow struck his rib cage. "Ouch." He cradled his ribs with a hand. "What was that for?"

"You didn't answer my question."

You never asked a question. "Oh."

The lights dimmed, leaving only the stage light on. The woman stepped in front of the preschoolers and tapped her microphone.

"You want to tell me you haven't noticed her eyes?" Katie whispered. "The flawless skin?"

Ryan let out an exasperated sigh. How could he put an end to this? How could someone as beautiful as Katie be so insecure at times? "Hadn't noticed."

"Thank you for being here!" the announcer introduced the songs that the four-year-olds would be performing to.

Ryan took a deep breath, relieved not to answer Katie.

What was he supposed to say? *Yes, she's beautiful, but I haven't paid attention because I'm trying to fix our relationship. You don't date your employee. She's way too young and might have a boyfriend.*

Laughter erupted when the kids walked in a zigzag instead of the straight line, their instructor was trying to redirect them in. They danced and walked off the stage before the song stopped. So hilarious.

Another group of kindergarteners danced to a ballet song before Zoe's group made it on the stage. Ryan caught movement through the corner of his eye. Destiny was scrambling with the baby in one hand and phone in the other. She needed help.

Crouching, he edged past Katie, keeping his head down so he didn't block the people in the back.

"I'll take the pictures on my phone since you're holding Carter," he whispered.

Destiny handed him her phone. "Have Josh take the video on my phone so you can snap the pictures on yours."

As Ryan returned to his seat and set Josh to work, Carter started wailing, earning Destiny glares. She slid her hand in her purse and pulled out a granola bar. Once Carter stuffed the treat in his mouth, he remained quiet.

They met Zoe in the lobby after the concert, and Destiny handed her a single red rose. How had she, someone who'd never taken care of kids, thought of that?

Several parents handed flowers to their kids while they took turns snapping pictures in front of the colorful Concert Night banner. He gave Destiny a curt nod and mouthed his thanks, the stiffness leaving his neck as she smiled back.

Destiny slid out her phone when it was their turn to take the picture. "How about you all line up, and I take your picture?" She handed him Carter.

Sounded good. He hoisted Carter over his hip, close to Katie.

"Oh my!" Katie jumped, stepping out of their picture line. Her brows furrowed. "My hair is all filled with slobber."

Apparently, Carter thought Katie's hair was a good snack; Ryan winced as he wiped at it. "I'm sorry about that."

She didn't respond.

With Katie not interested in being a part of their group picture, he asked Destiny to join the kids and took the pictures himself. Then Zoe wanted another picture of just her and Destiny.

"Wanna grab a bite?" Ryan suggested, hoping to stretch out their evening and let Katie get to know the kids.

"Destiny brought us dinner before we came." Zoe grabbed Destiny's hand and danced a bit around his side. "She brought you dinner, too, from the Greek place. You'll love it."

Ignoring the extra details, Ryan winked at Josh and Pete. "Ice cream then?"

"I can take Carter home." Destiny slipped her hand free from Zoe to tuck strands of hair back into the girl's ponytail. "You guys go grab a bite."

Her face downcast, Zoe pressed her lips together as she clung to Destiny's dress. "But I want *Destiny* to come with us."

Destiny bent down and whispered in Zoe's ear, and his niece eyed him, uttering a hesitant okay. When he passed Carter on to Destiny, she high-fived the boys, then gave Zoe a side hug. "Have fun."

With the boys complaining about getting their homework, Ryan drove to the nearest restaurant, an old diner with outdated furniture.

The kids ordered cake and ice cream while he and Katie ordered the only healthy thing on the menu—a garden salad.

"This place needs to be shut down," Katie grumbled as she picked at the salad with her fork. "It doesn't even taste fresh."

The salad wasn't too flavorful, but it was fresh. "There's not many options around this late."

With the late hour, the restaurant had only two other tables occupied.

When the boys finished their treat, they razzed each other, hands flying as they squirmed in their seats.

"What grade are you in boys in?" Katie shoved her full salad plate aside. At least she was interacting with the kids.

"Ouch!" Zoe shrieked when her brothers bumped into her. Another elbow knocked into a glass, tumbling it down, and water trailed over the table.

"Uncle, Josh squeezed my neck!" the girl howled.

"Let your sister be." Ryan gathered the few napkins on the table and stacked them over the water. "Go get more napkins."

Josh left and returned with several more. While Ryan cleaned the mess, the boys giggled and whispered to Zoe.

"The boys said burn to me," Zoe whined, her voice screeching. "You guys are mean!"

Ryan tossed the wet napkins over his half-eaten salad and wiped his hands with the last dry napkin. "You need to apologize to your sister, boys."

His heart was racing, tension rising. Couldn't they have behaved for *one* night? Should he have bribed them? Katie was getting a reality show from the kids.

"Sorry." Pete's insincere apology grated on Ryan's ears, but it would get them through the next thirty minutes.

Ryan pinned Josh with a look, like the tough parent he acted to be, and motioned with his chin. "Your turn."

Josh smirked. "Sorry you're being such a baby."

"You're mean!" Zoe's brows furrowed. She hunched back in her chair and crossed her hands over her chest, rumpling up her recital costume.

Ryan ran a hand through his hair, not ready to prolong the dilemma.

The server returned, and Ryan patted his pants for his wallet.

He stood and called the boys to follow him to the far corner. There, he tightened their circle, not wanting Katie to hear his parental failings. "You guys need to do me a favor."

Josh cocked his head to one side while Pete nodded, wide-eyed and solemn.

"My friend is..." Ryan stopped himself short, unsure if he could use Katie as an excuse. "Anyway, you need to behave when we're in public."

Yeah, sure. Just in public. Bree would kill him.

Josh nodded. His face fell, and his words surprised Ryan. "I'm sorry, Uncle."

Now that he had their attention, Ryan continued, "You're gonna go back there and give your sister a genuine apology."

"Okay," Josh said and Pete started back. When they did as Ryan asked, Zoe wrapped her brothers in a hug.

"I'm ready to go." Katie spoke before Ryan could.

"School night, I guess." Ryan called the kids to lead the way out, and for Katie's ears alone, he said, "sorry about that."

She didn't respond. As she sat, silent in the front passenger seat through their drive back to her Denver loft, he kept eyeing her in his peripheral vision, trying to read her. But her bland expression offered no insight. Picking her up after work hadn't been out of the way, but it was further from home as he dropped her off.

"'Nite!" She hopped out of the car before he could step out and hold her door open for her.

He jumped out, his steps unsure as he forced one foot in front of the other, in an attempt to catch up with her.

"Katie." He caught up to her at the glass-doored entrance and thrust his hands in his pockets. The breezy night sent a chill through him—just the brisk night. The chill had nothing to do with the woman before him or the cold doubt in his heart. "Listen, I know things have been different with the kids."

She let out an exasperated sigh and crossed her arms. "Ryan, I don't think there's anything we can do about that."

She was right. She didn't want kids, and that wasn't going to change.

"Unless your parents have decided to be the legal guardians."

Ryan's stomach lurched, and he suppressed the urge to talk back. He'd never raised his voice at Katie, and he wasn't about to start. One thing was certain though—"They're *my* kids."

How foolish he'd been trying to change her mind. He pulled one hand out of his pocket and waved. "Good night."

"You're a great guy, Ryan, and I had my hopes up. But... it's time for us to..."

"Break up?"

She shrugged and let out a mirthless laugh. "We've been together for five years, and our relationship never got anywhere. We barely had time for each other before you had kids—and now?" She threw her hands up, her voice cracking. "Where do *you* think that leaves us?"

Nowhere. He needed to take his kids home. He gave Katie a curt nod, a mix of emotions stirred up in his mind as he walked to the car and found the kids' heads pressed against the back window.

Surely, they hadn't heard his exchange. He drove home in silence, wrestling with a strange relief. He didn't have to divide his time between Katie and the kids any longer, didn't have to hope for something he knew couldn't be. Yet he'd just lost his girlfriend—someone he'd *bought* an engagement ring for, someone he'd planned to spend the rest of his life with. How could he feel...relief? What was wrong with him anyway? Where was Bree to talk to? Man, he needed her insight tonight. *Maybe I'm not boyfriend material.* At what point did he keep pursuing and hitting a dead end?

He turned onto his quiet street with homes spread acres apart. His house was the last on the street and closest to the boulders.

His stomach tightened as he thought of all the things that needed to be done before the kids went to bed. "You guys should've gotten your homework done before the concert."

"I got mine done," Zoe piped up and hopped from the SUV.

Of course, she had. Sometimes, she reminded him more of Gavin than her mother, who'd always had to be prodded to do her homework.

"I need help with math." Pete slouched back further in his seat, making no move to unlatch his seat belt. "Destiny said she didn't know math and wanted me to wait for you."

That girl was honest. Ryan loosened his tight grip on the steering wheel, smiling a little.

"I need to study for tomorrow's history quiz." Josh slammed his side door and strode toward the door to the back hallway.

Ryan ushered Pete inside, and his heart jolted when he sighted Destiny's warm smile. She greeted them as they walked into the kitchen.

A smile like that could temporarily make him forget the last chaotic hour.

"Did you guys enjoy your dinner?" she asked.

While Zoe gave a detailed analysis of what everyone ate, Ryan rounded the boys to get their homework done. A surge of contentment coursed through him as he helped Pete with his math and Josh sat not too far from them studying for his quiz. Destiny and Zoe had their backs to them as they made the next day's lunch at the island.

Realistically, Destiny was fixing lunch while Zoe chatted away, swaying and singing all sorts of tunes. Exhibiting her usual patience, Destiny praised Zoe for her unusual tunes.

She's exactly what Zoe needs—someone who's emotionally available.

It felt like they were a family or what he remembered of a family. Mom would work in the kitchen, and Dad helped him and Bree with homework or vice-versa.

When Ryan joined Destiny to pray with the kids, he remained a silent listener to their prayers. After saying good night to the kids, he pulled out his laptop and set it on the counter. He needed to go over the CT scans again before he met with the patient for consultation tomorrow morning. He never took his laptop to the bedroom. If he had, he'd be tempted into looking at one more email or researching some diagnosis.

Ignoring the clatter of pots and pans while Destiny cleaned the dirty dishes, he adjusted the blue-light-blocker glasses to study the X-rays.

Although they worked several feet apart, Destiny's presence filled the entire room. In the sudden silence, he sensed her gaze on him, and her sweet scent suggested she wasn't standing too far away.

He slid off his glasses and closed the laptop. Pushing it to the side, he swiveled his swivel chair. "What's up?"

She cleared her throat and sauntered even closer. She then hopped up on the counter inches from where his laptop had been. "I don't want to interrupt your work, but I wanted to ask a question."

"Ask away." His voice sounded raspy.

"Pete needs new uniform pants, and Josh needs new shoes." She kicked one foot as she talked. She was barefoot. Of course. The shoe-sales girl, too free-spirited to wear shoes in the house. "We also need to send money for school pictures."

In other words, he needed to go shopping. His chest rose and fell more rapidly than usual, and he suppressed a shudder at the thought of hitting the mall or wherever. He hadn't needed to shop for the kids' clothes since he became their guardian.

As if sensing his dread, she stopped kicking her feet and reached as though to touch his shoulder. But dropped her hand to her lap instead. "I can order the uniforms and shoes online, but I needed your permission to spend the money."

What a relief. "That's why I gave you the credit card."

Besides the receipts she stored for him, she always sought permission before she spent anything over thirty bucks.

"I was also wondering if we could buy the kids a trampoline."

A trampoline? He scooted back on his stool and rubbed his eyes. He had no time for intricate projects. "How are we going to assemble it?"

She looked down at her dangling feet as they swayed back and forth. "That's the beauty of the internet, I found a store that delivers and assembles."

They had plenty of space in the front yard. Why not get a trampoline? "Whatever helps the kids burn off their energy sounds good." Pete needed more exercise anyway. That boy thought too much. Sometimes the kid made him nervous. He didn't have to ask how much it cost. She'd probably price matched ten different websites to find the best deal.

She gestured to the computer. "What procedure are you performing tomorrow?"

"I'm meeting with a patient I removed a tumor from two years ago." His heart was beating a million miles per hour. "She needs a heart transplant, and we need to make sure her body can handle it first."

"Oh..." The word whooshed out in a gasp as compassion softened her features and those amazing eyes went all dewy. "That must be hard for her body to take in."

"That's why I have to do extra research."

"I'll be praying for her." She planted her feet on the floor. "I better let you get to work." After a few steps, she came back. "By the way, how did things go tonight? With Katie, I mean."

He grimaced. "The boys spilled water all over the table." He relayed the argument he'd broken up.

"Ouch, I'm sorry..." Destiny scrunched her face. "Next time, don't take the kids on your date."

He was done trying, but he didn't have to tell her. He peered into her warm eyes, and they shared a moment where they stared at each other. His heart pounded, and he lowered his gaze.

It was high time he got to know her better. "We take up a lot of your time here." He shifted, unsure where to start. "Tell me about you. I'm sure you have a boyfriend you'd rather spend a weekend with."

Her smile vanished. The sadness wobbling in its place didn't sit well with him. "No boyfriend, but I had one once."

That should end their conversation, but her face expressed such a painful memory. Did her boyfriend die too? "What happened?"

"I was a fool." She fixed her gaze on the closed computer. "He was married, and he decided not to disclose that when we started dating. Six months into our relationship, he tells me he'd split up with his wife when he met me, but they wanted to give their relationship another shot."

That jerk didn't deserve her. His gut tightened, his jaw clenched, and one hand fisted beneath the counter. The urge to protect her from any jerks surged through him. "He's the fool for not being honest. I'm sorry things didn't work out."

She shrugged. "I'm not. Glad I found out before I pursued the wrong guy." Then her chin jolted up, and her curls bounced as she chuckled. "I did something else that still surprises me."

His lips curled at the laughter in her tone. "What's that?"

"We were in the restaurant when he told me, and I hurled the Italian bread in his face, then chucked the glass of water at him."

Kinda hard to imagine her doing so, but the mischievous glint in her eyes insisted she had. "No, you didn't."

"I wouldn't do it now. That was before...before I knew I have to answer to God for my actions."

Her face fell again when she talked about her friend, Timon's re-action after the breakup. "He stayed in jail for two days from tres-passing and breaking the man's nose."

Did it make him a bad person for feeling relieved the jerk got what he deserved? Someday, hopefully soon, he'd love to meet all her friends. He shook his head, suppressed laughter carrying on his voice. "You're something else, Destiny Brown."

She waved a hand, changing the subject. "Your mom called me yesterday."

His mom could get carried away with phone calls. He winced. "I forgot to tell you I gave her your number."

"I'm glad you did. She needs to talk to her grandkids anytime." Destiny hugged her arms across her chest. "I ordered her some flow-ers for Mother's Day and signed it for all of us, I hope that's okay."

She was out of this world. "Are you kidding me? I forget Moth-er's Day almost every year." Unless Bree called to remind him. "She will know I had nothing to do with it."

"Well"—she took a step backward—"I better let you do your...thing."

Thing, huh? "Thanks for everything."

For trying to fix his relationship with Katie. For taking Zoe a flower. For being a comforting presence in the house whenever he came home.

"You pay me to do that." She edged another step backward, then turned and spoke over her shoulder. "Don't forget to take your beef kabobs for your lunch tomorrow. Hope you like leftovers."

He rarely ate leftovers, but he'd make an exception. She'd thought of him like she had since *Disney on Ice* when she bought him water.

Did the furnace kick up? He unbuttoned his top button, he'd already lost the one below it.

He stayed up for another thirty minutes or so, looking at the X-rays, before he made it back to his room. He stripped off his clothes, tossed them in the half-empty hamper, and stepped into the shower.

Even though he'd told Destiny not to clean his laundry, she'd dismissed his instructions and had been washing his clothes for the last week. Arguing with her was no use—plus, he was relieved not to worry if he had any clean underwear in his drawer when he stepped out of the shower.

The exhaustion should have made falling asleep easier, but his mind replayed the day. He and Katie had dated for five years, should he let that slip away?

Yes. She doesn't need you anymore.

Katie's words rang in his mind—*Haven't you noticed her gorgeous eyes? Or her flawless skin?*

He may not have thought much about Destiny if Katie and Lucas hadn't insinuated he was.

He lifted his pillow over his head, fighting off thoughts of Destiny. He clutched it, frustrated his feelings were shifting toward his nanny.

He closed his eyes to think of Destiny.... Ugh, no Katie. *Katie. Katie.*

How annoying that he had to repeat Katie's name. Each time his eyes closed, Destiny's warm face swirled behind his eyelids.

The monitor crackled when Carter fussed. His cries rose, and Ryan jumped out of bed. He might as well take care of the baby, so Destiny didn't have to wake up.

Just as he threw a T-shirt on, her soft voice came through the monitor. "Hey, little man. Did you have a bad dream?"

Ryan flopped back onto the bed, his head on the pillow and face to the ceiling. Destiny's voice soothed him as she sang to Carter. His body relaxed, and his eyes felt heavy. No wonder the little guy fell asleep easier when Destiny tended him.

Katie. *Think of Katie.* Five years together. Why was he not as troubled over their breakup? He ground his teeth. There had to be a reason besides her intelligence and physical attraction for him to have been with her all those years. He liked an orderly lifestyle, but he needed a reason—any reason why he was about to marry her.

Racking his brain and finding none, he flopped onto his side. It had been a long day, and nothing was ever clear when you were exhausted.

CHAPTER 10

Five weeks was long enough for a normal person to adapt to a routine, but it seemed more challenging for Destiny because her mornings still sent her heart into an uproar.

She'd set a few things in place to have the kids get their uniforms out the night before. She and Pete took their showers at night because they were slow waking up.

"Josh, will you please start the car?" she asked while she added cheese sticks to each of the lunch boxes.

"Got it," he responded.

She opened and closed the cupboards in search of a backup water bottle. "I don't know where I put Zoe's bottle." She'd refilled their water bottles last night and tucked them into the fridge to avoid this situation.

"Found it!" Zoe declared, lifting a purple water bottle in front of Destiny.

A glance at Zoe's tangled messy hair reminded her she was far from getting out of the door. "Go get my spray bottle and the wide-tooth comb from the bathroom." Zoe would know she meant Destiny's bathroom across from her room. "Don't forget the hair ties!" she shouted over Zoe's back. A bun would have to do this morning.

She zipped up the lunch boxes, and a handwritten note slipped out of Zoe's box. She picked it up and squeezed it back in. Since she was only off once a week, she held off on renting her own place. Jia didn't mind her staying in the extra room on Saturday and Sunday afternoons. During her free time, she wrote Scriptures and encouraging quotes to tuck in the kids' lunch boxes.

She almost sent Ryan's lunch with Josh until the boy frowned at the big lunch bag she handed him.

"Sorry." Pulling it back, she exchanged the lunches, then tucked Ryan's in the refrigerator.

Ever since he helped her make the kids' lunches, Destiny made his lunches whenever making the kids' the night before. His lunches were a bit technical since she made him salads, three times a week and sandwiches the other days.

Seeing Ryan's lunch in the refrigerator reminded her of their conversation. He'd said he wouldn't be going in to work until ten today.

Strange. He usually left no later than six a.m.

After spraying leave-in conditioner in Zoe's hair, Destiny wrung it up in a frizzy ponytail. She leaned her head to the side, impressed by the fast results. "You look beautiful." She patted Zoe's shoulder.

The girl's brown eyes lit up. "Thank you for fixing my hair."

"It's my pleasure." With the right conditioner and hair routine, Zoe's hair no longer had the dull look it had when Destiny met her.

With no time to put away the hairbrush and spray bottle, Destiny left them on the island. She'd clean up later. She fastened Carter in his infant carrier and adjusted the milk bottle in his hands so he could steady it in his mouth.

"Don't forget your sweaters!" she reminded the kids. Springtime in Colorado brought unpredictable weather.

Breathless, she hoisted Carter's car seat in the crook of her elbow and walked to the spacious garage.

The place could fit four cars, but Ryan was content with his Mercedes. With it parked at the opposite end of the Highlander, Destiny didn't have to fret bumping into it.

Josh and Zoe had taken their seats. Pete walked in the garage barefoot, his hands loaded with a sweater, socks, and a backpack.

Destiny's shoulders inched toward her ears. "Why don't you have your shoes on?"

He motioned at the things in his hands. "I have them here. I'll put them on when I get in the car."

"Great idea." Her tense shoulders loosened.

The garage door went up when she pressed the button, and she focused on the back-up camera built into the car. Otherwise, she didn't trust herself with reverse driving.

Rays of morning sun pierced the windshield as she drove the winding road. She prayed with the kids, something she'd begun on their morning commute.

"Can you turn on K-LOVE?" Destiny asked Josh after prayers.

"Hold on tight" by Mercy Me played in the background as they hit the highway.

Josh shifted in his seat. "Do you think we will make it on time *today*?"

According to the dashboard clock, they still had twenty minutes before drop-off. "We should be there at the exact time."

They were almost halfway to school when Pete's voice rose over the music. "I can't find my other shoe!"

Destiny blinked. They'd be late if she had to pull over and look for it. "You've got to be kidding." She glanced over her shoulder. "Keep looking."

"I did and can't find it."

The few weeks she'd been with the kids, she'd learned they didn't have the attention span to look for anything longer than one minute. At least she was approaching an exit. "Wait... let me pull over."

"Why didn't you get your shoes on at home?" Josh snapped. "What's the point of me waking up early if I'm going to be late *every* day?"

Just like Ryan, if Josh wasn't ten minutes early, he declared himself late.

But the boy had a point. Destiny needed to adjust her morning alarm for another fifteen minutes earlier.

"Let me help look." Zoe wiggled forward in her seat.

After parking alongside some pine trees, Destiny swung open her door and climbed in back to search. Pete was right.

"We better go back home." Defeated, she slumped back into her seat.

"I hate tardies," Josh grumbled and started reminding his brother of all the reasons he needed to be up by six. Crossing his arms over his chest, he stuck up his chin. "Why can't you get it together?"

Pete fired back, "You're not perfect either, leave me alone."

"Boys, just drop it. Okay?"

"You're always bossing me and telling me what to do." Pete shook a finger at his brother, but his lips trembled as his voice dominated the entire car.

Carter, picking up the tension, wailed.

Destiny turned off the music, a dull pain throbbing at her temples.

"Pete," she called, maintaining a calm tone, despite her urge to kick up her voice too. "Your brother is done arguing. You need to drop it."

"I don't want to drop anything!"

She'd never heard the quieter boy raise his voice. "It's gonna be okay."

"No...it's not going to be okay. I need my mom, and you're not my mom!" The boy's sobs grew louder.

That stung. Aching for him, she took a deep breath to compose herself. "I know...I'm not your mom, and I'm not trying to be."

"I want my mom back, and my dad!" He sobbed, and her heart constricted for him and his now-silent siblings. Even Carter had stopped crying, the minute Pete started.

Her eyes tingled, and she blinked away the threatening tears when she pulled in the driveway. She ran into the house and found Pete's shoe in the hallway.

The kids were fifteen minutes late to school, and she had to walk them into the building to sign them in for their tardy slips.

The lobby was spread out, and Carter wiggled out of her arms, his gaze beelining the glass shelf with school trophies and awards in the lobby. "I'm sure you'd enjoy sticking your tongue to that glass."

She hoisted him on her hip and waved to Josh. In a hurry to get to his class, he probably had no time for goodbyes.

Carter's little fingers trailed over her neck as he tugged at the back of her hair.

Zoe flung her arms around Destiny's legs. "Pete and Josh will be fine. Have a good day," she said before she darted off.

Pete stood with sunken eyes and sagging arms. Keeping his gaze on the tiled floor, he walked to Destiny after his siblings left. "I'm sorry...I got upset and yelled at you."

Her heart melted at the genuine apology. If she didn't have Carter in her hands, she'd sweep Pete in a hug. It was probably for the best since the boy might hate her for embarrassing him in front of his peers.

She touched his shoulder. "Thanks. Don't worry about it, okay?"

His head jerked up. Dewy-brown eyes braved hers. "Okay."

She and Carter left the school. If they were going to make it to story time at the Golden library, they'd better not go home yet. She drove three miles to the library and fed Carter Cheerios from the diaper bag as they waited for the library to open.

WITH CARTER NEXT TO her, Destiny sat on the library's colorful rug with a few parents and their little ones as they sang repetitive
songs led by the young man—Patrick was the name on his badge.

Carter clapped and giggled whenever Patrick introduced a new
song.

After story time, Patrick reminded them to join him every Tuesday and Thursday for baby story time. "Feel free to hang out for another forty-five minutes so the kids can play. We have toddler time in
one hour."

He tossed several stuffed animals and books on the carpet. Then
he added cube pillows and random toys for the kids.

The three moms by Destiny discussed their babies' sleep patterns
and shared advice on how to get kids to sleep through the night. She
could use some of that advice but was busy yanking stuffed toys from
Carter's hand. He had his mouth open, ready to shove in a plush ele-
phant.

With the help of the pillow in front of him, Carter struggled to
pull up and stand to his feet. He took an unsure step forward.

Just like all the other days he'd attempted to walk, Destiny pulled
her cell phone from the diaper bag and scrolled for the camera app
to record.

She crouched in front of him.

A wide grin spread across his face as he held up both hands in
the air with each step. Three...four and five more steps. Exhilaration
quickened her blood, laughter bursting from her lips. Her cheeks
hurt from smiling as she kept her phone steady. "He's walking! He's
walking!"

"Yay!" Another mom clapped, and Carter flopped down onto
the carpet.

"He just took his first steps!" Destiny bounced on her knees, unable to contain her excitement.

"Congratulations!" Several parents joined her as they asked about Carter's age.

"He'll be one tomorrow." Destiny scooped him up and hugged him close to her chest, kissing his soft cheeks. "You're such a big boy!" She was so proud of him. "Your uncle and siblings will be so happy when they see that video."

"Ma–ma." Carter bubbled.

"He just said mama." Destiny spun around to the other moms. "Did you hear him?" He hadn't said it since the Greek restaurant, but he seemed to know what he was saying this time.

A red-haired woman eyed her like *duh?* "My daughter said mama when she was ten months."

Whatever. It was a big deal to Destiny.

"You're lucky your son finally said mama." Another mom patted Destiny's back. "All my son says is dada, yet I'm the one with him all day and night when he wakes up."

Your son. That sounded good, but not the truth. "I'm his nanny."

The woman cocked her head to one side, her brow scrunching as she studied them. "He looks just like you."

Destiny pressed the video to send it to Ryan.

On their way out, she met a mom in the lobby. Long brown hair swayed in her ponytail. Why did she look familiar?

The woman's smile when she sighted Destiny was a confirmation—they'd met before.

"Hi." Destiny gave a little wave with the hand carrying her diaper bag. "You look familiar, and I..." She shook her head, trying to remember where she'd seen her.

"Yeah." Above a welcoming smile, her hazel eyes were warm. "I've seen you at church."

That's it. "Riverside?"

The lady nodded.

Destiny hadn't been there long enough to know anyone's names.

"I'm Holly." She stooped to grab a little boy's hand, then sent the toddler off to the toy area.

"Destiny." She motioned to the curly-haired boy. "Is that your little one?"

"Yes, I let him run around the play place before story time."

Several toddlers ran and squealed in the lobby's play place where Duplo tables and a toy kitchen offered entertainment. "Burning off some energy, I see." Destiny hoisted Carter who was wiggly on her hip. His chubby fingers were rubbing over his eyes.

Holly touched Carter's soft shoe. "I know most of the parents who have kids in the nursery, but I haven't seen you or this little guy."

"I'm his nanny." Destiny cuddled him closer. "He has three siblings in school right now."

Her forehead crinkling, Holly studied Carter's face. "His hair...and his skin, I thought he's..."

"Mine. Yeah, I get that a lot."

"How old are the other kids?"

Destiny told her the kids' ages starting with Josh. Holly, who appeared about four years older than Destiny, said she had two other kids.

"You should sign up for Vacation Bible School and sports camp. It starts the second week in June."

She'd seen the announcement in the church bulletin. It was three weeks away, and the kids would be out of school by then. "I might look into it."

Although the kids loved to play on the trampoline, they'd need several activities to keep them out of venturing into their backyard.

"Thanks for reminding me about that."

They visited for another fifteen minutes as Holly suggested the different free summer activities. The conversation shifted to meal planning and all the basics related to kids that Destiny hadn't figured out yet. God had definitely sent a teacher to bump up her learning.

After exchanging phone numbers, she returned to the car and fastened Carter in his car seat. "We better go home and eat before your doctor's appointment."

Her phone chimed an incoming message just as she fired the engine.

Ryan: That smile is priceless! Wish I was there to see the first steps.

She smiled as she typed her response.

Destiny: Hope he will walk for you soon.

Ryan: Thanks for the video. You're the best. What time is the appointment?

A warmth went through her at his mention of her being the best. It was nothing, but it wouldn't stop her from shaking when she typed a response.

Destiny: noon

Ryan: wanna stop by? I don't have patients, besides my follow-up calls this afternoon.

She wouldn't miss it for anything in the world.

Destiny: sounds good

Ryan: Text me as soon as you're done.

Destiny: Got it.

She added a wink emoji.

A schoolgirl giddiness surged through her at the thought of seeing Ryan at work. Her heart fluttering, she smiled.

He's into his girlfriend. A brutal reminder popped into her mind. *He's not my type.* Not another man who was chasing after his ex—actually, Katie wasn't even an ex. Their relationship was just rocky for the time being.

His invitation has nothing to do with you, but his nephew. He wants to see Carter take his first steps. She tightened her grip on the steering wheel, chastising herself as she drove to the clinic across from Ryan's hospital.

After giving Carter the infant Tylenol his doctor instructed, Destiny held him while they poked needles on his thigh. As his screams pierced her heart, she felt like a traitor.

When the nurse put the neon bandages over the areas she'd poked, Carter let out escaped gasps, buried his head in Destiny's neck, and sucked his thumb.

"I'm so sorry, sweetheart." Destiny's throat tightened as she bounced him on her hip, planting kisses on his forehead. She'd bought lollipops last week for when Carter cried while she drove. She wasn't driving right now, but it was an emergency. She dug in the diaper bag and retrieved one.

CHAPTER 11

Ryan met Destiny and Carter in the hospital lobby and took them to the doctor's lounge, where they sat at the corner table.

He unbuckled Carter from the stroller and kissed his forehead. "Are you going to walk for me today?" His admiration for Carter and all his kids always created a warm sensation in Destiny's heart.

Carter was still not himself. The lollipop hadn't lasted long before it fell out of his hand in the clinic elevator. "I don't think he's in the mood to do anything."

"How did he do?"

She winced. "I think he doesn't like me right now. I betrayed him." When had he *ever* cried that much? "If I'd known how painful that would be, I would've made you take him."

"He'll get over it." Ryan patted Carter's hair. "Won't you, bud?" He then squeezed Carter tight and sat in the chair across from her. "You're sure you don't need anything to eat?"

Not wanting to incur unexpected expenses, she gestured to the water bottle he'd handed her while they walked. "This will be enough, thanks."

Men and women in white lab coats and scrubs walked in and out of the lounge. A few greeted Ryan. The scent of their lunches and snacks surrounded them.

A man about Ryan's age strode toward their table. The wide grin on his face indicated they were pals.

"Hey, my man." He smiled at Carter as he set his chicken and pasta dish on the table. Crouching, he bent and patted the baby's back. "I can tell you won't give Uncle Lucas a smile today."

"Not until he smiles for me first," Ryan said, rubbing Carter's back.

Lucas. Ryan's biking buddy. He'd said his name when he opted for biking instead of a date with Katie. He looked athletic, his build muscular compared to Ryan's lean frame.

Lucas's blond hair was combed to the back and his eyes were warm as he extended his hand, but addressed Ryan. "Don't tell me this gorgeous lady is your nanny! I'm Lucas."

Before she could respond, Ryan—still cooing at Carter—did. "That's Destiny."

"Destiny?" Lucas repeated, testing out before concluding, "What a cool name. Right, Harper?"

"Yeah." Ryan fidgeted with Carter's fingers.

Lucas's handshake lingered longer than necessary before he took a seat next to her. "Did Harper tell you how your lunch saved us from starving?"

Ryan had told her how relieved they'd been to have lunch.

She looked at Ryan, then back to Lucas. "He did. I hope it was a nice ride?"

"Ryan's told me so much about you."

He had? She eyed him. He shook his head and almost rolled his eyes at Lucas. What could Ryan tell his colleagues about her, except that she was his reluctant nanny? That she'd almost sent *two* of his kids to the ER on her first day? That she couldn't seem to get them to school or bed on time? "I hope nothing scary."

"Don't worry. They're all good things."

Hmm. Those she'd like to hear. She sipped her water as Lucas bragged about beating Ryan up the hill during their bicycling outing and shattering his golf score.

"Are you planning to tell her you cheat?" Ryan pinned Lucas with a look of a man teasing his best bud, not intimidating him.

Lucas cupped his hand over his mouth and stage-whispered to Destiny, "He's lying."

Destiny laughed. Then, seeing Ryan's attention back on Carter, she asked Lucas if he was also a surgeon.

"That's for boring people." He waved a hand at his friend. "I'm the anesthesiologist, and I work with Ryan a lot. Gives me the chance to keep him in shape."

"You mean distract me?"

Carter nibbled at the hem of Ryan's scrub shirt, whining when Ryan shifted him. Destiny walked to the stroller. He needed a teething ring, but he deserved another lollipop as a special treat after he'd endured those shots. Plus, she still needed to earn his trust back. "He might like this better."

Ryan arched a brow but didn't protest when Carter grabbed the lollipop out of Destiny's hand and it found its way into his mouth.

"Seems somebody knows what this is?" Ryan commented.

Destiny grimaced. "For emergencies."

"Hey, Katie, over here." Lucas's deep voice bellowed toward Katie retrieving bottled water from the vending machine.

His brows furrowing, Ryan narrowed his gaze at Lucas. "Are you insane?"

Lucas chuckled at Ryan's hushed question and shrugged. "I'm saving you the after-breakup awkwardness. Trust me, you'll thank me later."

Breakup?

Katie joined their table, taking the last chair next to Ryan and across from Destiny.

"Hi again." Destiny waved in greeting. Katie's long blond hair was now cropped short. Surely, she hadn't cut it after Carter had slobbered in it? Her disgusted expression had seemed like someone had puked all over her hair. "Nice haircut."

"Thanks." Katie peeked at Ryan. She then snapped the lid open from the glass container, revealing vegetables with all sorts of grains. No wonder she stayed slim.

Although Destiny didn't eat salads, she wasn't fond of sweets either. But she was fond of Zumba, and that qualified for the healthy category.

"Hi, cutie." Katie squeezed Carter's toes. "Candy is terrible for your teeth."

"It's good for emergencies," Destiny explained, even though she'd already done that to her boss.

"Looks like someone is into kids now." His tone sarcastic, Lucas pinned his gaze on Katie. He then whispered to Destiny loud enough for Ryan and Katie to hear. "They broke up because she doesn't like kids."

Katie rolled her eyes, her words barely a whisper. "That's not why we broke up."

Ryan gave Lucas a look, his jaw twitching. "Are you in here to eat, or what?"

"Both." Lucas forked some of his pasta. "You've met Katie, I see."

"We met at Zoe's concert."

When did they break up? Ryan hadn't shown any signs of heartbreak—no puffy eyes, downcast gaze, or slumped posture. All she'd noticed were his chiseled features, broad shoulders, and well-rested eyes. As if he'd never slept better.

Lucas, finally silent, took his first bite of chicken.

Katie, her face flushed, shifted in her chair, and Destiny scrambled for anything to make her comfortable.

"Kids can be challenging." Maybe a story from a nanny blog would distract everyone? She told part of it, then shrugged. "The kids thought it was funny to put a snake in her dresser."

Katie gasped, and her hand flew to her mouth. Lucas laughed, and Ryan's lips were twitching into an almost smile.

"Your kids wouldn't do that, I'm sure." Carter clapped like he did at story time, and Destiny's heart warmed. She could handle the job—no matter what—but if what she read was true, she could understand Katie's fears.

As silence settled over them, Destiny ignored the jealousy tightening her gut whenever Katie stole glances at Ryan. It was probably time for her to get Carter home for a nap before picking up the kids. Though not the right place to ask, she had no idea how to get rid of the company before them, and she was running out of time.

She laid both hands on the table as if getting ready to rise, then said, "Before I leave, I want to talk about Carter's birthday. I thought it would be nice to have a party for him."

Ryan jerked his head and blinked. "He doesn't have friends."

"He has family, though." Ryan's birthday was coming up, too. The kids had told her when she'd asked, as a good employee should. When his mom called to talk to her grandkids, Destiny had enlisted her help in planning a present. She suppressed a shiver. The woman needed something to focus on when that day used to be one she celebrated with *two* of her kids.

"With your birthday in two weeks, what if we combined yours and Carter's birthday party?"

He eyed her, his expression unreadable, making it even harder to know what was going on in his brain. "I don't need to celebrate my birthday."

He didn't seem the type who liked parties. "We can invite your friends and have the kids' friends over too." She then gestured to Lucas and Katie. "You guys are officially invited, and maybe tell Ryan's other friends."

Katie's gaze collided with Ryan's. She set her fork over her half-eaten grainy salad. "That would be fine with me."

"Let's do this! I love parties." Lucas rubbed his hands together and winked at Destiny. "You're my kind of person."

Talking about parties brought to mind a commitment she'd made to Josh. "By the way, Josh's friends are coming for a sleepover this Friday."

Ryan was quiet as if letting her words sink in. Then he let out an exasperated sigh and ran a hand through his hair. "You mean next week or tomorrow?"

"Uh..." She hadn't thought things through. She bit her lower lip and spoke through gritted teeth, hoping he wouldn't hear. "Tomorrow."

The muscles in his temple twitched, and he shook his head, obviously composing his calm. There was a reason he was a surgeon. "Of all things, why did he want a party?"

Um...would this make things better or worse? She ducked her head and eyed the tabletop. "I was trying to get the kids to work like you suggested." She swallowed. *Was he angry?* "I told them, if they cleaned up their mess, they could get a reward for anything they wanted."

"And Josh wanted a sleepover?"

Destiny nodded.

"That's not the way you train kids to work. In fact, we need to sit down and come up with a chore chart." He bounced Carter on his lap. "How many kids are we talking?"

"I don't know." She knew. It turned out Josh was Mr. Popular and had friends from the two classes in his grade. Her throat closed over the words. "All the boys in his grade. Thirtyish, I think?"

His brows wrinkled, and he slapped the table. "Absolutely not."

She hadn't been thinking when she asked the kids what they wanted. How was she to know family rules when she remembered her dad's laid-back manner?

Focus. How could she tell Josh she'd made a mistake? She would crush his excitement. She'd agreed to this on Tuesday, and by Wednesday, she was receiving RSVP texts from parents. That meant all those parents had made plans for Friday night without their boys. How many date nights would she be canceling? They'd be furious, the kids would be disappointed, and Josh would face the humiliation for the rest of the school year.

But there was more. So much more. Losing both parents... Josh was trying to survive the unthinkable. But his parents weren't all he'd lost. She'd seen it in glimpses at school, heard it in snatches of his conversation. The once-popular boy was being left out and retreating further and further into his imaginary book worlds. His friends didn't know how to respond to his loss and probably avoided him.

It wasn't the same with Zoe—*no one* could ignore Zoe! Besides, kids her age were less self-conscious, less awkward and socially aware. They felt sorry for her, then moved on. And Pete? Well, he would rather be tinkering with his experiments, robots, and Legos. He had school friends interested in the same things, but he didn't *need* them, not the way Josh did. And whether he knew it or not, no amount of getting Josh to school on time would help him back into his world.

She *had* to host the party. She needed to show those boys that Josh was still one of them—approachable and fun, as he used to be.

This party...could change everything.

Convince Ryan that this is a good thing. Forgetting Lucas and Katie, she put on her pleading face. Time to relay Josh's exact words. "Ryan?" When he focused on her, she continued, "He says he hasn't been able to hang out with his friends since..." She stopped herself. Talking about Josh's parents might stir up pain.

"We need to talk about such things first." Ryan's brows unwrinkled, and his face softened. "You can't invite a bunch of kids to my house without asking."

Better late than never. "That's why I'm asking."

Those blue eyes bore into hers. She ignored her thundering heart as he spoke. "What you're doing right now is telling me your plan, not asking—big difference."

He was right. She'd messed up. "I thought it was more important to ask about the financial stuff."

But that was no excuse. She clasped her hands together. "I'm sorry. I'll ask next time."

"What's the big deal anyway?" Lucas swirled his drink. "You've hosted adult parties before. Kiddie parties are just the same. Thought that's why you bought the big house."

Ignoring him, Ryan hammered one finger on the table, facing her. "My backyard is not designed for kids. I could easily get sued if a kid gets hurt. Like you already know, I won't be home until late tomorrow night. With such short notice, you'd be on your own."

"Not a single child will go anywhere near the backyard for even a second."

Though she'd failed with Pete her first day, she'd kept the kids safely out of the back since. She could lock the back door and set the alarm he'd installed. Maybe even set up a camera over it so she could see it if she wasn't in its physical line of sight. And staying Friday night wasn't a problem. She stayed through Saturday mornings because she made the kids hot breakfast—her way of compensating for granola bar breakfasts in the car most of the week.

She crossed her fingers in front of him and made a show of a promise. "I promise to not bother you with anything. Thank you so much."

With that solved, she let out a breath and wiggled in her chair. *Just get it over with, girl.* "Um...I might have told Pete he could have a puppy if he cleaned his room."

Ryan's eyes widened. His mouth slid open. His lips moved. No sound came out. He exhaled and inhaled a few times, then shook his head. "Listen, Destiny."

She loved how her name rolled off his tongue. *Focus.* She stilled and gave him her best innocent look. "Uh huh?"

THE DOCTOR'S NANNY **113**

"There's not going to be a puppy in my house. I'm barely around for the kids, who do you think is going to take care of a puppy?"

She lifted her hand as if she was in a classroom. "Me?"

He shifted Carter to his shoulder. The little guy had fallen asleep and missed out on all the fun. His sticky red fingers left marks on Ryan's immaculate scrubs. "Not happening."

"I love this girl." Lucas grinned.

Katie typing on her phone, was thankfully ignoring their conversation.

"I hate to break my promises to the kids."

"You're gonna have to tell him it was a mistake."

Could they settle for a bunny? If they could, she'd have to bring up the issue later. At least they got tomorrow's sleepover.

"What did you promise Zoe?" The corners of his mouth twitched, and his eyes twinkled. Surely, he couldn't be amused by her crazy mistakes?

"She wants us to make slime and do our nails."

His tight posture relaxed. "God knows we don't need any more slime stuck to the walls."

She'd overstayed her welcome. Destiny rose and brought the stroller to Ryan's side. "I better let you get back to work."

His warm fingers brushed her shoulder as he eased Carter onto her chest.

As if feeling terrible for his reaction, he spoke for her ears alone. "I didn't mean to come down so harsh on you."

He'd handled it well, given her crossing the line. "Don't worry about it." She hushed her tone to match his.

"I'll walk you back to the car." He spoke a bit louder this time.

"I can do it." Lucas rose, setting his dirty plate on the cart. "If you don't mind."

Ryan opened his mouth as if to counter, then gripped the back of his neck. "I'll be home late—more like midnight. Tell the kids good night for me."

"I will."

That explained why he came in late today. He had a late shift today—and tomorrow. During her sleepover party. She really should have talked to him about it first.

She eased Carter into his infant seat clamped to the stroller. After saying goodbye to Katie and Ryan, she walked out of the lounge, assuming Lucas would follow. Not that she needed an escort, but this was one big building. If she got lost, she'd end up being late to get the kids from school. Bad enough getting them a tardy slip today. The last thing she wanted was to have them waiting for her this afternoon.

Lucas caught up with her. "Do I need to carry a bag, push the stroller, or something?"

"I'm good, thanks. You don't need to walk me out, just point me to the right elevator." She'd been so distracted checking out Ryan in his form-fitting scrubs, she hadn't paid attention to what wing they'd crossed.

"I don't mind walking with you." Lucas gave her a sideways glance. "Where are you parked?"

"Garage C." She'd even snapped a photo of the sign—just in case she forgot it. "This place is huge."

"Did you come through the café entrance?" At her headshake, he named all the possible entrances leading to the clinic she'd taken Carter.

"Yes...I came through the back door and into the dining area."

"Success!" He snapped his fingers. "I know where to go."

His smile held such energy. Hard to believe the guy made his living putting people to sleep. "What do you do on weekends, Destiny?"

If she wasn't at Ryan's house, she was at her friend's studio teaching Zumba. "My weekends are pretty busy." That was honest. She preferred hanging out with the kids and helping Ryan on Saturdays if he needed her. "I go to church on Sundays. Then I rest before I go back to work. What about you?" she asked to be polite.

"I'm usually done with work by four. But some days, surgeries get delayed, and I work late." He held open the heavy door for her. "My schedule is more flexible than your boss's."

She'd wasted enough of his time. "Thanks again for walking out with me."

"The pleasure is all mine." He set his hand on his chest and bowed. "It was nice to meet you."

"Nice to meet you too."

"See you at the party." He winked. "I'll get on Ryan's nerves to keep me posted after you pencil in the date."

"Sounds good." He was kind of cute, but she wasn't searching—unless her boss was available.

IT SEEMED LIKE A GOOD time to make his departure, now that Destiny was gone, but Ryan stayed and sipped the rest of his water. It was his only escape from scrambling for conversation with Katie as she scooped her final bite of salad.

He had to say something. "How's everything going?"

Katie tucked a strand of her hair behind her ears. "Good." She half-smiled. "You're a typical family man now."

That he was. As silence settled between them, he ran his hand over the water bottle rim. The way things stood between them, he had no idea what else to say.

"My nanny..." He cleared his throat, stalling. "She drives me crazy sometimes." In an oddly interesting way.

"Oh yeah?" Katie's shoulders stiffened. "I can't believe she talked you into having a bunch of kids at your house."

He'd started it by publicly reprimanding Destiny earlier, but Katie's accusatory tone rankled. "She's doing her best."

Everything she did was in the kids' best interest.

Katie's phone buzzed, and she gave it a cursory glance before sliding it to the side and setting her hands on the table. "You guys are having a domestic argument. Like any normal couple. Kids this and kids that—that's exactly what it looks like with you two."

Is it? "Don't be ridiculous." He gulped more water than he needed. Was Katie right? Was that what parents and couples did?

He and Katie never had time to argue. In the limited time they spent together, they had to make plans for their future rather than squabble.

Katie pushed back the chair and stood. "I have to meet with a patient here soon."

Thank goodness their conversation was over.

"I hope we can still be friends?"

Friends would be awkward, but what else could he say? "We work together, of course."

"See you around."

He lifted his hand and gave her a curt nod before walking back to his office. There, he retrieved his lunch from the small refrigerator while replaying Katie's words. *You guys are having a domestic argument.*

Destiny came to mind as he ate the spinach quinoa salad she'd made. She didn't eat salads, but she figured out how to make intricate ones for him—fancier than he ate from the hospital café. She was everything he needed, yet he couldn't pursue her. Unless he wanted to lose a nanny by messing things up.

A smile curved his lips when he remembered the lunch-box note he'd tucked in his desk. He opened the desk drawer, his heart thrumming as if he'd tucked away a deep secret.

Warmth rushed through him as he reread Destiny's scribbled writing for Josh.

"Count each day's blessing. Always remember: You're loved and you're important. *The Lord says I will instruct you and teach you the way you should go...* Psalm 32:8"

In her fast-paced way to get the kids' lunches ready, she'd tossed the note into his lunch instead of the kids'.

Enough daydreaming. He tucked the note in the drawer and stowed his container in his lunch box. He needed to make follow-up calls. The first week home after complex surgeries was the hardest for patients.

Depending on a given week, Ryan worked in emergency settings, performing urgent surgeries, like the one they beeped him for before he finished his calls. He extracted a .22 bullet from the patient's skull. The successful GWS surgery took three hours.

He was grateful for his late lunch. It held him up until he got home, a little after eleven.

The house was quiet and the lights turned off, except for the floor lamp in the living room.

Heavenly smells teased his nose as he passed the kitchen. A hint of bread and garlic. Whatever she'd made for dinner made his stomach growl for a midnight snack.

After setting his bag and keys on the counter, he walked to the living room to turn off the lamp, but Destiny was curled on the couch, head tilted back and a wrapped-up bundle on her shoulder. Her eyes were closed.

Carter was out, his little hand fisted in Destiny's locks. The lamp-light cast a golden glow over them, creating the most beautiful sight he'd ever seen.

With one hand protectively on the baby's back, she'd tucked him under her chin. Carter's mouth slightly parted.

Not wanting to frighten her or wake up Carter, he whispered. "Destiny?"

Nope. Deep breathing followed.

He eased the baby from her. After laying Carter down, he would cover her with the soft throw on the couch. She'd likely stay asleep there until morning—unless Carter fussed. Then she'd beat him to the baby's room.

He lingered to rub Carter's back, since the squirt moaned when Ryan set him in the crib. When Carter's chest fell and rose, accompanied by his steady breathing, Ryan exited the room, closing the door.

A body barreled toward him and crashed into his chest, catching him off guard when a fist struck his side. "What're you doing here?!"

Ryan jumped a step back. Destiny? Was she sleepwalking? She hurled a hand at him, and he swerved his head to dodge it.

"Where's my baby?"

When she crouched to unplug the hall night-light, probably to swing at him as a weapon, Ryan reached for her, wrapping his arms around her while taking both her hands in his. She tried to struggle out of his hold, but he had a good grip to keep her in place.

"Destiny, it's me...Ryan." With her racing heart beneath his, the touch became so intimate and close his heart started racing. Her delicate warmth melted into him, even as the sweetness of her scent teased him.

While Destiny's thundering chest had to do with her assumption she was fighting an intruder, Ryan's was for an entirely different reason.

When she slumped in his arms, finally registering whom she was fighting, he let go of her. Once she stepped back, he spoke, his voice hoarse. "I put Carter in bed. He's okay. Didn't want to wake you."

"Oh!" Her hand flew to her chest. "Sorry for hitting you."

The mother hen, she is. "It's okay."

Leaving her, he showered and changed into his pajama shorts and a T-shirt. Movement rustled downstairs. Something bounced off the tile, a spoon perhaps.

If Destiny reopened the kitchen, maybe it wasn't too late for a snack. Forget not eating past midnight, he was hungry, especially after wrestling with her.

A glass of almond milk would be perfect. He could also help her with whatever she was doing. *Yeah, right.* Like the good boss he was, or was this an excuse to see her again?

Before he thought it through, his bare feet hit the bottom step. He winced at the cold tile. She was attuned to the sandwiches she was making.

"Shouldn't you be going back to sleep?"

She jerked, and her wide eyes found him. "Carter woke right when I was getting ready to fix lunches."

"I'll help."

"You have work tomorrow."

Ignoring her response, he reached for the Ziploc bags and slid in the sandwiches she'd already fixed. He could see himself making lunches with her daily, and not tiring of doing so.

"Don't worry about my lunch." He'd eat at the hospital.

"Too late. I already made yours." Her chin notched up. Her green shirt proclaimed "I dare you" in bold white letters.

"I made you something different." She snapped the lid back on the peanut butter. "You'll like it."

Huh? Confident was she? "Is that so?"

A smile curled her lips into her cheeks. "It's healthy. Don't worry."

He was already looking forward to his lunch. "Can I have it now?"

"Oh, are you hungry?" Frowning, she swung open the fridge. "I still have some lasagna leftovers."

"I'm fine. I was teasing." He reached for a glass from the cabinet and filled it halfway with almond milk.

After he helped put things away, she sat with him at the island. "I'm sorry for hitting you—"

"That's what I get for separating a lion cub from its mother."

She chuckled, her laugh playing havoc with his insides.

Well, fact was, she'd said, "Where's *my* baby?" She defended the kids like her own. She'd dived down after Pete from the fall, and then protected Carter, even if it meant facing a possible ax murderer.

He wished Bree were here. She and Destiny would be the best of friends—both were the life of the party. *If Bree were here, your path never would've crossed with Destiny's.*

Her fingers tapped on the table, interrupting his thoughts. "What're you thinking about?"

You. "Tell me more about this sleepover?" He leaned back in his chair and folded his arms across his chest. "It's been a very long time since I had one. You'll need to walk me through so I know how I can help."

"Deal was for me to handle it—you're working."

Same reason he wasn't supposed to be falling for her, but his heart wasn't getting the memo. "I found someone to cover the last three hours of my shift. I'll owe her a huge favor, but no way was I leaving you alone to supervise that many kids. They're going to be a handful. I remember not sleeping all night when I went to a friend's house. I'm pretty sure that will be the case."

"I don't know what boys do, but I looked up some ideas about slumber parties on the internet."

Somehow "slumber parties" sounded girlie. He didn't say so. "What did you find out?"

"I'll go shopping for junk food...." She continued sharing her plans for a successful sleepover.

They talked about parties they'd had as kids. She'd stopped having parties when her dad died. She didn't dwell much on her loss, and shifted the conversation back to party planning.

"Earlier today, I met a woman from my church. She told me about the children's museum and Costco. If it's okay, I'm going to get a Costco membership tomorrow. It should save our family money on groceries."

Good thing she knew she was family, because Ryan felt the same. "Do whatever needs to be done."

She was so careful with spending, he gave her authorization to use his account and pay for the credit card bills at the end of the month. She'd enrolled in some credit card that earned them cash back for their spending.

Wanting to keep her talking, he asked more about her day, the time she hadn't been visiting him.

She gave a detailed analysis about Carter's first steps and lit up when she said he called her mama. "Of course he doesn't know what he's saying, but..."

"He knows." She treated him like her son. "I think even babies have great instincts."

She lifted a shoulder, then shared Pete's outburst. "It was worth it, because he ended up apologizing, and I think we bonded."

"I know you did." He repeated the kids' counselor's words. "When the kids can express their feelings, it means they are comfortable with you."

"Oh." She sat up straighter, kicking her dangling feet. "Guess another reason we should get him that puppy."

"Having a puppy is like having another kid around." They were barely managing with four. "You're gonna need to tell Pete there will be no puppy."

Her smile vanished. "He'll be so disappointed."

"Kids can't get whatever they want."

She had that adorable puppy-dog pleading look again. "Can we settle for a bunny?"

Knowing her, she wouldn't take no for an answer. "A goldfish." He smiled at her. "Way less maintenance."

She grinned as if he'd just donated an organ to her. Her hand covered his. "You're a great guardian."

"I doubt that." Otherwise, he wouldn't be yielding to all these requests.

"One more request, and I'll back off."

Another one? Hadn't she practically gotten her way on everything? "Oh, brother." He ran a hand over his face, his eyes starting to feel weary, not from requests, but exhaustion.

"Can we get Fortnite for Josh's sleepover? He wants his friends to be able to play a game they enjoy."

Though he had no idea what Fortnite entailed, he trusted her research. "Sure."

She blinked. Her mouth slid open before she snapped it closed. "That easy?"

"Sure." He shrugged. "Why not?"

GOOD THING THEY'D GOTTEN Fortnite come Friday night. The boys stayed down in the basement playing, talking, and eating for most of the night.

He climbed up the stairs to join Destiny in the kitchen as she finished refilling another popcorn bowl. The scent permeated the house.

"You don't have to make them any more food." He slid onto the stool across the counter from her and rested his arms on the marble countertop. "I just told them to get to bed."

"They polished off the last pizza box, and I figured I better be prepared with more stuff." She shook the last kernels of corn into the party bowl, added more salt, then raised her brows at him. "You better go get some sleep. Zoe is hogging my bed, so I'm pretty sure I'll sleep out here on the couch."

"She didn't want to sleep on the air mattress?"

"That thing's so uncomfortable." Destiny swept a curl off her forehead with the back of her hand, then gave the popcorn another hefty shaking of salt. "I think she asked me to read her *Pocahontas* so she could fall asleep in my bed."

With a bunch of boys downstairs, Zoe had moved into Destiny's room for the night. He could offer Destiny his bed and take the couch. He wouldn't mind having her scent on his pillow, but she might feel awkward.

He pushed away from the counter. "The alarms are all set. The boys may or may not sleep, but they won't be getting out in the backyard without us knowing. We'll need all the rest we can get."

She glanced at the stove clock. "I need to wake up in three hours to make breakfast."

"I will help."

She gave him a raised eyebrow. "Don't you want to pretend you're not here?"

Glad he'd found someone to cover the last three hours of his shift, he shrugged. "Do I have a choice?"

CHAPTER 12

Ryan and Carter's birthday party day started with a hearty breakfast Destiny cooked. Pancakes, eggs, and bacon for the kids. She'd whipped up egg whites, turkey sausage, and a protein smoothie for him.

"Slow down." He grimaced at the calories from the syrup Pete's pancakes were swimming in. The three kids sat in the breakfast nook across from the island.

"It's a special day." Destiny chopped tiny pancake chunks and put them on Carter's high chair tray.

Special day! Yes, he shouldn't worry about the kids clogging up their arteries.

Destiny prayed for their food. She thanked God for protecting Ryan over the last years of his life. His chest felt heavy at the convicting prayer so applicable to his life.

But Bree... This year, for the first time in his life, his sister wasn't sharing his birthday. He was a year older; she never would be. He'd been protected; she hadn't been. Why?

Or had she been? Had God tried to stop her from going out that night, canceling her sitter to keep her home, and Ryan intervened?

"Amen," the kids said, and Ryan drew in a shaky breath, responding with an amen a second later.

The forks clanked when the kids bit into their pancakes. Ryan cut into his sausage and lifted a fork, the first bite all but melting in his mouth. Closing his eyes, he savored the deliciousness.

"Where did you get these sausages?" he asked when the last remnant of flavor had slipped off his tongue.

Destiny poured orange juice into the kids' glasses. "At a meat market. I figured you'd want the fresh stuff."

She'd gone to a lot of work. The house was decorated when Ryan woke up at five. Birthday banners glitter-glue painted with Ryan's and Carter's names hung around the living room. Balloons and streamers were strung across the kitchen and sunroom.

She slid a glass of juice in front of him.

"Thanks, but I'll stick with the smoothie." He pointed to it. A smoothie she'd made specifically for him.

His cell phone rang. A glance at the stove top made Ryan wince. Only one person would be calling right now on this day.

"I got it." Destiny brought it to him, and he put the phone on speaker.

"Thirty-nine years ago, at nine twenty-eight, a special baby boy was born..."

Ryan dragged a hand through his hair while listening to Mom's enthusiastic voice and the familiar words she said every year when she wished him a happy birthday. She'd be saying the same to Bree, only it would be a baby girl and she'd be born at nine forty-seven.

Not this year. His stomach clenched, his throat closed, and his heartbeat thundered.

Destiny giggled before adding tiny pieces of strawberries to Carter's tray.

She couldn't begin to fathom how hard this day was for him. He and Bree would call each other on their birthdays just to laugh about Mom's birthday calls. He'd never call her again. Never answer his phone to her ringtone. Blood whooshed through his head. Light-headed, he pressed both hands to the counter to keep from wobbling, passing out. Breathe. He had to breathe. How could he do a birthday without talking to Bree?

"You're still there?"

"Yeah," Ryan barely whispered. "You want to talk to the kids?"

Anything to get her off the phone. She had to be hurting almost as much today. But she wanted him to have a good day.

"Yes..."

Destiny was at his side, taking the phone and setting it on the kids' table.

"Hi, Grandma," the trio spoke in unison.

"Hi, sweeties."

"Destiny made us pancakes," Zoe piped up, Bree's voice in her sweet singsong. "We're also having a party this afternoon with Uncle's friends...."

A party. He couldn't do this. Couldn't *celebrate* this horrible day that he and Bree should be together—they *would* be together if not for him.

Focus. Listen to the kids. Think of how happy Bree would be to know how well they were doing. Just listen to them. He closed his eyes. If Bree could hear them...what would she hear? Would she hear Zoe's endless energy? Pete's mumbling? Josh's take-charge attitude? And how, similar to the other days when the kids spoke to Mom, they brought up Destiny.

"You'd like her, Sis. She's good for them."

From across the room at the kids' table, Destiny glanced up. Probably wondering if he had spoken and whom he was speaking to. But she couldn't hear him any more than Bree could.

Zoe continued to speak on her siblings' behalf. Mostly about Destiny and the day's plans. "Uncle is going golfing, and we're going to clean the house before people come over."

"This Destiny sounds amazing!"

His head snapped up. *Yes, she is.*

Destiny scrunched her face as she scooped mixed berries onto each kid's plate.

"Is she there?" Mom asked.

"Hello, Mrs. Harper." Destiny bent closer to the phone. "You're amazing, too."

"Oh...hi there." Mom laughed. "I can't wait to meet you when I come for Thanksgiving."

It was almost July, and Mom was already talking about Thanksgiving?

"Can't wait to meet you, too." Destiny then brought the phone back to Ryan after Mom said goodbye to the kids.

Ryan turned the speaker off, just in case Mom said anything she shouldn't.

"I like this Destiny. She's good for the kids... and for you too."

He didn't tell Mom he'd broken off with Katie, so why was she playing cupid? "Mom..."

"Katie doesn't like kids, and now you're a parent." Her huff interrupted his protest. "Anyways, Zoe says Destiny is very pretty."

"I'm going to hang up here soon." If she kept talking about Destiny.

"Do you like her?"

He was falling for her, but she was his nanny. Plus, Lucas was now interested in her. It wasn't Mom's or anyone's business what he liked and didn't. His body was starting to feel warm. "Mom, I gotta go."

His face flushed, he gulped the rest of his smoothie and polished off his breakfast.

Thankfully, Destiny was too immersed filling up the kids with more drinks to be paying attention to his color transformation.

After helping her load the dishes and wiping down the kitchen countertops, he went golfing with Lucas and two other buddies. Another generous gift Destiny had initiated, and sacrificed her Saturday to ensure he had fun.

After almost four hours of golfing, he drove home.

An hour before the party started, he pulled into the driveway. So many scooters and bikes littered the two-acre lawn, he had to look twice before proceeding. The place looked exactly the way it should. Kids live here. Destiny had bought the scooters and toys from the community garage sale.

Her smile sent his heart racing as she pointed the biggest soaker toward the kids, who were running from her. Their happy squeals were too loud for them to hear Ryan's car engine as he drove past them into the garage.

Just like the yard, the house was in disarray—worse than when he'd left. Darts, socks, and flip-flops cluttered the floor.

I could start by cleaning up. But the kids needed to clean up their own mess.

When he stepped out front, he took in the sight of Destiny. He expected kids to be kids playing. He hadn't expected Destiny to be part of the game and enjoy every minute of it. The kids were all drenched, but Destiny's tank top worn over jean shorts was as dry as could be. Huh.

He ducked when water shot over his head.

"Oopsie!" Destiny put her fingers on her lips. The smile underneath those fingers... She wasn't sorry at all. "Did you have fun?"

"I did."

Josh shot water at her from behind, and she winced and spun around. She then squeezed her gun at him, and he sprinted toward Ryan.

"Hide me, Uncle!" Josh squealed.

Zoe yelped when Destiny streamed water at her. She ran to refill the gun by the toolshed inches away from the trampoline.

Pete aimed his gun at Destiny, and her hand made fast work squirting out a flood of water at Pete's back as he ran toward Ryan.

All three kids were hiding behind him. "She has the biggest squirt gun, Uncle." Zoe gripped his athletic shorts.

"I need to refill mine." Josh shook it, showing the empty toy.

"Hiding all my people, aren't you?"

Her eyes met his, and the air left his lungs like someone sliced a punch through his chest. No denying that she was gorgeous—not just pretty, spunky, and sweet, but the most beautiful woman he'd ever seen. Her eyelashes long and thick, boldly framing expressive blue-green eyes. Her lips perfectly round. Lord have mercy, the kids were around, and he was having the wrong thoughts about their nanny.

She blasted the last water at him, reeling him back to focus. "Sorry again." She lifted her gun in surrender. "I better go get a refill though."

She was so darn cute, and begging for what was coming to her. "I'll protect you guys." Ryan snagged Pete's and Zoe's guns and sent Josh to refill his. "When she comes our way, I'll pummel her before she shoots at us." *Bring it on.*

Destiny returned, armed and grinning. Ryan bombarded her top before she could aim.

Finally, her hair was wet, clinging to her forehead. She let out a dramatic sigh. "Aha! The war is on, Dr. Harper."

Water seeped through his T-shirt when she squirted him, and his two water guns were now empty.

She lowered her weapon. "You asked for it."

Ryan grinned. The cold water felt good after sweating during golf. "We need a refill. Come on, guys, to the hose." He ushered the kids just as Destiny splattered whatever was left in her gun and ran to the house, possibly to refill her water.

The kids giggled. Exhilaration energized him. When was the last time he'd been this silly, playing for the fun of it? Even Bree wouldn't have been able to answer that.

The kids loaded their water guns, and he had the hose ready when Destiny emerged.

While the giggling kids shot at her, Ryan aimed the hose and re-leased a stream of water.

Hands up to protect her eyes, she laughed uncontrollably as he hosed her down.

"You took it to the next level, Dr. Harper." She wiped at her face after Josh turned off the water. Her hair drenched, her tank top cling-ing to her, she folded the hem into a ball and squeezed the water out of it.

"You left me no choice, Destiny Brown." Victory thrilled him. The kids were already back to jumping on the trampoline.

"I'm going to plot my revenge." She wagged a finger, mischief crinkling her eyes. "Very soon, too."

What revenge could that be? "It's my birthday, don't forget." He turned for the house. "I'll go get you a towel."

He returned with several, handing one to her and reminding the kids to dry off before they went inside.

"Still having that party, are we?"

"All your friends know you have kids, right?"

"Yes, but we don't want them to trip over toys and break a bone. We'll end up having someone in the ER." He gestured to her doused clothes and hair. "Since you're soaked the most, you can shower first while the kids and I clean up."

"You think you're getting away from payback?" She flounced away.

He and the kids picked up the toys. The house smelled clean, de-spite the darts and Nerf guns. He sent the kids to shower and sprang upstairs to clean up.

Carter's cries sounded muffled through the baby monitor. Ryan worked the button on his jeans and adjusted his short-sleeved shirt before walking down the hallway.

Sitting in his crib, Carter hugged his soft blanket tight in his grasp. A wide smile opened his mouth, revealing new teeth he'd worked hard to produce. Waving his hands, he babbled. "Da-da...da...da."

"Yes, I'm your dada." He scooped him up, kissing his forehead, and smoothed a palm over his soft skin. As they trekked down the stairs, Carter's little fingers crawled at the back of Ryan's neck, and tenderness filled every part of him.

Slow music played from Destiny's phone. Warm and savory smells penetrated the kitchen. Foil pans filled with food arrayed the island—buffet style. She'd ordered the meal from her friend's Greek restaurant. Ryan ogled their salad.

Beyond the food, Destiny was mixing powdered beverages in a glass pitcher. His breath caught at the sight of her. The ankle jeans hugged her curves, and an orange tank top—vibrant enough for Lucas to spot her every move—offset her gleaming hair and sun-kissed tawny skin. "Guess who I found awake?" he said, announcing his presence.

She jumped and spun around. The fondness altering her face and posture when she looked at Carter tugged at Ryan's heart. She walked toward them and clapped her hands. "Hey, cutie."

"Mama..." Carter lifted his hands and all but jumped out of Ryan's grasp. When she caught the squirt, Carter nestled his face into her shoulder and stuck a thumb into his mouth.

She rubbed his back and swayed side to side. "Are you going to help me mix the lemonade?"

She had a tender way with Carter and the kids. No wonder they depended on her. *I rely on her, too.*

He could help her finish with whatever she was doing. But guests should be arriving, and he needed to tend to his friends. "I'll take him downstairs so the kids can play with him while you finish up."

She kissed Carter's cheek and ruffled his curls before handing him back. "Go back to Dada. I'll see you soon."

The doorbell rang as Ryan returned from downstairs, and he let Lucas in.

Jorge, the lab technician, stood behind him with two six-packs of beer in hand. He hoisted the beer. "Planning to get wasted tonight."

"This is a kids' and adults' party." Ryan mock scowled at Lucas. "Who invited this guy?"

"He has a crush on your surgical assistant."

"I need to be out of my mind to work up the nerve to ask her out," Jorge said.

"You're not drinking beer in front of the kids." Ryan needed to lead by example.

"I'll keep them in the car. If I need them, I can just run back and drink there." Jorge lugged his beer to the car.

Ryan rarely drank, not enough for him to have any around the house. He needed to stay alert and ready to fill in at the hospital if he got called in at the last minute.

"I'm here for your nanny." Lucas winked as he walked in.

Something cringed in Ryan's stomach. "Her name's Destiny. And she's not your usual one-night stand."

"Maybe I'm tired of one-night stands."

He scrubbed a hand over his face. Destiny was an adult, and he wasn't in charge of her.

Several people joined them.

From some of Ryan's favorites to movie theme songs, Destiny's playlist provided background noise as twenty-plus of his coworkers chatted. He had no idea how she'd found out his taste in music.

He half-listened to another surgeon discussing his engagement party while his eyes focused on Destiny. She wove through the guests as the women snagged Carter from her, passing him around. They oohed and aahed at how cute he was. Carter gurgled and giggled, soaking up the attention.

"What a sweetheart. His hair looks exactly like yours," Sally, a hospital receptionist said.

Ryan couldn't hear Destiny's response since Jorge chimed in. "I think he has Harper's lips."

Katie stood a few inches away from Destiny's circle, immersed in a conversation with Ryan's surgical assistant, Becky. She'd started some diet plan last month, and it was all she spoke about lately.

The kids left for downstairs after dinner, where they hung out with their friends.

Lucas had followed Destiny and helped her in the kitchen. Ryan cringed every time Lucas made her laugh. Then Josh called Lucas downstairs. The boys needed help with a game Ryan had no idea about. Being a kid at heart, Lucas spent half his time playing Fortnite with the boys until the kids' friends' parents picked them up.

When they sang "Happy Birthday" to Ryan and Carter, Destiny cut the cake. While everyone enjoyed the treats, Ryan recorded Carter smothering his face with cake.

"Ready to taste some ice cream?" Destiny lifted a spoon to Carter's mouth.

He winced at first, likely from the cold, while testing whether he liked it or not. Then his brows unfurrowed as he stuck out his tongue and swiped it at his lips.

"You like that?" Ryan asked.

Carter responded by kicking his legs and pointing his hands to the ice cream for more.

Carter and Ryan opened their gifts. Gift cards for Ryan.

Carter giggled when Ryan helped him open his gifts. All kinds of noisy toys. Ryan gratefully thanked everyone.

While Destiny took Carter for a bath and got him ready for bed, Ryan went to say good night to the kids downstairs.

The boys wanted to stay up and play video games. "Until your friends leave," Josh suggested, one brow rising hopefully. But they'd had enough TV for the night.

When Ryan refused, they started wrestling with him, stretching out their bedtime. "Okay, guys." He untangled himself from them, then ruffled Pete's hair. "Seriously, it's time for bed." He still had company waiting upstairs. Panting from the sudden workout, he stood with his hands on his hips. Destiny had gotten Pete's hair cut. It looked good.

"Can you come to my room, please?" Zoe said after they prayed in the boys' room.

Stuffed animals occupied half her bed. The twinkling LED lights strung from one corner to another over the pink walls added a special element. More personable than the gray it had been when the kids moved in.

Destiny had offered to paint the room when Zoe asked. He moved a unicorn to clear a spot on her bed. "Do you like your room now?"

"I love it. Destiny took me to Ross, and we got some pictures." She pointed at the canvas unicorn on the wall.

Mom had brought the hand-me-down dresser when the kids moved in. He'd used it when he was young. "Did Destiny paint the dresser too?"

"Yes."

A different primary color adorned each drawer. He walked over to pull them out. He'd been torn between donating the beat-up dresser and hurting his mom's feelings. Destiny had replaced the bottom of the drawers with new boards—amazing work.

"It looks new."

"It sure does."

He sank on to the clear spot on Zoe's bed, and she slid her small fingers into his big ones. "Did you have a good birthday?"

He'd never made a big deal about his birthday until today. "You guys made it special."

"Destiny wanted you to have a special day."

And he'd had one. "I need to go back and entertain my guests."

"Is Destiny coming to pray with us?"

With Lucas awaiting her return from putting Carter down, Ryan wouldn't be surprised if he was lurking for her by Carter's room. "I don't know."

"She said she'd read us a Bible story and pray with us."

"If she said it, then I'm sure she'll be here."

Back upstairs, people started saying their goodbyes, and the crowd was thinning.

"How does it feel to be almost forty?" Katie asked, sipping her coconut water.

"Still the same." He scratched his shaven jaw.

"Is Destiny coming back?" Lucas reappeared in the kitchen.

As if on cue, Destiny walked down the stairs; Ryan's heart jolted, and then his jaw clenched when Lucas adjusted his button-up shirt and squared his shoulders.

"Here you are." Lucas fell in step with Destiny. "Now that the kids are sleeping, we can have some adult conversation."

"I still need to read and pray with them."

"I'll be waiting."

Ryan suppressed the urge to remind Lucas it was past eleven and visiting time was over.

"Lucas and your nanny seem to have hit it off." Katie peered at him over her drink.

"I don't have a problem with that." His edgy tone sounded like he had a problem with it. He didn't. Or did he?

"Was just pointing out the obvious."

Whatever.

When people left, he organized his birthday cards into a stack as Lucas's deep laugh rumbled from the porch. What could they be talking about? The view couldn't complement their romantic evening. After minutes that stretched like days, Lucas's laughter thundered as the deck door opened, and two figures stepped back inside.

Ryan busied himself, packaging the leftovers into Tupperware. He stilled when Lucas asked for her number.

"Ryan will get it to you."

What he will be getting is the end of the blade in the OR.

"I need to get a few things done before I go to bed." Destiny walked through the kitchen. "Bye, Lucas, thanks for coming tonight."

"Can't wait to catch up." Lucas's final words bounced off her back as she disappeared into her room.

Lucas motioned for Ryan to follow through the front door. "Man, I think I'm falling in love."

"There's a big difference between lust and love." Good, that came out neutral enough. He thrust his hands in his jeans pocket. "She's not your typical kind of fling. Destiny is—"

"Religious, I know." Lucas rolled off his toes, bouncing a little as he stood there as if warming up for a workout. "She will only go out with me on Sunday."

"She's off on Saturdays." Some Saturdays at least.

"She said she keeps Saturdays open, in case you need her, but she also teaches on-call ballet classes or was it..." He scratched his head, then shrugged. "Some kind of dance—I don't remember."

Zumba. Good, she was too busy to date.

"So, you want me to play matchmaker. Is that why we're having this conversation?"

Lucas blew a deep breath out. Ryan had never seen him struggle when he went after a girl. He folded his arms across his chest, even more disturbed. If a girl turned Lucas down, which was rare, given his charm and easygoing manner, he'd move on to the next.

"She'll go out with me if I go to church with her. In other words, we can go out to lunch after mass, or what did she call it?"

Ryan chuckled. Lucas Matthews would not step inside a church—even for a girl. Problem solved. He slapped Lucas's shoulder. "I guess you move on to the next chick."

His friend was silent, and Ryan was ready to say good night when Lucas rubbed the ridge between his brows. "I need her number, bro. Looks like it's time for me to go to church."

He had to be kidding. Why did she want Ryan to give out her number, rather than do it herself? His heart thudding a jumble through his body, he reluctantly uttered Destiny's number—one of the two phone numbers he now knew by heart. The other number was Mom's.

Bree's had been there once. He recited it silently. A number he'd never dial again.

"Well, my friend"—the porch light highlighted Lucas's wide grin—"since you're still stuck on getting Katie back, I guess I'll roll forward into uncharted territory."

Ryan lifted a hand to wave at Lucas who hummed as he strolled to his Mustang.

DESTINY WAS WIPING down the counter when Ryan reentered the kitchen. She'd changed into a neon pink T-shirt and cotton shorts. "You've been working all day."

Water dripped from her hands as she grabbed the dish towel to dry them. "It's your birthday."

She then swung open the freezer, pulling out a clear quart container of ice cream, not just any ice cream, his weakness. "Mint chocolate chip?"

Her smile mischievous, she set the carton on the island. "Time for my revenge. I get to watch you eat sugar at midnight."

"No way." She couldn't be serious. He rarely indulged in ice cream. He settled onto the stool, planting his elbows on the white marble counter.

She didn't pay attention to him—goodness, when did she ever take no for an answer? Not from him anyway. She pulled out the drawer and retrieved two spoons, then handed one to him. "Okay, I'll have a bite so you don't have to feel bad. Let me get some bowls."

Might as well give in. He reached for her hand to stop her. "Let's not get the dishes dirty."

She wriggled onto the barstool across from him and ordered him to take the first bite because he was the birthday boy.

He closed his eyes to feel the cream melt on his tongue. Man... just the way he remembered, but this was creamier and more flavorful. Either that, or it had been too long to remember what it tasted like. "Where did you get it?"

Pleased, she arched one eyebrow and dipped her spoon in the container. "I did my research for the best ice cream in town."

"I usually don't eat this late." Contradicting his strict words and schedule, he spooned another bite.

"I know." She narrowed those amazing eyes at him. She was his other weakness. "But it's your birthday, and payback for hosing me down."

He chuckled at the fun memory. Playing with her and the kids was something he'd never forget. "I'm sorry?"

She wagged her spoon in front of him. "Sorry with a question mark? You're not sorry at all."

She took another bite, smiling. "Were you able to reconnect with Katie? You think tonight helped ease the dilemma from Zoe's concert?"

Ryan shoveled out another spoonful, buying himself time. Even though Lucas blurted their breakup, she'd misunderstood if she was asking about Katie. If he didn't tell her, Lucas with his unfiltered mouth would.

"Thanks for trying." He eyed the melting mint. "It's over between us. At some point, you have to let go."

He loved the kids too much to try to force them on someone who didn't want them.

Her spoon clanked when she set it on the counter, and her warm hand covered his, leaving every nerve tingling in its wake. "I'm so sorry." The concern glowing in her eyes made Ryan feel all sorry for himself. But he put on a strong mask.

"I'm good." His lips twisted into something hopefully resembling a smile. "Did you have a good time?"

She eased her hand from his. "I did."

Probably chatting with Lucas. But Ryan didn't want to ask what they'd talked about, afraid to know.

As if reading his mind, she scooted back on her stool and started kicking her dangling feet. "I had fun watching you, Carter, and all the kids have a good time."

She was the most selfless person he'd ever met. Zoe's words rushed back to his mind—*Destiny wanted you to have a special day.*

He scraped the bottom of the now-liquidy ice cream. "By the way, I gave Lucas your number."

"Oh." She swallowed. "I didn't think he'd ask for it right away."

"He said you invited him to church?"

She dismissed him with a wave. "Kind of... you're welcome, too, if you like. I wanted to ask if I could take the kids every Sunday, but you only have a short window with them, so I don't want to take that time away from you."

"I'll pass on the church, but you can take the kids."

Bree and Gavin used to take them. Bree had to have known he wouldn't when she gave him guardianship. But she'd still be saddened by it. "I'm sure they'd love it."

"I also signed them up for Vacation Bible School next week." She told him about the five-day church camp. "If they don't like it after two days, I can cancel."

"If the kids are okay with it, I'm fine."

He didn't want to talk about church. He wanted to know about her—how she came to live with his counselor, how she got into dancing, how she'd learned so much about kids. Too many questions, but he needed to start somewhere. He slid aside the empty container. "How did your parents die?"

Those dewy blue-green eyes peered at him, pure earnestness in their depths. "Do we have to talk about death on your birthday?"

It didn't occur to him it would be a touchy subject. "I mean, you don't have to talk about it...."

"Mom had complications during labor." She shrugged, keeping a calm tone, but the light dimmed in her eyes. "My dad—he took care of me. H–he died of some heart disease when I was twelve."

She slumped forward in her seat, plunking her chin in her hand, her dangling legs slowing their swinging. "I spent most of my time in one foster home or another. Don't let me fool you—I wasn't the easiest shell to crack." She talked about a foster home the foster boys burned down, and landed her in a group home. "Timon and I ambushed two of those boys at night, beat them up, and threatened them that, if they didn't report themselves to the police, we'd beat them again."

Ryan sucked in a sharp breath, surprised she'd done such a thing.

"I'm not proud of my actions." She shook her head. "That's why I'm grateful God has given me a second chance."

Then she smiled, easing the tension he'd built upon her tragic story. He touched her shoulder. "I'm glad you're here now."

"Not for long, though," she reminded him.

He'd not had much time to think of Destiny being here temporarily. He hadn't had any word from Valeria, and she never left a contact number.

"Do you have a dance studio?" That was if she had someone managing it for her.

She laughed, bolting upright in her chair, and his insides warmed. "That would be nice, but I'm not sure I want to be a business owner." She made a face. "If I could make enough money from it, that would be my dream job. Don't get me wrong, I love you guys, but...you know what I mean?"

She was passionate about dance. "I understand."

"Before I forget, I got something for you." The chair scraped the tile when she stood. "I'll be back."

Minutes after she'd left for her room, she returned with a medium-sized wrapped box with ribbons bouncing on top. She plunked it before him and clapped, bouncing on her toes. "Open it! I hope you like it."

He would have to like it if she were that excited. Anticipation tingling through him, he tore off the shiny blue wrapper.

"I know you have something like it by now, but I didn't know what else to get you." She brought the knife for him to cut the tape.

"You made this hard to access." He cut through the tape and flipped open the box, pulling out a blue dress shirt.

"My hair got stuck on your shirt, and you lost a button."

He smiled, feeling like it was yesterday—how his entire body heated up at the debacle. Their eyes locked, and his breath caught. "You could've just bought a button."

She nibbled on her lower lip. "The shirt was cheaper."

He eased the black leather-bound book resting beneath it from the box. He ran his hand over its smooth surface before opening the first page. *Special Moments* embossed the inside cover.

Curiosity sped his hands to the next page. A smile lifted the corners of his lips at the sight of him and Bree as babies side by side in a crib. He looked at Destiny, her smile wider than his own.

He tapped the photo. "Where did you get this?"

She motioned for him to proceed. "Keep opening."

Bree and him as toddlers dominated the next page. He kept flipping. Him and Bree fishing with Dad—displaying Bree's first fish. She was so full of life. Like Destiny. He touched her face, his throat closing. Then laughter loosened the clog. He read a note Destiny scribbled to the side—"Ryan's almost first fish."

Still standing, she edged closer to peer over to the page.

He touched Bree again. "Did Mom tell you the story behind this?"

Destiny cackled with a slow nod. "It was your sister's fish, and you wanted to show off that it was yours."

"No...no, that's not true."

"Is that so?" Destiny folded her hands on the island.

"My sister got the fish, but she was too freaked out by it to hold it for the picture. So I volunteered."

As he flipped through pictures of him throughout his life, he paused to tell stories whenever Destiny asked about the details. Pictures of him graduating from kindergarten all the way up to college—Bree there for every special moment in his life. Pictures of him holding his nephews and niece after they were born.

He'd made it to the hospital for each child, surprisingly.

Emotion lodged in his throat, not only over the memories of his sister, but also how Destiny would never know what the gift meant to him. He lowered his chin to meet her gaze, her eyes dancing beneath the pendant lights, her vibrant soul shining through. Where did she find the time to do all that?

With her gaze so intent on him, he swallowed and opened his lips to say thanks. But the words choked in his throat.

"You're welcome." She shrugged a shoulder and swept a wayward curl away from her eyes. "Wouldn't have done it without your mom."

It was probably Destiny's idea. Her time she'd invested to make the copies. He suppressed the urge to sweep her up in an embrace, forget he was her boss, or whatever he told himself.

Except his best friend was interested in her. His chest rose and fell. Hugs were not a good idea either. He was too jumbled up and would end up kissing her.

"How did your sister's procedure inspire you to become a surgeon?"

How like her to notice his weirdness and move things along. He cleared his throat to get rid of the lump. "Yeah, the tumor she had at twelve. I remember being so scared—I'd never been apart from her, not for more than a few days. I couldn't lose her." Still wasn't ready to be without her. "And when she survived, I decided I wanted to be the doctor who helped other people like Bree." But she still died.

"Death is inevitable." She hopped up on her stool. "That's why we have to depend on God all the time."

Hmm. She was right. He'd depended on Bree all his life. He sought her every time he needed advice, companionship, and solace. But wasn't that what he was supposed to turn to God for? His job was a constant reminder that he needed God's help to have successful procedures, and people needed God's help to survive.

She stood and tossed the ice-cream container into the trash. "We polished off the ice cream at..."

Ryan checked the stove top. "One."

"I have church tomorrow."

"Are you taking the kids?"

"Is it okay if I do?"

"Fine with me."

Because of the party, she'd stayed the night on her day off. She put a hand on his shoulder, zapping his entire arm and quickening his heart. "Happy birthday. Feeling older yet?"

"I guess not if I'm up this late eating ice cream." He couldn't help grinning. "I'll wake you and help get the kids ready for church."

She never set alarms on Saturdays. The kids stormed into her room to wake her in excitement for their Saturday breakfast. She probably wouldn't set one on Sundays either.

"That will be great." She slid her hand away.

Ryan was due for a church visit, but he needed to recover from tonight.

"Good night," he whispered and watched her walk away until she closed her door. One thing became clear—something he hadn't thought about after breaking off things with Katie. By letting go, he'd come to grips with the realization that some people were a part of your history, while others were meant to be your destiny.

CHAPTER 13

Between parent-teacher conferences and the end-of-year school programs and classroom parties, Destiny welcomed the last school day.

Ryan had worked through Memorial Day weekend. He'd scheduled several surgeries at the volunteer hospital.

The rainy first week of June made it tricky to keep the kids engaged inside. Josh read the entire Lord of the Rings series, Pete went through several Life Savers candies and multiple sodas to test which soda created the best lava launch. Zoe made various types of slime. They were all looking forward to the church camp so they could get out of the house.

Vacation Bible School was set to start at nine. A lot later than school normally started, but the I-70 stretch from Genesee to Denver made Destiny second-guess their five-day commitment.

Thank goodness there's no tardies for church.

"Did you just run a red light?" Pete's voice rang from the back seat.

"It was sort of yellowish." Not exactly a lie. It had been yellow but switched to red when she hit the intersection. "We should be there soon."

She turned from Federal to another street leading them to the park where the church camp was taking place. They used the park so they could reach out to the surrounding community.

After parking the Highlander in front of the studio apartments, she unstrapped Carter from his car seat and slid him into her kangaroo-style baby carrier.

Pete sped ahead, and Josh scolded him for running in the street without first looking.

Zoe stayed by Destiny's side before they crossed the road to the freshly cut lawn and headed to the white canopy.

The air smelled of grass and spring. A middle-aged man in a red T-shirt boldly lettered *VBS* ushered them to the three check-in lines.

The lady explained what sports they offered so each kid could choose what they wanted to play for the rest of the week. Josh signed up for soccer, while Pete chose basketball, and Zoe the arts and crafts.

"We will be done at noon," the lady said, and after Destiny received additional instructions about pickup, she escorted the kids to their respective groups and introduced herself to their leaders.

She drove Carter to a nearby library for ten a.m. story time. Afterward, she took him to the library playground.

He giggled as he kicked his feet in delight when she pushed him in the swing. "You like the swing?" She crouched and made a funny face, adding vroom-vroom sound effects.

Carter laughed heartily. His adorable laugh invoked the urge to snuggle with him. She scooped him up and held him tight, swinging him from side to side.

"Ma...ma," he burbled.

She held him on her lap as they went down the slide until he fussed.

"You must be hungry." She kissed his tousled hair. "Let's go back to the library and change your diaper first."

By the time she finished feeding him, she needed to pick up his siblings.

They sat on the grass to eat the lunch she'd made last night.

"I did a slam dunk." Pete rocked back on his haunches, miming a throw. "It was fun."

He still seemed a bit short for basketball, but it was good to see him interested in something active.

"Can we come back tomorrow?" Josh asked as he reached for a carrot stick.

"I signed you up for the whole week, so yes."

Zoe hopped to her feet and thrust her backpack in front of them. "I added this flower. Do you like it?"

Destiny took the bag in her hand, touching the fluffy silk flowers now embellishing the soft purple. "I love it."

Children's happy screams rang from the playground, and Josh shoved the rest of his sandwich into his mouth. "Can I go shoot some baskets?"

"If they can let you borrow their ball, I don't see why not."

"Going with Josh." Pete stuffed the last of his sandwich in his mouth and scrambled to his feet, then sprinted after his brother. They made quite the pair—sciency and awkward versus lanky and athletic. Pete didn't stand a chance against his brother at basketball, but with the way Josh looked out for his siblings, she wouldn't be surprised if they came back and told her Pete won their spar.

Destiny ran after Carter as he toddled toward the boys. Zoe followed her, chatting about her favorite things about camp.

"What are we going to do today?" Zoe asked.

"As soon as you finish your sandwich, we can walk to the playground. Carter will love the swing."

"I love the monkey bars."

At the playground, Holly stood talking to two other moms. She smiled at Destiny and beckoned her over. "Hi, Destiny," Holly greeted before she introduced the two moms. "They're both in my small group at church."

She hadn't joined a small group yet. "Cool."

"My kids are over there." Holly pointed to a brown-haired boy playing basketball with Pete, Josh, and two others. She then waved at Zoe, asking her name. "I'd like to introduce you to my daughter, Tessa."

Zoe, her eyes big, looked at Destiny for permission to go with a stranger.

"It's okay, sweetie. I'll be right here." Zoe would have more fun playing with someone her age than with her baby brother.

Before long, Zoe beamed, waving at Destiny whenever she went down the slide. Her new friend was adorable in her pigtails.

They stayed at the playground for almost two hours, way after several parents and kids had left.

Holly talked about her family and all the things they did during the summer.

"Do you have family in Colorado?" Destiny asked.

"No, we moved here from Florida fifteen years ago when my husband's company moved here."

Since she was easy to talk to, they spoke as if they'd known each other for years.

Holly plopped on a bench. "Tell me more about your boss."

"He's a nice man...." The urge to share her feelings for him with someone who had a godly perspective pressed down on her. "He works so hard at the hospital." *And I have a crush on him.* She kept that to herself. "How long have you been married?"

"Sixteen years."

So marriage could last. Except she and Ryan had several reasons hindering their relationship. Faith, for one. Plus, he was well educated. No way would he fall for a high school graduate. Having said bye for the day to Holly, Destiny shook off the crazy thoughts as she walked the kids to the car.

The kids were sweaty and thirsty by the time they scrambled into their seats. She hadn't thought of packing their water bottles, except for the Izze drinks they'd guzzled with their lunch.

"Can I play with my new friend tomorrow?" Zoe buckled herself in.

"Can we stay and play afterward?" Josh asked, wiping perspiration from his forehead.

"Can you pack us some chips for lunch tomorrow?" Pete said.

"Yes." Destiny smiled, grateful they'd had fun.

The rest of the week went way too fast with the kids having a blast.

On Friday, the church put on a barbeque. Kids sang some of the songs they'd learned during camp. The pastor suggested everyone come back on Sunday and listen to the rest of the VBS songs. First through fifth grade were the only ones singing.

That afternoon, all Destiny wanted was fifteen minutes of quiet and cool down. Engaging with the kids nonstop made her forget about her problems. It helped her catch up to the childhood she wished she'd had.

When Carter was down for his nap, Pete cleaned his fish tank, then engaged in an experiment of ice cubes, timing how fast they could melt on a warm stove top. Josh was reading *The Hobbit* he'd started last night. Zoe was cutting all sorts of papers.

With everyone doing something, Destiny went to her room to lie down—not exactly napping, unless she wanted Pete to light the kitchen on fire.

She'd just relaxed her head when a loud screech stiffened her spine. "Stop!" Zoe demanded and feet pattered. Destiny's bedroom door swung open. "Josh put ice down the back of my shirt." She crossed her hands on her chest, her chin quivering. "I told him to stop but..."

"I'll talk to him." Destiny swung her tired feet off the bed. Zoe rarely got upset, but her brothers knew how to get under her skin.

Rest would have to wait. Unsure of how to solve the dilemma, Destiny strode out of the bedroom.

Josh met her with a mischievous grin.

"Shouldn't you be reading?" That was a better start. Maybe she wouldn't need to play judge.

"I finished the book."

She couldn't keep up with books for him and his avid reading level. "Your sister says you shoved ice under her shirt."

Josh shrugged. "I was just having fun."

She tried to recall the mom blog she'd read in a similar situation. Time out? Hah, not gonna work. Last time she tried it with him, he'd used it to read.

Ryan's voice rang in her mind. *Age-appropriate consequences of misbehavior.* She tapped her head. She had to think of something.

"Do you think she's having fun?"

His grin spread wider, his chuckle exacerbating the situation. "It's funny, but she doesn't know how to joke."

"Stop!" Zoe yelled, hurling a hand toward Josh.

He ducked.

"You owe your sister an apology," Destiny told the preteen, wondering if he'd comply.

He did—sorta. "Sorry that you're being such a baby."

Zoe snarled at Josh, but tears welled in her precious eyes. "Leave me alone!"

That didn't go well. Destiny rubbed her throbbing temples. She'd always hated being made to clean the bathroom for misbehavior. She could make Josh do that, but using chores as consequences didn't seem right. Plus, she hated being the bad guy.

She'd have to seek Ryan's counsel on what to do next time.

Change of plan. "Okay, let's clean up the mess and go for a walk after Carter's nap."

The promise of an outing made cleaning up easier. After she blended smoothies for their snacks, they were all eager for the walk. They ended up on a trail they discovered while aimlessly wandering the neighborhood.

It was dinnertime when they returned. After they'd all cleaned up and dressed in pajamas, Destiny ordered pizza for their Friday pizza night. She bathed Carter after dinner, then read him a story before putting him to bed at eight.

The three kids flipped through the Disney channel in search of a movie and argued about what to watch until she intervened.

"Who chose the movie last Friday?"

"Not me..." they all chorused.

It would be a while before they got a movie started. Destiny took the remote from Zoe and scrolled through the movie streaming options. "*The Greatest Showman*." She'd heard about it but had no idea if it was kid-friendly.

"Can we watch that?" Josh asked.

"We're not going to watch it until I review it," Destiny said. "Let's find something else. *Tangled*?"

"Oh please! Can we not watch that?" Pete rolled his eyes. "That's boring."

He'd probably rather watch *Frozen* after spending the afternoon melting ice-cubes. Destiny kept the thought to herself.

Zoe was already jumping up and down, clapping. "That's perfect."

Josh didn't say anything, so he was probably okay either way.

To be fair, Destiny said, "Next week, Pete and Josh will choose the movie."

"Let me get popcorn." Zoe skipped to the kitchen. The salty popcorn scent filled the house when she returned shortly with a bowl full.

It wasn't Destiny's favorite popcorn, but she had a bag of SkinnyPop tucked away for her emergency munching. She turned off the lights, leaving the corner floor lamp on as the opening credits rolled in.

Tense music played as guards scurried for the magical flower. Zoe sat next to Destiny on the sectional couch, and Josh perched on the white lounge chair. Pete flopped on the rug and propped his head over several cushions.

Destiny and Zoe scooped handfuls of popcorn from the bowl before passing it to the boys.

They were almost halfway into the movie when Ryan walked in, looking tired. His button-up was still tucked in, and the sleeves rolled to his elbows.

Destiny froze, a popcorn kernel halfway to her gaping mouth, and her heart beat faster. The lamp cast a golden glow to his thick hair. Was it as soft as it looked? That's how she imagined it when she thought about him.

He lifted a hand to wave when he met her gaze. The kids' eyes were intent on the movie.

"Hi." She spoke over the TV sound before pausing the movie.

"Oh." Zoe realized what was happening. The three of them darted over to him and engulfed him in a group hug, then started telling him about their day.

"Can I sign up for basketball?" Pete asked.

Ryan cuffed him on the back of his head, then left his hand cupped there. "That's a winter sport, buddy."

"We're going to sing all the songs we did this week at VBS." Zoe bounced from foot to foot. "Will you come to church and listen?"

He scratched his jaw as if thinking about it. "I'll be there."

"Uncle, Destiny made a killer smoothie." Josh strode toward the kitchen. "We saved you some."

Her breathing quickened when his gaze sliced through her. "She did?"

"We saved you dinner too," Destiny said. Her knees felt weak as if they could buckle if she stood.

"Can you watch the movie with us?" Zoe clasped his hand, her "please" face shaping up. "We're watching *Tangled.*"

"I'll need to shower first." Ryan eased away from them.

When he returned, Zoe patted the space to her right side for him to sit, leaving her in between him and Destiny.

Destiny brought over his kale and apple salad. Upon Josh's insistence, Ryan had to drink the smoothie they'd saved him.

When he finished eating, Destiny took his plate to the sink before they resumed the movie.

Zoe held the bowl of popcorn, and sometime during the movie, Destiny and Ryan reached for the popcorn at the same time, and their hands brushed.

"Sorry," they said in unison, both pulling back their hands with no popcorn.

Ryan stretched his arm along the back of the couch behind her shoulders. Her body broke out in goose bumps when his fingertip brushed her neck. She peeked at him to see if it was intentional or accidental.

His gaze was intent on the TV. And that's where she turned hers until the movie ended.

They prayed with the kids and said good night to them. Zoe wanted hugs and kisses—and a few last-minute answers about tomorrow's plans.

"I'll make breakfast for sure," Destiny assured her.

"Go to bed, Zoe," Ryan said.

In the kitchen, Destiny rinsed their dinner plates to put them in the dishwasher.

Ryan leaned against the counter. "I take it tonight's movie is your favorite?"

She frowned, confused.

"Zoe said you chose the movie."

She snapped the dishwasher shut and wiped her hands. "Yes and no. It's my favorite Disney movie, but the kids were having a hard time deciding." She wiped her hands with a dishtowel, curious about the kind of movies he watched. "What's your favorite movie or TV show?"

He dragged a hand through his hair. "It's been so long since I watched TV." Which made sense. He barely had time to himself. "I always found the *Mountain Men* series quite interesting. I tried to record, but never got to watch them."

His tired eyes were ready for bed, but a crazy thought slipped past her brain to her lips. "Would you like to watch an episode with me?" Whatever *Mountain Men* was, she was intrigued to know what he watched. "I've never seen it before." *Good grief, does that sound like a date?*

"Now?" He stretched his arm and yawned.

Ten thirty was way past Ryan's bedtime, but she enjoyed his company. She shrugged. "Sure."

"Really?" One brow rose, seeming to balance his off-kilter grin. Then, with a wave, he walked toward the living room. "Don't blame me if I fall asleep during the show."

He didn't have to work the next day. "Is the show so boring it will rock you to sleep?"

He laughed, shaking his head. She opened the pantry for her stash—a half-empty bag of SkinnyPop—and brought it to the living room.

Ryan looked up the reruns of the show as she flopped down, leaving a couple of inches between them. She slid the bag toward him. "This is the best popcorn you will ever have."

"I'm so stuffed." He eyed the bag. "Okay, I'll just taste it."

The narrator introduced the individuals in different mountain towns. An Alaskan seventy-year-old man and how he survived the long winter months.

They watched the entire episode and started another. They talked about the best skills to have if you lived in seclusion. During the final half of the second episode, Ryan's spicy scent distracted her. She sneaked glances at his chiseled jaw and hoped he wouldn't quiz her on how the man preserved his salmon.

Four episodes later, they were both yawning as Ryan turned off the TV. "This is way more TV than I've watched my entire life." He peered at her. "What do you think?"

"It was interesting. I think I prefer buying my meat from the store after someone has done all the hard work for me."

They talked about their favorite places featured in the show before Ryan shifted the conversation. "I know you invited me to church last time, and I couldn't come. Is it okay if I come to see the kids' program this Sunday?"

"Of course." Anticipation coursed through her. "Would...would you like me to pick you up?" What was wrong with her tongue?

"Maybe we can pick you up instead. You live way closer to the church than we do." His lips lifted into a smile—was that a wink? "Plus, I'd rather not be late on my first day at church in a long time."

She wouldn't have been late. Well, maybe she would've. Pushing away her protestation, she settled back in her seat, her heart rate kicking up speed.

It's just church, not a date. Either way, her mind was already processing her Sunday outfit.

CHAPTER 14

Ryan arrived at Jia's house, where Destiny stayed during her brief time off work. He parked at the wide street in front of a ranch-style home. Though earlier than she'd suggested, he sent her a text.

Ryan: We're here. You can come out whenever you're ready.

Destiny: Did you have to show up twenty minutes early?

He laughed and peered over the seat to address the kids. "She's not ready yet."

"She's probably just waking up."

Ryan could only agree with Josh. He refocused on his phone.

Ryan: Take your time.

Several minutes later, the screen door swung open, and she stormed out. A turquoise dress danced around her knees as she sprinted toward the car with black heels in her hands.

Ryan fired the engine and reached over the steering wheel to open the passenger door. Josh had offered to sit in the back to let Destiny take the front.

"Hi, guys." She spun her head to the back when she settled in.

Carter squealed, kicking his legs in excitement at seeing her.

She gave his foot a gentle squeeze. "Sorry to keep you waiting."

"It's okay." Zoe and Josh spoke in unison.

"It's your uncle's fault for getting you here early."

Ryan suppressed a laugh. "Church starts in fifteen minutes."

Leave it to her and they'd be thirty minutes late.

While Destiny patted her loose curls and inspected them through the passenger mirror, he tried to ignore her tantalizing scent, and Pete pointed out the coolest cars on the road to church. When Ryan stepped into the spacious atrium, a gray diaper bag resembling a purse was slung to his shoulder. Destiny hoisted Carter to her hip, and the three kids walked in step with them. Random people chatted and sipped coffee in the lobby.

"Destiny!" A woman in her mid thirties smiled warmly when she patted Carter's shoulder, then greeted each kid by name.

"Hi, Holly." Destiny touched his elbow. "This is my boss."

Was that how she addressed him—as her boss? *Yes, you're her boss, in case you entertain the wrong ideas.* Too late for that.

He outstretched his hand. "Ryan. Destiny has said a lot about you." Whenever she talked about her church and the kids' friends, she'd mentioned Holly.

Holly shook his hand. "My hubby is somewhere." She lifted onto tiptoe to scan the group shuffling in the doorway. "Guess I'll have to introduce him to you later."

A tall woman joined them. "Hi, guys. I'm Stacey, the children's director." She shook Ryan's hand. "It's been so wonderful to have your kids this week at camp." Then she praised Josh for lending a hand with the kindergarten soccer on Thursday. "What a blessing for you to have such a wonderful family."

A blessing. It had been a long time since he'd used the word. His sister and mom used it all the time. His sister...

After checking Carter into the nursery, they entered the worship center. Josh sat on one side of him and Destiny on his other side. The kids sang the opening music. As usual, Destiny made him take pictures while she recorded the kids' songs on her phone.

When the kids were taken to their respective classes, the pastor walked onto the stage and read Bible verses displayed on the wide screen. He talked about doubt, and something about seeking God wholeheartedly. Random words grasped Ryan, somewhat familiar. Perhaps from his Sunday school days.

He hadn't yet bothered to pray to God, let alone wholeheartedly—besides the questions he'd grumbled to himself about God taking Bree and Gavin. His chest tightened at the conviction. Perhaps he could ask God directly. Would He answer?

When the song played after the pastor's final words, he could hear Destiny's pretty voice. She sang the words as if she knew them by heart.

A husky man made an announcement asking first-time guests to stop by the lobby and meet the pastor.

Ryan didn't feel confident connecting with the church group—not today anyway. That would only add another commitment to his already busy schedule. To his relief, Destiny didn't ask. She pushed so many things, but she never pushed her Christianity on anyone. Only when Ryan asked her a question did she speak of her faith.

Without thinking, he put his hand on the small of Destiny's back as they made their way through the crowded aisle. Three people offering greetings stopped them before they made it to the nursery. They picked up Carter and the kids from their classes.

They had lunch at the restaurant not far from church, just across from the Denver aquarium.

Looking at the spilled water and Mexican rice on the table, the black beans Carter had dumped on the floor, Ryan cringed. Yes, a 25 percent tip was a necessity.

Destiny suggested they take the kids to the children's museum. "It's just across the street, and we have membership."

He frowned at her. "But this is your only day off."

Her eyes were genuine and warm. "I love spending time with you guys—as long as I get my sleep at night."

He chuckled. "You don't have Carter tonight. Your sleep is guaranteed—rest assured."

They started back where the kids spread out to play.

His shoulder brushed her arm when she shifted, and he felt her warmth through his button-up shirt. The electrical jolt charged his entire body. Like Destiny, he tried to keep his eyes on the kids as they played at the museum's outdoor theme park.

The boys were scaling rocks, while Zoe played beside Carter in the water streaming below the rocks.

"What did you think of the salad at that restaurant?" she asked, breaking the silence.

"It was different, but I loved it."

"I guess you like any kind of salad."

"Pretty much."

She gave him a sideways glance. "You're quite unusual, Dr. Harper."

He hoped in a good way, but he didn't have time to dwell on it. Not when a kid screamed as she ran past them. A man he assumed to be her dad was chasing her.

While the kids played under their parents' watchful eyes, Ryan wondered what Destiny's childhood was like. "In what part of Colorado were you born?"

"East Denver." She crossed her legs and scooted back on the bench, smoothing her blue dress. "After dad died, I was all over the place." The blue brought out that color in her eyes. The color highlighted the sadness in them as she continued. "I used to not like change very much. After we left the home that burned down, I caused trouble whenever I moved to a new home. I had no idea what I wanted."

With her so sweet and gentle, he could scarcely picture her as a troublemaker.

"What about Timon? When did you first meet?"

"That foster home where we stayed for two years." She picked up a ladybug, letting it crawl over her hand. "He and I had a similar story. He'd lost both parents, and his distant relatives in Greece didn't want him."

As she shared how sometimes Timon protected her from harm, compassion tightened Ryan's gut, and his jaw clenched. What would have happened to her without Timon...? He didn't want to consider those alternatives any more than he knew whether to be jealous of or grateful to the guy.

Several kids squealed as they ran through the grass. Others climbed the zipline, their laughter zinging through the air faster than the cable carried them.

Returning his gaze to Carter a few feet away, Ryan watched a pudgy toddler yank a toy out of Carter's hand. Carter started to cry, his bottom lip quivered. Zoe consoled him when she handed him a rock she picked up from the water.

Destiny bounced her knee as a woman Ryan assumed to be the toddler's mom pleaded with her son.

"Give back his toy, sweetheart."

The little boy drew his lips in a pout. "Mine."

"One. Two. Three..." the mom counted, and threatened to leave if he didn't do as asked. When her son wasn't bothered by her threats, she lifted her hands in surrender.

Destiny's warm breath tickled Ryan's ear when she whispered, "What happens if he doesn't give back Carter's toy?"

"We can always buy another."

"Carter may have to face bullies someday, but not today." She marched toward the little boy and crouched in front of the toddler.

Ryan couldn't hear what she was saying, but the boy sauntered toward Carter and slid the toy back into his hand.

Mother hen. She'd jump at anybody's throat to protect the kids.

"Thank you." Destiny smiled at the boy and strode back to the bench.

"How did you get him to listen?"

"I told him he needed to give it back." Her eyes twinkled. "I might have gritted my teeth and put on a scary face. Whatever works."

As she winked, Ryan's shoulders shook. He threw his head back, chuckling.

The boys returned, panting. "It's so hot." Josh fanned himself with a hand. "Can we go play inside?"

Pete revealed the rocks in his hands. "I want to start a fire with these." He rubbed the lava rocks together. "If you can start a fire with flint rock, I'm sure lava rock can do it too."

"I think it's possible." Ryan addressed his curious nephew. "But that might take us all night because we're using the wrong rock."

He took the kids inside the museum for the indoor exhibits before dropping off Destiny at her house.

"Can we stay with you?" Zoe asked as Destiny stepped out of the car.

"No," he spoke up instantly. "We've already taken her entire day." The Saturdays when Ryan didn't work were Destiny's days off too, but lately, he and the kids had invaded them.

"I'll see you tomorrow, though." Destiny kissed Carter's cheek and waved before closing the back door.

Zoe bolted out of the car and threw her arms around Destiny. As Destiny crouched to return Zoe's third goodbye hug, he wanted to trade spots with his niece.

"Only a few more hours, and I'll see you again," she promised while Zoe told her she'd be missed.

Ryan already missed her the moment she'd stepped out of the car. He lifted a hand to wave, then gripped the leather steering wheel as he watched her swaying back to the red door. As if aware of him ogling, she waved to him one more time before entering the house and closing the door.

CHAPTER 15

Saturday was the perfect morning for Destiny to sleep in and not worry about jolting out of bed to a blaring alarm. She didn't have to stress about being late for school.

Scratch that, she couldn't sleep in while at Ryan's house. A creaking door confirmed that thought. Soon, cold air slapped over her shoulders when the edge of her covers lifted and another warm body slid next to her.

"Destiny," Zoe whispered. "are you awake?"

I am now. Destiny blinked and rubbed her groggy eyes, then rolled onto her stomach. "Zoe." She stifled a yawn. "Shouldn't you be sleeping in?"

"It's already seven." Zoe pulled the covers to her chin. She then flopped her head to the extra pillow.

"Zoe," Pete called at the doorway, imitating a whisper. "Come back. Destiny is still sleeping."

"She's awake." Zoe beckoned Pete to the bed.

When Destiny sat up, the gray comforter was now at her feet. She caught Josh poking his head through the door.

He ambled forward. "I told them to not wake you." He spread his hands apologetically as he sat on the edge of the bed next to Pete.

"It's okay, Josh. You guys can wake me up anytime." She wanted them to feel comfortable to talk to her whenever they needed to.

It was the third Saturday in a row the kids showed up in her room. Not to count the times they woke her up in the middle of the night. At times, Zoe crawled into Destiny's bed because she had nightmares. Josh and Pete showed up if they had a headache or on nights they missed their parents the most and needed to talk.

162

"What's for breakfast?" Josh asked.

The obvious response would be cereal, since they knew how to get it themselves, but it was Saturday breakfast. "What do you guys want?"

Josh shrugged. "Whatever is easy for you to cook."

"French toast." Zoe hopped up and clapped.

"We ate that last week." Pete scowled at her, scrambling out of her way before she bumped into him. "How about pancakes?"

"Is there a party going on in here?" Destiny's heart jolted at the sound of Ryan's deep voice. A wide grin lit his face as his frame almost filled the doorway. Carter bounced against Ryan's hip, his feet rubbing against Ryan's gray sweats.

Suddenly self-conscious, Destiny shoved a couple of strands of hair back.

"Come join us," she said, but no way would Ryan walk over to her bed. It was for the best. Knowing he had sat on the bed she slept in would interfere with her sleep for days.

"Yes, come, Uncle." Pete scooted aside to make room.

Ryan's gaze held Destiny's captive for a second or so, appearing so relaxed with his rumpled hair and casual black T-shirt. Whereas she... not a bit of her was relaxed with him in her room!

"Mama!" Carter wiggled out of Ryan's hands, and he set him down on the floor. His little feet beneath footie pajamas slapped over the tile and onto the rug next to the bed. Destiny scooped him up and smiled at him. "Hey, little guy."

His fingers crept over her cheek, and she kissed his wild hair.

Carter sucked his thumb and dropped his head over her shoulder the way he usually did, all but filling her heart with joy. She squeezed him tight.

Zoe patted the bed. "Uncle, come sit with us." She waved him in. "There's room for you."

He seemed to be thinking about it. Destiny nearly gasped when he walked over and sat on the edge of the bed.

"What should I make for breakfast?" she asked him, even as Zoe and Pete yelled their responses.

"French toast."

"Pancakes."

"I'll eat anything." Ryan shrugged. "Looks like it's between pancakes and French toast."

"I have gluten-free flour in there somewhere."

"I'll be okay with the regular." He stood and swept his hands toward the kitchen. "Let's all help out. What do you think, kids?"

The kids rose.

"It's family time," Zoe sang out while Ryan herded them out of the room.

"We'll give you a few minutes to wake up." He swooped up Carter, then pressed a kiss near the little one's ear. "Won't we, little squirt?"

Destiny brushed her teeth, washed her hands, and changed into shorts before joining them in the kitchen. Carter hunkered beneath Ryan's feet as he yanked at the cabinets to pry them open, but the child safety locks stayed intact.

After convincing Zoe she'd make French toast next Saturday, Destiny scrolled through Pinterest on her phone. "IHOP copycat recipe," she said to Ryan, whose hair brushed her forehead when he leaned in to look at it. She swallowed. "This one only has four ingredients. What do you think?"

Ryan nodded as he studied the recipe. "We can pull this off."

She asked Josh to slice up the strawberries, Pete to rip open the sausages and put them in the pan, and Zoe to get Carter's bottle with a promise she would mix the batter after.

Destiny worked beside Ryan, doubling the recipe. The original recipe served four pancakes, which wouldn't even dent the boys' growing appetites.

By the time she flipped the pancakes onto the stack, they'd spilled batter, shattered plates, and turned the kitchen into a disaster zone. A beautiful mess, a sense of fulfillment with a family she would always remember.

After the feast, Ryan had the kids load the dishes in the dishwasher and wipe down the counters. And they didn't argue. Huh. One request from him, and they complied. She, on the other hand, had to throw an entire speech and stoop to bribery to get them to do anything.

She'd made a chore chart with him, but doing their jobs was so much easier than spending an entire hour reminding them what they should do.

She'd planned to leave after breakfast, but the boys coerced her into a game of Frisbee.

While Carter took his midmorning nap, she and the boys played in the front yard. Zoe opted to stay in the house and practice handstands. How long would it be until she was trying out for cheerleading?

A tank top was a perfect summer outfit, but not enough protection from the midmorning sun as she ran after the Frisbee.

Halfway through the game, Ryan joined them, and somehow her body temperature kicked up another twenty degrees as they took turns tossing and catching the red flying disc.

"Okay, guys." She fanned herself with a hand when the game was over. "I need to get going."

"Can you first jump with us on the trampoline?" Josh asked, which was rare because Zoe always asked on behalf of her siblings.

"We need to let Destiny go." Ryan swiped his glistening forehead with the back of his hand.

"Okay." Josh's shoulders sagged, and turning him down bothered her. It might be the only time he'd ever ask.

All right. She jammed her hands on her hips and nodded. "I'll only jump for five minutes."

Ryan turned to leave. "I'll let you guys do that."

"Please, Uncle, come jump with us." Pete grabbed his hand and hung on it, swinging their arms.

"Really?" Ryan lifted his free hand, questioning. "We'll break the trampoline."

Pete stood in front of his uncle and gave him a breakdown as to why he should get on the trampoline. "Our trampoline can hold up to five hundred pounds. Let's pretend you and Destiny have at least..."

"Two hundred and eighty pounds," Josh called over his shoulder as he climbed the trampoline.

"Josh and I have one-eighty I think." Pete slapped his forehead. "Okay, so maybe not very accurate but close enough."

Ryan exchanged a glance with Destiny, trapped by his nephews' determination. He slapped Pete on the shoulder. "I think you and Josh will make good salesmen someday. It's not very safe with so many people on it, but it's a risk I'm willing to take as long as no one gets too wild—deal?"

When they nodded, he grinned. "Okay, salesmen, let's go jumping."

"Or surgeons," Destiny whispered for Ryan's ears alone. "Smart like their uncle."

A fresh hint of color mottled his neck as he shook his head. "I don't know where you get that information."

"I'm a great observer."

They jumped as they tossed a football to play catch, which lasted way longer than five minutes. She wasn't complaining, not when

Ryan's hands brushed over hers when she fought him off for the ball he tried to steal from her.

It was almost two when she said goodbye to the kids and promised to see them at church tomorrow.

"I won't be able to join you tomorrow." Ryan grimaced an apology. "I need to get some research done."

He'd said he had an early surgery Monday morning. "Don't worry. I'll come get the kids."

He rubbed the back of his neck, the grimace becoming a full-on cringe. "You're sure?"

"You'll get a lot more done when the house is quiet."

"You're the best!" His smile reminded her of his youngest nephew, full of innocent delight as he waved at her.

The kids stood beside Ryan, watching her hop in her car. She felt a deep hole—a gap widening as she peered at their faces through the rearview mirror. Oh, how she missed them already!

She needed to remember her job was temporary. Pretty soon their nanny would be back.

Uneasiness settled in her heart as thoughts of not being around Carter, Zoe, and the boys—Ryan—twisted things inside her.

There's a time for everything.... The Bible verse echoed in her mind. One day at a time was all she had to live for, and the assurance of seeing them early the next morning calmed her nerves. It also got her through the night until the next day when she returned to pick them up for church.

"HOW CAN I HELP?" RYAN asked as soon as he swung open the glass door for her.

He had enough to deal with. "You need to get your work done." Destiny followed him to the kitchen, then glanced next to his opened laptop by the wall counter, where several folders were spread wide open.

"I already woke up the kids. I just hope they're getting dressed."

"Don't worry." Despite not wanting to interfere, she could use the help. "I'll get their cereal ready if you don't mind calling them up to eat?"

"Got it."

Destiny poured cereal in the bowls and set the milk jug on the island before bounding upstairs to get Carter.

He was lying on his back, his eyes closed. He looked so peaceful, she dreaded interfering. She crouched, lifting him up, and rubbed his back slowly before changing his diaper and dressing him.

The kids were eating when she buckled Carter in his high chair.

Even though Carter had a bib, he still smeared his face and shirt with oatmeal. Note to self—feed him first, dress him later.

"Okay." She sighed. "Let's get you changed again."

His hair needed a rinse. She hefted him out of his high chair. "You got food in your hair too?"

"How can I help?" Ryan repeated and closed his laptop.

"Check on the kids to see if they're getting dressed." She could hear a ball bouncing off the wall and thumping back and forth.

After several minutes, with Carter cleaned up, she met Ryan downstairs. "The kids are already in the car." He then handed her a to-go coffee cup and an energy bar. "Just in case you forgot to eat."

She scooped it from him, touched by his thoughtfulness. Of course, he knew she skipped breakfast on fast-paced mornings when she had to rush out the door. "Thank you."

By the time she hoisted Carter in his infant seat and to the car, the older kids were already buckled in their seats.

"Can I go back and get my headband?" Zoe asked.

Destiny had taught her how to fix her own hair, which helped on rush mornings. "I'll go get it." She'd forgotten to bring Carter's milk.

She returned to the house, huffed downstairs to Zoe's room, and grabbed the first headband from the stash in her top drawer.

"Carter's milk," she mumbled to Ryan as she passed him.

"Church starts in five minutes." He eyed her, one brow rising. "Take your time driving."

Worry edged his eyes. Having his sister die in an accident gave him a good reason for his concern.

"I'll be careful." And she meant it. At least she tried not to go over the speed limit, even when she reached the stop signs in the church neighborhood.

Take your time driving. Ryan's face and his warning words rang in her mind. She stopped and waited at least two seconds at each stop sign, long enough to take two sips of her delicious coffee before lifting her foot off the brake. She made it to church twenty minutes late.

After taking the kids to their respective classes, she remembered Lucas was coming today. That's if he followed through as per his text last night. Retrieving her cell phone from her purse, she winced at two missed calls from him.

God, I really need help with this time-management thing. Not the best impression when I invited someone. She read two texts he'd sent.

I'm waiting in church. Hope you didn't stand me up on our first date.

She scurried to the sanctuary and peered over several heads as they listened to someone make announcements. One of the ushers asked if she needed help finding a place to sit.

"I'm meeting someone."

"Destiny."

She jerked, turning toward a hushed voice. Lucas's.

"Sorry I'm late," she whispered stepping beside him as he led them to where he'd been sitting before joining her.

Her heart raced, and she fanned herself when she sat. She needed to cool off from all the scurrying around.

Lucas was attentive through service. He even peered over to read through her Bible when the pastor prompted a reading.

"I'm so sorry again for being late," she said after church was dismissed.

"Seriously, don't beat yourself up." He adjusted the collar on the white button-down shirt he'd tucked into dress pants.

She relayed her morning dilemma as they waited in line to get Carter.

"You're very brave to take care of four kids."

Brave? Huh. Interesting way to put it.

Carter beamed. "Maa...ma...ma!"

When she reached for him, he dove from the child carer's hands and into Destiny's arms. "You missed me, little guy?"

He babbled, flapping his hands.

"I missed you, too."

"Somebody is excited to see you," Lucas said as they pressed through the crowded hallway of kids running and the parents she waved to when they got past.

After they'd gathered all the kids, Lucas left his car in the church parking lot and rode with her. He and the kids played a Would You Rather? question game on the way to meet Ryan at the gas station. They'd agreed to meet so he could take the kids home.

The kids remained in their seats while he walked her and Lucas to his Mercedes.

"Have fun." He handed her the keys. Carter's car seat base took up plenty of room in the back, which made it impossible to fit all the kids.

How he trusted her so much with his stuff baffled her. Good thing Jia and her husband were visiting her mom in China. Since they'd parked her car at the airport, Destiny could park Ryan's in the garage.

"Have fun playing Uncle Mom." Lucas wagged a warning finger. "PS, don't call Destiny if you have any questions. This is her day off."

"Just shut up." Ryan's tone was light. "Have fun eating whatever today because I'll be whipping you in golf on Wednesday."

Destiny tried to encourage him to do something fun for rejuvenation. Hence his Wednesday afternoon golf.

"There's a jar of food in the diaper bag. Carter can have that before his nap." She gave him last-minute reminders of Carter's schedule. "Don't hesitate to text if you need to."

"Don't you dare text." Lucas gave him a look.

"Watch out for this guy." Ryan addressed her. "If he's not afraid to threaten my life in front of you, that's a red flag right there."

Destiny chuckled, amazed by Ryan's easy manner with his friend. "Thanks for the warning."

He punched Lucas on the back before he strode back to the Highlander.

Finally alone with Lucas, she asked where he wanted to eat. Letting him choose the restaurant was the least she could do after making him wait for her at church.

"There's a Red Robin over there." He pointed to the restaurant sign in the nearby shopping center.

The dimly lit room buzzed with an afternoon crowd. They didn't wait long before a teenage girl with Goth-black hair matching her black outfit walked them to their table. Destiny's heels clicked on the hard floor as she settled into the booth. The loud Pac-Man pictures on the wall beside them made her think of the boys.

"So, that's what church life is all about?" Lucas smiled, leaning back and stretching his arm across the back of his booth. "It's not as bad as I thought."

She smoothed her yellow summer dress beneath her and tucked her feet together at the ankles. "What did you think it was like?"

"I used to think it was all judgy."

She'd sort of thought the same—until the day she was forced to step through those doors.

Their server brought a red basket of french fries and glasses of water before she took their orders.

Lucas ordered a mushroom burger with Swiss cheese, and she ordered a croissant sandwich.

"Can I have ranch for my fries, please?" she asked the server.

Lucas's eyes widened, and he slapped the table. "I can't eat my fries without ranch dressing!"

It wasn't a big deal for her because she rarely ate fries. Plus, she didn't know very many people to learn how they liked their french fries, but she had to be polite. "That's interesting."

Not making a show of praying, she closed her eyes and bowed her head. She then reached for a couple of fries from the basket, dipping one in the small cup of dressing.

The restaurant smelled tangy, scented with grilled meats and fried food, all making her excited for her food. She shifted more comfortably in the hard booth seat and asked about his work and his family.

"Haven't seen my mom in a while, but I think she's okay."

"Any brothers and sisters?" She wiggled her feet. The open-toed pumps she'd worn were pinching.

"I have an older brother, and a young sister who's still 'finding herself.' " He made air quotes. "She travels all over the world. How about you?"

She told him about Timon and their journey of group homes. "He's like a brother to me, though."

When their food was served, Lucas bit into his juicy hamburger. He closed his eyes and moaned in satisfaction.

She laughed, picking up her croissant. "I thought all doctors ate salads and lean meats."

"That would be your boss, not me." He spoke over a mouthful.

Talking about Ryan made her wonder how he was doing with the kids. She'd forgotten to ask if he'd had enough time to get his work done.

Would it be rude if she texted him? *Lucas wouldn't mind, I'm sure—they're friends after all.*

She dug her phone out of her purse. "Sorry, I need to text Ryan. I forgot to tell him Carter won't drink his milk cold. He prefers it warm."

"He'll figure it out."

"You're right." She set the phone back on the table and took her first bite.

When her phone vibrated, she leaped for it, assuming it was Ryan but the call from an unknown number stopped before its second ring.

Her disappointment that it wasn't Ryan must have shown.

Lucas shrugged. "Go ahead."

She winced at being rude. "I...also needed to ask if he needs me to watch the kids so he can finish his research, you know?" That was the truth.

"Trust me, he needs to figure out juggling things by himself. He will then appreciate all you do while he's at work."

Maybe she'd better let him figure things out. "I know he appreciates what I do." He'd told her several times.

"You know what?" She lifted her sandwich. "Forget Ryan. He'll be okay."

"I agree." Lucas nodded. "I'm glad you're having a break."

She'd better explain why she invited him to church. "I hope you don't feel like I trapped you into coming?" she said. "When you said you'd never been in church before and had no reason to, I thought I'd invite you." She'd wanted to put an end to his date request. "I didn't think you'd come."

He raised a brow hopefully, scratching his clean-shaven jaw. "Good. Because this is not my idea of a first date."

Destiny arched a brow and sipped her water. Surely, he wouldn't take things too seriously? She wasn't ready to date yet. Lucas was charming and handsome with that killer smile, but her boss was the only one who made her long for a relationship.

She readjusted her feet beneath the table, taking the pressure off her toes. The yellow patent leather pumps weren't broken in yet. An impulse buy with her former employee discount. "What kind of date did you have in mind?"

His face serious, he folded his arms on the table and leaned into her, wide brown eyes searching hers. "If it's okay, we have this banquet in a couple of weeks. It's our annual staff party. We do it in July instead of December. There's dancing...." He continued with the list of things the party entailed, but he'd lost her when he said dancing.

If only Ryan had invited her. He would always see her as the nanny he could join in and play with and make a great team with the kids. Nothing more.

"Is this where we break up before our first date?"

Lucas's words pulled her from her thoughts and she formed a quick smile. "Did you say there's dancing?"

"A lot of dancing." He swayed his body from side to side. "I love dancing. This is the only time I get to show off my moves. Unlike Ryan, who never makes it to the dance floor every year."

The corners of her lips lifted, picturing Ryan on the dance floor. What would it be like to get him to shake it up a little?

"I guess the smile means that you like dancing too?"

"Love it." Hopefully, she was giving the right response since Ryan consumed half her brain.

"Plus, I promised you a date if you came to church with me." Lunch had been her idea. "Except I have to ask Ryan and make sure he's okay with someone else watching the kids."

She would take them to Holly's house—if she was available and up for watching four more kids. After the banquet, she'd make things clear between her and Lucas. Her heart was with someone else, and if she kept her hands busy, it would only lessen her chances to get the man of her dreams.

CHAPTER 16

The smell of nail polish remover permeated the bathroom. Destiny scrunched her nose and turned on the fan to tone down the harsh scent. In preparation for tonight's banquet, Zoe had helped Destiny paint her nails in a soft peach color. Destiny had painted Zoe's nails in return while the boys played Minecraft downstairs.

A closing door and the sound of footsteps on the stairs brought butterflies to her stomach. The confirmation of why the butterflies happened came when she looked up and her eyes collided with Ryan's.

Her body tingled when he slowed and held her gaze. She'd forgotten they had another person in the room until Zoe gushed, "Wow! You look very handsome, Uncle."

Ryan cleared his throat and patted at the suit that fit his lean frame so perfectly. "Thank you, sweetheart."

"What do you think?" He glanced at Destiny, lifting his hands in a gesture. His eyes popped with the blue shirt he wore underneath the dark jacket.

"Perfect," she whispered.

Zoe's knees hit the floor, and she spoke to Carter. She pressed a button on the toy, and it burst into a cow sound, sending Carter into a fit of giggles.

Ryan strode closer and crouched, patting Carter's hair. "See you later."

"You're leaving already?" Zoe sprang up and threw her hands around Ryan for a hug.

"I'll see you tonight, though. Have fun playing with your friend." When he turned to Destiny, he raised a brow. "See you soon?"

She caught a tag dangling out through his collar. He wore the shirt she'd given him for his birthday!

"Wait." She leaned over, running a finger around the inside of it. She could grab scissors, but she was thinking of efficiency. She tugged at the string to snap the tag, but it wouldn't budge.

"Maybe bend a little." Her tiptoes were getting tired with his extra height.

He did as asked.

Leaning to the side of his neck, she placed her mouth against the tag and bit it off with her front teeth. Her fingers brushed his warm flesh, and she tried to ignore his fresh scent. Was it eucalyptus? She pulled back when the tag tore off, then showed it off. "Got it!"

"Oh...I..." he stuttered. His neck colored a deep red.

"Uncle, your face is red." Zoe pointed out innocently.

He fiddled with his tie. "It's quite hot."

Without glancing at Destiny or Zoe, he reached for his keys from the counter. "All right. See you there." He reminded her to drive carefully.

Destiny spent most of the extra hour and a half in front of the mirror, fidgeting with her hair. She could only design her hair in so many ways, but with Zoe's interest in her evening, she insisted Destiny add a white ribbon flower to the side. How could she say no?

"I got it," Zoe said, clasping the silk fabric to Destiny's hair.

While Destiny twirled in front of the mirror, Zoe rummaged through her closet, spilling all her heels. Carter yanked her dresses from the bed and covered his face to play peekaboo.

"You should wear these." Zoe brandished a pair of high-heeled pink sandals.

"Did I tell you that I have to dance?" Destiny had already picked out her shoes, but Zoe wasn't content with her choice.

"How about these, then?" Cream wasn't too off, but they were still high for dancing. Being a wide heel, they might be okay. She stole the sandals from her. "You know what, I think these will be perfect. You should be my designer."

Zoe beamed, her big eyes lighting up. "I love all your shoes and your pretty dresses. When I get bigger, can I wear some of your dresses?"

She'd tried on Destiny's dresses earlier as if she was having a fashion show of her own. It would be cool to have a little girl to share her clothes with. Destiny responded "of course" before thinking about how short her time here would be.

Even though she'd had a decent salary before losing her job, she'd bought most of her clothes on end-of-season bargain racks. Working at the shoe store, she'd put her employee discount to good use and been able to pick out fabulous deals from discontinued products. Plus, showing off the newest trends had gotten her better commissions as the ladies fell in love with her shoes.

She stood before the mirror, the full dress hit slightly below the knee. She had Ryan to impress—uh, rather *Lucas*.

"You look so pretty." Zoe clapped. "Will you dance with Uncle?"

Did she read into Destiny's heated looks with Ryan? "Um... I'll be dancing with Lucas." If Ryan asked her to dance, though... No, he wouldn't. "But I might dance with anyone else who needs a dance partner."

She fed Carter an afternoon snack, grateful Holly had offered to feed the kids dinner.

As usual, getting out the door with four kids took longer than she'd planned. After retrieving the board games Josh wanted to take with him and unearthing Zoe's missing slime, she was going to be late. She glanced at the dashboard. It was five twenty-five. The event would be starting in five minutes.

With no intention to navigate downtown's one-way streets, she handed Josh her phone. "Can you look up the Uber app for me, please?" She rolled through a yellow light before hitting the highway.

She then gave Josh instructions on how to use the coupon to book an Uber to pick her up at Holly's house.

THE BANQUET TOOK PLACE in an exquisite downtown hotel ballroom. Waiters passed exotic appetizers and fancy champagne flutes, but Ryan declined every time. He shifted his stance.

Partially listening to one of their oncologists execute his retirement plan, which was three years away, Ryan kept from shifting his feet again. The other half of his brain coordinated with his eyes pinned to the entrance for Destiny's arrival. Seeing all his colleagues dressed up in suits and cocktail dresses, as opposed to the scrubs, was strange.

The announcer spoke through the microphone, urging everyone to make their way to the buffet, and Ryan joined the line to the savory scents. He'd need food to strengthen him for a torturous evening of watching Lucas with Destiny.

He scooped a salad and salmon onto his plate. No carbs, unless Destiny offered them. He added a couple of bacon-wrapped dates that he'd declined during cocktail hour.

He sat three tables away from the entrance for two reasons. One—to eat right away. Two—see Destiny walk in through the door. In a habit he'd learned from her, he closed his eyes, but then realized he had no idea how to pray. *Thank You for the food.* Yes, something along those lines. *Amen.*

He forked his first bite of smoked salmon and savored it as it melted in his mouth.

"You think Destiny stood me up?"

Lucas's voice sounded just as the chair scraped the floor. Ryan's plan to watch Destiny had just been ambushed. Lucas set his food and a glass of red wine on the table.

"By now, you should know she's a person of her word." Good, no edge crept into his tone. "She says she'll be here, so she will show eventually." *She never breaks her word, and she never keeps time.* But no need to tell Lucas.

Ryan was tempted to join the beverage line so he could drown himself in alcohol. Perhaps it would distract him from Destiny chatting and dancing with his best friend.

"You're sure you don't want to date her?" Lucas interrupted, narrowing his gaze on Ryan.

I'm in love with her. "I'm sure," he mumbled, shifting his gaze to the tea light candles in the center of their round table.

"When I first asked her out, I wanted to make you jealous, so you'd claim her." Lucas leaned back, tugged at his tie. "But if you're still waiting for Katie to fall in love with your kids, I'm going to kick things up with Destiny."

Lucas was never the steady guy in romance. "By kicking, you mean?"

His friend shrugged and sliced into his steak. "She's the real deal—the marrying type, you know? Plus, she and I have a lot of things in common." He lifted the fork to his mouth and spoke over a mouthful. "We both like our fries dipped in ranch. Can you believe that? What does that tell you?"

Both were great dancers, too.

Ryan's stomach dropped at the thought of his friend dating Destiny. Would his friendship with Lucas remain the same? What about his friendship with Destiny? She was his friend at this point. She was the reason he looked forward to getting home and talking to her before his bedtime. She was the person on his mind before he fell asleep and as soon as he woke.

The muscles in his temples tingled. Not a headache, he hoped as he forced his salad down in silence.

Two more people joined their table, and while Lucas engaged the couple in conversation, Ryan was in no mood to talk.

Just as his gaze wandered toward the door, she emerged. His jaw paused midchew, and his heart jolted.

From the way she was fanning herself with her hand, he could only imagine the evening she'd endured to get here. She'd probably run back to the house for Carter's bottle or Pete's missing shoe. How many yellow lights had she run through to get the kids to her friend's house?

As she scanned the crowd, her eyes cut across the room, then to the front to him. He held her gaze for a second, the chatter suddenly distant, except for the thumping of his heart.

Darn it!

Lucas slapped the table and sprang to his feet, interrupting the moment. "There she is."

Ryan shook his head, blinking back to his half-eaten plate. "Ah, Destiny...what?"

He was going nuts.

The server refilled their water glasses and cleared Lucas's plate.

"Man! She's beautiful! Got to make an impression." Lucas patted his hair. "How do I look?"

Ryan rolled his eyes in a way he hadn't since Bree had asked before her dates with Gavin. "Fine."

While Lucas walked toward her, Ryan's gaze swept over her, his mouth going dry.

The royal-blue dress fit her in all the right places as if it was specifically tailored. The lighting sparkled off the detailed sequined bodice, and the simple diamonds on her ears complemented her attire. She was the guest of honor for the night.

He could only agree with Lucas. Destiny was beautiful—Ryan already knew she held both internal and external beauty.

She finally recognized Lucas approaching her.

Ryan lifted his water and gulped it down. Better to drown his face in the glass than watch Lucas hug her or kiss her on the cheek—maybe even kiss her lips.

A wrenching twisted in his stomach as one more person joined the table. Before he could register, it was Destiny.

"Hey, Ryan."

He jumped to his feet, almost toppling the chair. Where was he going? Uh...

He gave a curt nod, pretending not to look at her vibrant curls and the white flower highlighting them. "Oh." He ran a hand in his hair and sat. "Hi."

Lucas pulled out the chair next to Ryan and ushered Destiny to sit.

"What did you order?" She slid into the chair and eyed Ryan's plate.

Her tantalizing scent and nearness made it hard to get his racing heart under control.

"Salad and..."

"This doesn't look like salad to me." Her gaze pinned on the two leftover appetizers, she chatted about the different foods she'd seen on people's plates. A nervous habit. "Can I try one?"

"Bacon-wrapped dates." He nodded toward the still heavily laden tables. "You could get a fresh one at the buffet."

She grabbed the white cloth napkin and reached for one of the pieces from his plate, then bit into it. Soft lashes fluttered against her tawny cheeks, and her throat worked as she closed her eyes to savor it. "Mmmm...this is so good."

Mesmerized, he watched her lick her full lips, wondering what it would feel like to kiss them. Man, there wasn't another woman in the room like her—another woman in the world.

Someone tested the microphone, and several chairs and tables were being moved to one side.

"Let's go get you a plate." Lucas touched her elbow. "If they ran out of bacon-wrapped dates, I'll hunt down the event chef."

Destiny pushed back her chair and rose, her amazing eyes alight. "What else do they have?"

"They don't have fries, but they have some roasted potatoes." Lucas mentioned the list of foods being served. "We better hurry before the dancing starts."

Ryan dared to peek long enough to see Lucas's hand hit the small of her back. He shifted in his chair when Tony, the dermatologist, called his name upon taking a seat at their table.

Twenty minutes later, music blared, and people danced underneath the dim lights. Ryan was fixated on Lucas and Destiny's location as they swayed at the edge of the circle.

It was either Ryan's judgment from being a terrible dancer, but Lucas and Destiny had a lot of things in common, dancing being one of them. Her full dress swayed when the song hit a crescendo. Lucas tossed her out and rolled her body back into him before he dipped her toward the ground. Even from here, Ryan could imagine her laughter and sense her delight.

Another song played, and Lucas swung her back and forth into its rhythm with a confident ease that made Ryan ache to learn to dance. Whistles and claps erupted from the onlookers. Destiny and Lucas were the center of attention—the couple for the night.

Ryan pushed back his chair, half rising in his seat. He couldn't bear this any longer. He was suddenly hot and bothered by the outcome.

He could go home and call it a night, but she'd be asking why he left early. He needed air.

On his way out, his gaze caught Destiny's. She smiled at him, and he consoled himself that her smiles with Lucas seemed less warm than the ones she shared with him. Finally on the balcony, he loosened his tie, welcoming the gentle breeze as he peered over the sky-line twinkling with lights.

"Taking a break?"

He jumped at the intrusion. "Katie?"

She brushed back her cropped hair and stood next to him, lean-ing over the railing. "Destiny can sure dance. Seems Lucas found his match."

"Yeah...he did." He spoke with less interest in the conversation.

"You look happy these days. Seems you have the parenting thing down."

Thanks to Destiny, he found himself smiling during the day whenever he thought of her quirky ways. "Yeah, the kids are pretty happy."

Katie cleared her throat. "I miss you."

Ahhh...what? Not the time or place. "I see you at the hospital." Much safer response than the truth. He'd been busy falling in love with Destiny. Without knowing it, Destiny had picked up his broken heart.

"You know what I mean."

"No...I don't."

She reached for his hand, and while he should feel the sparks he once felt, there was nothing. "I was thinking...maybe we should give things another chance."

He eased his hand free, sliding it out of hers, and stepped back to lean against the wall, then thrust his hands in his pockets where she couldn't access them. "Katie, I'm a parent now, and you don't want kids."

"As long as we have a nanny."

Ryan chuckled more sarcastically than he intended. As a family, there'd be times they took vacations and trips to give their nanny a break. He tried not to think of Destiny and Carter's relationship—a mother-son relationship. The way she protected the kids, took care of them *and* Ryan, always making sure he didn't go to bed hungry... The list was endless.

"Ryan?"

Right. "Yeah?"

"I was asking if you'd like to go out sometime this week—I mean the next time you get off early."

He looked forward to getting home early and playing with Destiny and the kids, whatever games they had planned. If he got home after the kids were in bed, he loved talking to her as they binge-watched *Mountain Men* while munching SkinnyPop. He'd even watched a couple of rom-coms with her after insisting they watch something she liked.

"I'm busy, Katie. You and I are..."

"Done?"

Exactly. "I have a family now." He drew his hands from his pockets and gestured toward the party. "I better go back inside." *To torture myself, ogling the woman I can't have.*

Katie followed him. A fast-paced song was winding down. The moment of his undoing was when Destiny walked toward him and tapped him on the shoulder.

"Come dance." As if she just realized Katie was there, she said, "Oh! Hi, Katie."

"Hi."

"That necklace is gorgeous." As she spoke, both hands clasped behind her back, Destiny swayed slightly—as if the music had a grip on her she hadn't shaken. "I wanted to talk Ryan into dancing."

Katie glanced up at Ryan, tight-lipped. "Yeah, I'm sure he could use some dancing."

No way. "I don't dance." He'd end up stepping on her sandal straps, or worse, squashing her toes.

Katie excused herself with an awkward half-wave, saying she'd see them around.

Destiny crossed her arms and arched a brow. "You mean like you don't know how to, or you don't want to?"

"Both."

She gazed at him, unconvinced. "You're wrong." Her hands dropped to the side of her dress, and she shook her head, swaying from side to side, keeping up with the music. She then leaned closer. "Everybody dances. *You* danced to the Spider-Man theme song with the kids."

Not one of his better moments. And *only* because she triggered something in him to let loose. "That was different." A silly song she and the kids had talked him into dancing.

He heaved out a heavy breath when she reached her hand out for his. She wasn't giving up. She *never* gave up.

The longer he ignored her outstretched hand, the more attention he drew.

"Dance with me, please." Her gorgeous face glowed in the light. Her eyes were dancing enough for the both of them. Who in their right mind could refuse her anything? That's if anyone could stay in their right mind around her.

Fine. He took her hand, and they joined the dancers on the floor. Lucas was currently dancing with someone else.

Ryan and Destiny spun around, her hands warm and soft clasped in his. Her presence was in the room's very air—her vibrancy was lethal.

She felt good in his arms, her hands now resting on his shoulders. He breathed in the coconut blending with the exotic spicy scent she always wore. It teased his senses. It was the sweetest kind of torture....

"You're dancing just fine."

"You're just being nice."

The song ended, and it was practical for him to let go of her. But he didn't want to. She didn't attempt to move either when another slow song started.

She met his eyes once, and something—a mix of curiosity and longing—flared in hers, stirring the same emotions in him. For a moment, he forgot to breathe.

"I forgot my deodorant." She spoke breathlessly. "I hope I don't stink."

She was probably as nervous as he was. If she smelled this good with no deodorant, then he didn't want to find out what she smelled like with it. "You smell...amazing."

His hands started shaking, his nerves tingled with fire, and when she rested her head on his shoulder, the action warmed his senses. Relief and regret waltzed through him when the final notes died away.

"See? You did good." She patted his shoulders, then brushed at them as if sweeping away all evidence that she'd held on to him. "You're a great dance partner, too."

She had no idea his feet were about to fall off. He fumbled with his loosened tie. He was sweating profusely, and it had nothing to do with the music. "Thanks. You're a great dancer, too."

"Do you think you can give me a ride to Holly's house?"

His eyebrows shot up. "How did you get here?"

"I took an Uber. Didn't want to drive downtown."

He didn't want to ask why she didn't ask Lucas. He was too selfish to want her and Lucas in the car alone—plus, he'd seen his friend drinking. "I can drive you."

"I'm going to say goodbye to Lucas and tell him we'll get going in a few. Will that be okay?"

It wasn't okay to talk to Lucas, but...Ryan was driving her back. It was far better. "Perfect."

He wiped sweat from his forehead and returned to his table, gulping the entire glass of water that was refilled in his absence. He'd never danced through an entire song in his whole life. He shook his head, surprised at the things Destiny talked him into doing—dancing, jumping on trampolines, playing with water guns, going to church....

The drive started with a contented silence. Ryan was very aware of Destiny's nearness, if his heated body was any indication. It didn't matter that the car was blasting cool air.

He should never talk when nervous, but he did. "Are you and Lucas getting serious?"

Too late to take that question back.

"He's a neat guy," she said. "But...you should ask him that question."

Was that hesitation in her tone?

He decided to drop that conversation when she asked if he and Katie reconciled.

"We work together." He tightened his grip on the steering wheel. He never should have dated someone he worked with. If it was going to be awkward in the hospital, how horrible would it be if he tried to date Destiny? "It's a work relationship and nothing more."

"Oh..." She shrugged. "I'm...sorry you broke up?"

"An apology with a question mark, how genuine." He used her words from weeks ago.

She chuckled and reached for his phone from the console, lifting the light to his face. "Let me see if your eyes are swollen. Any sign of a broken heart? Hmm..."

Ryan kept his gaze on the road. His cheeks almost hurt from grinning as he suppressed his own chuckle.

After dropping her off at Holly's house, it being Destiny's evening off, he let her take his Mercedes while he drove the kids home in the Highlander.

"We'll pick you up in the morning for church," he said.

"I'll be ready."

He doubted it. He put the kids to bed when he got home. He then took the longest shower, thinking of Destiny in his arms while they danced. He could still smell her scent on him. Should he tell her how he felt? He was pretty sure she felt the same way, but Lucas stood in the way.

She'd dodged Ryan's question when he asked if they were dating. *He's a neat guy.... But you should ask him that question.* Her voice echoed in his mind. Huh!

He'd better wait in silence, and if he and Destiny were meant to be, things would work out in the end.

Instead of going to bed like he should, he grabbed his phone when he thought of the pictures he'd taken of Destiny and the kids. His screen saver was the picture of her with Zoe and Carter on the concert night.

His phone chirped an incoming text, and his heart leaped. *Destiny?*

His smile vanished. His former nanny, Valeria, texted instead.

I'm home. If it's okay, I can return to work on Monday.

He dropped the phone on his nightstand. He hadn't heard from Valeria since she'd left the country. Hopefully, her dad was fine. But no matter what, she'd just have to enjoy some extra time off.

He needed another week or two to let Destiny know she didn't have a job anymore.... Good grief, he needed eternity with Destiny.

He flopped his head to the pillow. *I can tell Destiny how I feel now that she won't be working for me.* He shifted his body to the side. *She's with Lucas.*

Ugh...

Conflicting emotions stirred his mind all night. How was Carter going to manage without her? What about Zoe and the boys? They might be okay, but Destiny had changed everything.

I can't keep both of them. He couldn't afford to give two nannies decent pay. He'd have to tell Destiny about Valeria tomorrow.

CHAPTER 17

Destiny's week flew by. Her welling emotions rising with each passing day didn't help. The thought of leaving the kids, being away from them for a week was hard enough—but forever? She'd find a job and may not have time to visit whenever she wanted to.

Even though Ryan said he'd talk to the nanny and let Destiny see the kids anytime she wanted to, she didn't feel comfortable interfering with the other woman's schedule.

Besides Ryan helping her write her resume, she'd done all the kids' favorite things and made their favorite meals this week, cherishing each moment as if it were her last—because each moment was building toward her last.

Sitting on a rocking chair in his room, she clung to Carter. His soft face glistened beneath the dim night light. He looked so peaceful as his chest rose and fell in a steady rhythm.

Lately, she put him down before he fell asleep so he could put himself to sleep, but tonight, she'd let him fall asleep in her arms.

The thumping footsteps clambering on the stairs reminded her of the other kids needing her attention.

Besides eating their favorite foods, they'd also been going to bed much later than ten, wanting to play board games or family icebreaker questions.

Tonight the kids wanted to play hide-and-seek.

Even Josh— being twelve didn't hinder him from playing any given game. Destiny was taken by how polite and delightful the kids were.

She planted a soft kiss on Carter's forehead and lifted him to the crib, laying him gently on his back. He would eventually flop to his tummy in the night.

Zoe, humming one of her special tunes, was waiting outside Carter's room when Destiny stepped out and closed the door. "Ready?"

The girl beamed, her hair bounced off her shoulders as she nodded.

They met the boys in the living room. "We can't hide upstairs." Destiny prepped the kids so they didn't wake their brother.

Just as they decided who was counting first, the back door shut. Her heart soared, and her stomach tightened into a ball of anxiety. Warmth flooded through her, the same way it did every time he came home lately.

"Uncle Ryan is home!" Zoe rushed after her brothers as they dashed for the back hallway, no doubt hugging their uncle.

Destiny suppressed a twinge of jealousy since she couldn't freely throw her arms around him for an embrace. She could still smell him ever since the dance. She'd replayed their conversation that night until each word they spoke to each other was engraved in her mind. She still imagined his arms wrapped around her. Twirling around in his arms like some kind of fairy princess was like pouring lighter fluid on a slow-burning fire. Her feelings for him were getting out of hand.

Surely, by now, Lucas had told him they weren't dating.

At the dance, she'd told Lucas she didn't want to mislead him. He'd chuckled and said, "I know...I have a confession to make myself. You see...I think you're beautiful, and I'd have you in a heartbeat. But...I might ruin a friendship by doing so."

Confused, she'd pressed to know why he'd asked her out then.

"I wanted to make Ryan jealous. He won't admit it but..." He'd shrugged. "I don't need to tell you this because you already know."

She knew where the conversation was going, so she didn't ask any more questions. Despite the signs that Ryan liked her, he'd not attempted to say or do anything.

Maybe it's all in my mind, and he doesn't look at me in the romantic way I imagine him to.

She set the daydreaming aside to fix him a light meal. A spinach-avocado salad. Thank goodness for Pinterest where there was always a new recipe. After learning he didn't have time to eat dinner at the hospital, she started fixing dinner for him and storing it in the refrigerator. In fact, she rarely went to bed until he was home—unless he worked night shifts, which was rare.

"Hi." He loosened his tie and clanked his keys in the porcelain bowl.

"How was your day?" Her voice sounded off.

"Good, yours?"

"Can you play hide-and-seek with us?" Zoe asked, saving Destiny from sounding odd.

"Destiny is playing, too," Josh chimed in, taking Ryan's hand in his.

"The more the merrier," Pete added.

With the look of adoration he gave the kids, he wasn't going to say no.

"Let me shower first."

"Eat, too." Destiny set his salad on the island.

"Thank you." His appreciative smile turned her way.

Unable to maintain his gaze, she filled an empty glass with ice and water from the fridge dispenser.

Thirty minutes later, the game of hide-and-seek began.

Destiny counted first, then Ryan, and before long, it was Josh.

Destiny ran to the hall closet—a great hiding spot because it was small enough for her to hide behind the hanging coats. Once inside, she eased the door closed and scooted behind the coats.

"Careful."

She jumped, and a shiver rippled through her spine at the fresh familiar scent—Ryan's.

Unsure where he was standing in the dark, she moved backward to the far corner, only to land into a warm body. Strong arms gripped her bare arms. If she'd expected this encounter, she would've worn a long-sleeved shirt rather than a sleeveless top.

"I didn't want to startle you," he whispered against her neck.

She'd dreamt of being in his arms, but now, she had no idea what to do. With her heart beating wildly, she broke out in goose bumps at the light drag of his fingertips trailing on her arm. His heart thumped against her back—either that or she was hallucinating. Probably from dehydration. She needed a glass of ice water as soon as she left the closet.

"Looks like we have the same hiding spot," he said.

Her tongue was frozen, her mind slush. She had no idea where she was. Except for the feel of her knees threatening to buckle.

She swallowed, leaning back her head. Then she closed her eyes, sniffing his soft breath one more time before she managed a breathy whisper. "I...Josh will..." There'd be some explaining if Josh found them in the closet together.

"I'll go instead." Having the same concern as her, he dropped his hands. Destiny beat him to it and walked out of the closet just as Josh announced, "Ready or not here I come."

He grinned at Destiny, wagging a finger. "Found you!"

Needing a moment to calm her racing heart, she tried to play dumb as if she'd been looking for a hiding place.

In the kitchen, her hands shook as she filled her glass with ice water. Something happened between her and Ryan in the closet. She had no idea what to call it, but she had the feeling their relationship was in the early stages of becoming something more. When she went to bed that night, despite the day's exhaustion, she lay awake wondering how she could survive another day without knowing what Ryan thought about her.

EVER SINCE RYAN HAD attended the children's program at church, he'd made it a habit to attend church on Sundays whenever he wasn't scheduled to work.

This Sunday was emotional as he listened to the pastor extend an invitation after his sermon. "Today is the day of salvation. What are you waiting for? Raise your hand if you want this new life."

His heart thundered at the conviction. Everything in him shouted for him to raise his hand. He could only attribute the emotions to this being Destiny's last Sunday. It ignited all the things he'd learned from her. She was transparent in her mistakes and openly shared how much she needed God's help to get her through life's challenges. He was fine before she came along, but boy, was he going to miss her!

Ever since their moment in the closet three days ago, he'd decided to ignore it like nothing had happened between them. Seemed she'd decided the same thing. Yet her very being seemed to be in the air he breathed.

He turned to look down at Destiny. Her eyes were closed, but then everyone around had their heads bowed. If he lifted his hand, nobody would ever know. But... He swiped at his forehead as he broke out in a sweat. He then rubbed his hands up and down over his thighs.

He exhaled when a man in his late twenties stepped up to the altar to strum the guitar and announced the church service was over.

At the kids' request, Destiny agreed to spend Sunday afternoon with them. They ate at a fast-food joint before heading to the east side of Denver and driving past the house where Destiny grew up. She pointed out the homes where she used to play with friends.

While passing by the zoo, the kids wanted to stop by and see the animals. Destiny thought it was a good idea, though Ryan protested taking her day off. But, just like the kids, he didn't want her to leave. She'd merely shrugged and pointed out that she was about to have lots of days off.

Indeed, summer was winding down, and Destiny's last day with them would be tomorrow. Would he see her again?

Not unless you tell her how you feel.

Lucas had told him he and Destiny broke up, saying Ryan was the only reason he was backing off. "When we went biking and you described Destiny by the warmth of her eyes," Lucas had said, "I knew you liked her. You don't notice a woman's eyes unless you have a thing for her."

Whatever. Ryan still hadn't believed his friend would give up Destiny without a fight. But Lucas's words haunted him—"If you let her slip out of your hands, we'll never be friends again."

Then Lucas revealed his dirty trick of why he'd initially pursued Destiny.

Now that she wasn't dating anyone, Ryan had no idea how to go about it.

He'd pleaded with her to stay, planning to pay for two nannies. But she said he was just being nice and she didn't want him to incur extra expenses on her account.

The next day, he performed a minor surgery at the volunteer hospital, called patients, went over patient charts—all the while dealing with conflicting emotions and counting down the minutes to get home.

During his lunch break, he texted Destiny to remind her not to cook anything. He wanted to take her and the kids out to dinner.

He got home just after seven—later than he'd planned. As usual, his kids' happy squeals sounded through the house. A warm smell of something homemade teased his nose. The sight in the kitchen tightened his chest—come tomorrow, everything would be different.

Carter babbled in his high chair, his voice competing with the gospel music playing through Destiny's phone. All three kids were leaning into Destiny, their heads touching, as they looked at the pan on the counter.

"Hey, buddy." Ryan touched his head to Carter's, and the squirt giggled before his wet hands found Ryan's cheek.

"Hi, Uncle!" Ryan turned at the sound of Josh's voice.

Destiny, beautiful in her orange sundress, spun around. His gaze held hers, and she smiled before voicing a breathless welcome home.

Zoe and Pete hugged him. Ryan crossed over to set his bag and keys on the counter.

"Check it out." Josh pointed to the pan. "We made Rice Krispie treats."

Ryan exchanged a glance with Destiny. "I hope I can still take you out tonight—it being our last night together."

When she smiled playfully, he couldn't hold back his own smile.

She tilted her head to one side. "You make it sound as if I'll never see you guys."

Good. She intended to see them again.

"Ready to go?"

"The restaurant will rob us of our time." Destiny gestured toward the clock. "Let's order pizza instead."

"Pizza!" the kids chimed.

Unable to argue, he reached for his phone to order through Uber Eats. "I'll go shower and be back before the pizza is delivered."

After dinner, Destiny put Carter to bed at almost eight. They all gathered around the island to play a UNO card game as they gobbled the Rice Krispie treats.

The kids dragged the night by asking to play one board game after another until Ryan put an end to it. "Looks like I won the most games tonight."

"Oh, yeah?" Destiny's brow shot up. "I see who's competitive around here."

Josh slammed his hands on his hips. "If we play two more games, I will win."

Ryan knew the trick. The kids didn't want Destiny to leave, and he didn't want her driving back to Denver this late.

"It's getting late for you guys," she told the kids, urging them to brush their teeth. Then to Ryan, she said, "And it's a work night for you."

He touched her hand. "Stay the night." Oh! That didn't sound right. "I–I mean, it's past ten and it's not safe driving and your room's still..."

Her head shake stopped his pathetic babbling.

"It will be easier if I leave tonight." Sadness seeped through her eyes. "Everything has a beginning and an end you know."

He closed his hands over hers, squeezing tight as if he could hold her there. "Now who's talking like we will never see each other again?"

When they prayed with the kids, tears were streaming down Destiny's cheeks. Zoe clung to her arm throughout the kids' sweet prayers thanking God for Destiny. Ryan's throat felt like a piece of glass was stuck in it.

Watching the kids say goodbye was unbearable. Surely, he could tell Valeria she wasn't needed anymore. But he couldn't do that to someone mourning her father.

"Please don't go." Tears welled in Zoe's eyes. "I love you."

"I"—Destiny's voice cracked, and her delicate throat worked as she swallowed—"love you too."

The boys hugged her, and their sad faces crushed Ryan's heart.

With the kids in bed, Ryan and Destiny returned upstairs. He would be performing an eight-hour procedure tomorrow, the more reason to be asleep by now, but he didn't want to go to bed—or be anywhere without Destiny.

"I already made lunches for you and the kids tomorrow."

"You shouldn't drive this late." The idea of her driving in the dark—the idea of her leaving—left him ill.

Her eyes, the blue-green color so fluid already, were wet and shining, and the sight gripped his chest.

"I'll go grab my stuff." She left for her room and returned with a neon-green duffel bag—Zumba written in dancing letters on its side.

His hands brushed with hers when he took it out of her hand. "I'll walk you out."

He pulled out an envelope from his pocket and handed it to her. "Thank you so much." His gruff voice rasped against the emotion closing his throat. "We'll miss you around here."

"Same here." She wiped tears from her face. "You shouldn't pay me when I didn't work the entire month this month."

"You still worked." With only one week left in July, Ryan paid her three months of her salary. He'd tucked the money in an envelope to avoid her arguing, yet she was still arguing!

He walked her out to the sidewalk by her yellow Bug and slid her bag into the passenger seat. He then thrust his hands in the pockets of his athletic shorts.

The security light illuminated her soft features. His fingers itched to touch her glowing face, the luxuriant skin he imagined to be as soft as silk.

She crossed the asphalt and stepped in his space, wrapping her arms around him. "Thank you...for everything." Her warm breath tickled his throat, awaking each nerve in him.

By the time he got his hands out of his pockets to return the hug, she'd dropped her hands and stepped back.

For a second, she just stood there, and his heart hammered. He studied her glossy lips, their shape outlined by the light. *Tell her.*

"Destiny..." he whispered and stepped closer, capturing her hand, He squeezed it, letting his thumb trace a slow circle on her wrist. *I'm in love with you.* That didn't seem right. What if she felt awkward at his confession? "I'm glad you came into our lives.... Please stay in touch."

"You can count on that." Her expression grew so soft, he gave in to the urge to cup her cheek.

Without meeting his gaze, she spoke, her voice as soft as her expression. "Please send me pictures of the kids. Have them call me whenever possible." She sniffled. "Carter..."

She swallowed, no doubt crying. This was not easy.

"We'll text and call you every night." There had to be some way he could convince her to stay! He'd always considered himself a smart man. How could he not figure this out? They stood without speaking until he glanced at the twinkling stars blanketing the sky.

Unable to utter the words he should, he breathed the sweet scent he would miss terribly. Before he told himself to walk away, he swallowed the lump in his throat and cupped the back of her head, pressing a kiss to her forehead. "'Nite."

If he didn't walk away, he was less than one second from kissing her.

She lifted her hand to wave. "See you around."

When she got in her car, Ryan watched her drive away, suddenly engulfed by emptiness, before he even walked back into the quiet house.

CHAPTER 18

Destiny's absence didn't go unnoticed during the following week. Everything went back to normal, both at home and at work. Normal meant a timely schedule for Ryan getting to work and a clean house waiting at the end of the day.

He'd seen Destiny at church last Sunday, and he'd intended to leave the kids with her so he could get home and catch up on notes from Saturday's hospital cases, but he'd ended up hanging out with her and the kids instead.

After church, she had them over to her house—Jia's house. Ryan's counselor was still visiting her family in China. Destiny grilled chicken, hamburgers, and corn on the grill for their lunch. They then went to one of the summer concerts in the park that afternoon.

The long summer evening stretched into the night as they sprawled out on a blanket listening to the eighties' rock music.

The kids sat on a separate blanket, munching all sorts of unhealthy food, including butter-covered popcorn and ice-cream cones they'd bought from the food vendors.

While they switched bands and the music stopped, Ryan was anxious to talk to Destiny. It was almost nine, the summer sky was giving way to full darkness, their time together was almost over. "Had any job interviews yet?"

"Yes, I interviewed as an admin at a law firm downtown." She grinned up at him. "I hope my boss is as nice as my ex-boss."

"Your ex-boss was nice?" Maybe this conversation could lead somewhere.

She wrinkled her face. "I'm not telling you more about my ex-boss.... By the way, I used you as my reference too."

"If your boss is a single guy, I'm not giving any recommendations." He should be happy for her new job, but why was he scared their interactions would be minimal when she started work full time? "Or you could come back."

"We've been over this. I don't want to interfere with your other employee. Plus, she'd take a pay cut, too."

So would Ryan, but he couldn't care less as long as Destiny stayed.

Saying good night to her wasn't any easier, as the kids wanted a slumber party at her house.

She laughed and tousled Pete's hair. "I don't have extra beds or blankets for you guys."

"We'll see her next Sunday." Ryan urged the kids to say good night.

Carter fell asleep on the drive home. The older kids sat in silence, seeming saddened and lost in their thoughts. He twisted his grip on the steering wheel, trying to think of something to say to ease their hurt. They'd lost their parents but been brave enough to love again—not that Destiny could ever replace their mother. But now, they'd lost her too. He'd let them down, opened them for more heartache.

Somehow, he endured a second week without Destiny in their family, yet she consumed his mind during every breath and step of it.

It was midmorning, and he'd just finished rounds and entered his office when an incoming text chimed. He slid his cell phone from the drawer.

His heart thundered, and a smile curved his lips when he saw Destiny's name. A picture of her hugging Carter while he kissed her cheek was Ryan's new screen saver. He'd captured it on Sunday at the park before the concert.

He slid his thumb to read her message, anticipation coursing through him.

Destiny: What's the prescription for separation anxiety?

Ryan shook his head, imagining what she was doing then. He pictured her smiling with a teasing smirk, sitting somewhere relaxing on the couch, except it was *his* couch he pictured. He typed his response.

Ryan: Separation from whom?

Destiny: Hmm...let's see, my family?

She didn't have family, except for Timon. But, to Ryan, Destiny was part of his family, so by missing her family, surely she meant his kids.

Ryan: prescription—go back to your family. I'm sure they miss you too.

Destiny: I intend to if I survive the pap smear. Ugh, please tell me I will survive.

A loud chuckle rumbled his chest. He imagined her at the doctor's office, waiting on the table with her phone. Upon adding her to his insurance, Ryan had learned she'd never been to a gynecologist. She'd been nervous when her doctor recommended she schedule an appointment, and she'd asked Ryan all sorts of questions on what the process entailed. He'd managed to picture her as a patient and give her a summary of what to expect.

Ryan: You will survive—you have to. The kids are counting down the days till they see you on Sunday.

Me the most. He couldn't stop smiling as he replayed the words from her text while he went to his afternoon rounds.

Ryan was double-checking charts outside the patient's room.

"Quit whistling, Harper!"

Was he really whistling? He turned at the sound of Lucas's voice. "I can tell you've finally made your move on Destiny."

Ryan shook his head to Lucas's arched eyebrow as he stood inches from him. "Why?"

"You're all flushed, and that grin hasn't left your face for three days."

Since seeing Destiny on Sunday, then texting her the kids' pictures on Tuesday when he got home early. "Try taking the stairs and see if it turns your face red." He'd only climbed one flight of stairs, not enough to create sweat. "Plus, I'm always smiling."

"Yeah right." Lucas snorted. "So... how'd it go when you told her?"

"We're just friends." He hadn't worked up the nerve to utter his feelings.

"Good grief, Harper. The woman spent seventy percent of our time together talking about you. She's into you... didn't know you're that messed up."

"Who's messed up?" Katie joined their circle.

Ryan scratched his jaw. Although he was trying to walk the friend line with Katie, they didn't tell each other stuff. Plus, how could he think of a response when Lucas just revealed Destiny talked about him during their date?

Several feet scuffled up, conveniently interrupting the moment. "Oh! Are we late?" One of the three interns fidgeted with her folder.

On taxing days, Ryan got after his interns if they didn't show up ten minutes early during rounds. He expected twenty minutes early if they were assisting him in surgery.

"Relax, dude." Lucas slapped the kid on the back. "We still have fifteen minutes before the cardiologist shows."

Ryan was consulting on the case—a woman whose brain tumor he'd removed two years ago. With her name at the top of the heart transplant list, they needed to discuss her CT scans, lab work, and medical procedure results.

With her husband in attendance, Ryan hoped a family member would be critical in helping his patient make the right decision.

When he returned home at almost eight, instead of the kids' thrills and shouts greeting him, the house was silent. The interior smelled fresh with lemon disinfectant, not baked foods or popcorn.

As usual, Valeria was good at keeping the kids' bedtime routine. A clean and quiet house should be fulfilling after a long work-day—something he'd always wanted. But somehow, he missed the mess and noise—the house with Destiny in it. He missed coming home to talk to someone way after the kids were in bed, to watch a TV show and gobble late-night popcorn.

He tossed his keys in the bowl on the counter and set his bag down.

"Hi."

He jolted at Valeria's voice as she walked from Destiny's bed-room—no, the guest room—with her handbag slung over her shoul-der.

"The kids have been having a hard time getting to bed lately. I told them to be quiet. I think they finally fell asleep."

He doubted they were, not after Destiny turned their schedule around.

"See you tomorrow."

"See you."

She'd always gone home to her family as soon as he returned. She only stayed the night on the days he worked overnight shifts.

Ryan went downstairs after she left. Whispers sounded through the boys' room behind their closed door.

If he went to the boys' room first, Zoe might fall asleep before he made it to her room. He walked down the hall to her door, rapped on its hard surface before letting himself in.

"Oh, hi, Uncle!" Zoe tossed her covers to the side and sat up. How could the girl sleep with the bright twinkle lights dazzling her room?

"Did Destiny text you today?" Was her first question when Ryan sat on her bed.

He stretched his arms. "My hug first."

Her warm hugs always lifted his spirit. After they embraced, he asked about her day.

"Can I first text Destiny to wish her good night?"

Destiny might get tired of their constant texts. "Maybe we better give her some space."

Zoe's face fell, and her shoulders slumped. She wiggled her fingers where remnants of chipped purple nail polish lingered. The girl had refused to let Valeria help her remove it, insisting quite voluminously that *Destiny* helped her apply it and it would stay until *Destiny* helped her take it off. "I really miss her."

She said the same thing every night.

I do, too. "I know." Forget giving her space. "You can Facetime her. I'll bring my phone when I go back upstairs."

"Can Destiny move in with us? She doesn't have to be our nanny, but she can live with us—can't she?"

It was as brilliant a suggestion as it was hard to ask her.

Can you move in as my girlfriend? Nope, not asking. He didn't enjoy complicated conversations, and this was turning into one. "I'd better say good night to the boys."

In the boys' room, Pete was fumbling with a Rubik's cube, and Josh was fixated in a book. He'd started reading a Michael Vey Series.

"Hi, Uncle." Pete plunked the cube onto his lap. He'd completed two of the sides and half of another. Someday, he'd get the whole thing—for now, he refused to "cheat" and look up the tricks.

"How was your day?" Josh slid a tissue to bookmark the page he was reading.

"How are you guys doing?" Ryan sat on Josh's bed.

Pete rolled the Rubik's cube from one knee to the other. "Is Destiny coming back?"

Ryan let out an exhale. It was high time he did something different, even if he had no idea where to start.

ON THURSDAY, HE HAD a complex brain surgery and spent
over eight hours in the Operating Room. Then he stayed after work
to catch up on patient charts, getting home past ten when the kids
had already fallen asleep.

The next morning, he left the house at five thirty, as soon as Valeria arrived. He told her they needed to talk when he got home.

An hour later, he met with interns for the scheduled procedure
of a patient with nerve damage. Even if he usually saw one patient
on days he had complex procedures scheduled, he still had to make
allowances for emergencies. For that reason, his day didn't go as
planned. Just like the way they paged him after a seven-hour surgery
to tend a gentleman who'd suffered a cerebrovascular accident.

His phone chirped as he entered the cafeteria to get a late lunch.
He pulled it out of his scrubs to answer. The law firm was inquiring
about Destiny. Ryan stepped outside to respond as they asked about
her reliability and dependability.

"We're considering her for the job, and her last management position indicates she's well qualified. As you can imagine, with the
high level of confidentiality and discretion we promise our
clients—"

"She's the best employee you will ever have." Ryan dragged a
hand through his hair. Why hadn't he worked harder to talk her into
staying with them? "Loyal to a fault. She takes her work seriously. In
fact, I made a terrible mistake letting her go." His last words came out
as a whisper. He doubted the man heard him.

"Sounds like our firm could use someone like that," the man said.
"Thank you."

Good luck. Ryan hung up. He was going after her before the law firm snagged her.

Intending to give Valeria three months' pay and an outstanding recommendation, Ryan hoped she could find another job in the twelve-week period.

On the way out of the hospital, he stopped at the gift shop to buy Destiny some flowers—a bribe, he told himself. But they'd run out of flowers, and he ended up getting a brown teddy bear with a red ribbon around the neck.

After driving through her neighborhood, a mix of ranch-style and two-story homes, he parked beside a Camry in the two-car driveway.

He hid the teddy bear behind his back when he took the final step and rang the doorbell. The bold color on the door was typical Destiny. Ryan could only imagine how she'd talked Jia into painting her door red.

The door swung open, and Ryan grinned, his heart racing in anticipation, but his smile vanished when a young man opened the door.

Tan skin, long dark hair, he couldn't be much older than Destiny. If he was Jia's son, his unfriendly face bore no resemblance to her.

"How may I help you?" An accent of some sort gave the only lilt to his flat tone.

Ryan swallowed, contemplated getting back to the car and texting Destiny. In his rush, he'd not thought of texting or calling her first. What if she had a boyfriend?

His stomach churned. "I'm here to see Destiny."

The man scoffed and crossed his arms over his chest. "And you are?"

He was a boyfriend, no doubt. He was too confident to be a guest.

Ryan gripped the teddy bear behind his back, wishing he could chuck the stuffed animal in the nearby shrub. Then he spotted Destiny over the man's shoulder. A few inches away, she was shuffling things off the couch and scurrying with blankets in her hands to another room.

He returned his gaze to the man in front of him. "I'm her..." What was he? "I'm the previous..."

"Timon!" Destiny shoved the young man aside, taking his place at the door. "Hey," she greeted, breathless as if she'd just run a marathon. "I didn't know you were coming."

"Sorry I didn't text." It was an impulsive decision. "I figured it would be a long text if I sat down to type."

"Don't get me wrong—I'm happy to see you." Then concern crumpled her face. "Are the kids okay?"

"Yeah." Ryan pulled out the teddy bear and handed it to her, hoping she'd like it. "I meant to get you flowers, but this is all..."

"I love it." She hugged the lucky toy close to her chest, erasing Ryan's doubts. "It's so soft. Thank you."

Warmth loosened his muscles at her genuineness.

"Oh, by the way, Timon is my..."

"Brother." The young man sidestepped Destiny and extended his hand. "Sorry for the rough intro."

Ryan's heart felt light. The guy wasn't her boyfriend. "No worries. I'm Ryan." He remembered the Greek salads Destiny brought him whenever she went to Timon's restaurant. "I like your food."

The guy grinned, his chest puffing. "Glad you like it. I'm catering for two of your doc friends. Appreciate the recommendation."

"Makes it easy when the food's good." They'd asked for the restaurant number after Ryan's party.

"You want to come in?" Destiny pushed the door wide open. "Movie night, Timon and I are going to watch *Mountain Men*...I have SkinnyPop too."

He exchanged a smile with her, wishing he could stay. "I didn't know you liked *Mountain Men* that much."

"I know, right?" Timon grumbled. "I was willing to torture myself with some chick flick or even *America's Got Talent*, but she insisted on watching some stranded men in the wilderness."

Destiny elbowed Timon. "Stop with the drama already."

"Please come talk her out of this creepy show." Timon made a show of putting his hands together in a pleading gesture.

"I have to get home to the kids." And talk to Valeria about her job. Ryan cleared his throat and gazed at Destiny. "Can I talk to you out here?"

"Let me put Teddy on the couch." She left, and Timon's friendliness vanished.

"Seriously, dude, even if you sent customers my way...if you hurt her." Timon's body frame wasn't the bodybuilder style, but if eyes could attack, Ryan would be struck to the ground. "I'm not afraid of the law."

He'd never forgotten Destiny's conversations, especially the one when Timon broke her ex-boyfriend's nose. Ryan raised his hands. "Trust me, I don't want to get on your bad side. Glad someone's watching out for her...."

"Ready?" Destiny frowned, looking at him, then Timon. She punched Timon's shoulder. "You better behave."

The late afternoon sun was low on the horizon, a perfect evening with a gentle breeze stirring Destiny's curls onto her forehead when she leaned against his Mercedes.

"The kids miss you." He thrust his hands in his pockets to keep them from fumbling. "They want you back."

Silent, head cocked to one side, she watched him. Was she going to say she'd already taken the job at the law firm? That's if they'd called her right away.

She clasped her hands in front of her. "How about the other nanny? I don't want her out of a job."

"I have a plan." He told her his intention to pay her until she found another job. "I'll put referrals in at the hospital for her, too."

She seemed to be thinking about it.

Panicked, Ryan felt the need to say something more convincing. "I miss you, too." He swallowed, hoping he'd opened up a little of how he felt. "When Carter wakes up at night, he calls for his mama...for you."

A smile softened her expression, and her eyes glistened. "He does?" Her voice wavered. "I miss you guys.... When do you want me to start?"

"Tonight." He was teasing, but if she showed, it would be a celebration at his house.

Her smile made him weak in the knees. She was a refreshing sight, and he couldn't wait to see that warm smile every night when he got home.

She raised a hand, saluting him. "I'm reporting for duty early tomorrow morning."

"By morning, you mean eleven?"

"Six, making breakfast for the kids."

"I'll give you a wake-up call at four." He'd let the kids be surprised when she showed. If he told them tonight, they'd stay up all night, just like he intended to do. He was like a kid again, on Christmas night waiting for Santa.

But that call he'd gotten... It wouldn't be fair if he didn't tell her what she'd be missing if she came back to work for him. "The law firm called for you. I think you might have a shot at it."

"Yeah. I got the job."

There went that. "I guess I should've told you first."

"I told them I'd think about it." Her head cocked sideways again, she eyed him. "Unless you've changed your mind about hiring me, I prefer my old boss." She winked. "As long as we can schedule monthly dance nights at the house, I'm all in."

"Just don't count me in your dance nights."

She playfully poked his chest, those shining eyes twinkling against rich skin. "We'll see."

She'd eventually make him dance, and he'd do it. There was no need for having the discussion besides him wanting to hear her talk.

CHAPTER 19

Saturday felt like a coming home party. For once, Destiny had kept time to be somewhere. By the time Ryan had sent a wake-up text, she was already up and dressed, since she kept checking the time on her phone.

Excitement and adrenaline had kept her tossing and turning for most of the night.

With no traffic on the highway, it only took her thirty minutes to get up to the mountains.

The moment she stepped out of her car, the front door swung open as if Ryan had been peeking through the window for her.

She could almost see through his heart when he greeted her. The gentle brush of his soft lips to her cheek sent a new set of butterflies to her stomach. "Welcome home," he murmured low in his deep voice as he closed the door.

Despite the cool breeze that chilled her outside, Ryan's peck warmed her entire body. The urge to pull him against her and kiss him warmed her neck, but she was here for the kids. "Glad to be home."

The house smelled of familiar scents of a home she'd gotten used to. Ryan's scent and the coffee all made for a day she was already looking forward to.

"I made plenty of coffee like you asked." He pulled out two mugs and poured the dark liquid into them. "Seems like we will both need an extra dose of caffeine."

Was his lack of sleep from the same reason as hers? Had he been too filled with excitement to see her, just like she was to see him and the kids?

When she lifted the cup to her lips, she closed her eyes and whiffed the precious smell before she took a sip. "How I've missed your coffee."

A sheepish grin crinkled his eyes over the cup's rim. "I'll brew you a full pot from this day forward."

They spent the next few minutes catching up while Ryan told her about his disasters with the kids. "I made the mistake of putting Carter down with no clothes on except for his diaper." He smiled, shaking his head. "When I picked him up after his nap, he'd taken off the diaper. The entire crib was smothered with his potty."

Destiny scrunched her nose, imagining the smell. "What a mess! Not the way you expected to spend your day off."

He dragged a hand through his tousled hair. "Two hours of cleaning, another hour giving him a bath. Lesson learned—always put clothes over his diaper."

If only she'd been around to help.

He looked at her, a glint in his eyes as if he could see right through her inner thoughts. Her mouth felt dry. "So glad you're home." He reached as though to cover her hand with his, then drew his back. "What's for breakfast?"

She'd left her tote bag in the car. After watching *Mountain Men* with Timon, she'd gone grocery shopping. "I bought some fruit and pancake stuff—I hope you have eggs."

"I'll get those out."

She retrieved her tote bag. Ryan was already whipping up some eggs. His strong muscles filled out the gray T-shirt he was wearing over basketball shorts.

"Scrambled eggs okay?"

She nodded. "I brought sausage and bacon too."

She and Ryan made a great team in the kitchen. As they cooked, they talked about all sorts of things until he brought up Lucas.

"Sorry things didn't work out." His smile was wide as he scratched the day's worth of scruff on his jaw.

"Why do I get the feeling you're not sorry?"

"Wow, is that the response I get when I try to show sympathy?" Winking, he reached for the plates from the cupboards. "What's wrong with people these days?"

The clatter of footsteps and voices kept Destiny from her response. She beelined for the stairs where all three kids emerged in their pajamas.

The look in their eyes was priceless.

"Destiny?" Josh blinked.

Pete scratched his eyes as if he needed to clear the fog to see clearly.

"Destiny is here!" Clapping, Zoe charged forward and threw her arms around her.

Destiny crouched and squeezed her tight. "So good to see you."

Not much for hugging her, even the boys came and hugged her. She fought off the welling emotion threatening to release a flood of tears. The kids *had* missed her as much as she'd missed them!

"Are you staying this time?" Josh asked.

"Like in forever?" Zoe asked. "Please don't leave."

"Guys, we'll talk about it during breakfast." Ryan glanced at her and shrugged as if saying, "We've all missed you."

"You want to wake Carter up?" he asked, and she didn't hesitate in climbing two steps at a time to his room.

Gently rubbing Carter's back, Destiny spoke in a soft voice, not to startle him. "Hey, little guy."

He opened his eyelids a bit, blinked twice, then gurgled a smile, melting her heart all over.

She scooped him up and breathed in the baby scent she'd missed since Sunday. "I'm home, sweetheart." For as long as Ryan would keep her.

As she swayed him from side to side, Carter yanked her hair in an effort to look at her face, so she lifted him to face her. "Ma...ma..." He flapped his hands.

As they ate breakfast, Ryan told them Destiny was back full time, and Valeria was gone. She was grateful they didn't seem bothered to lose their other nanny.

The kids spoke over each other when she asked what they did during the week. And what they wanted to do for the rest of the day. With their school starting after Labor Day, they still had another week left for their summer break.

"Biking!"

"Golfing!"

"Swimming!"

Each kid put in their request.

"We can't go biking." Ryan pointed his fork at Pete. "We don't have a bike carrier for Carter, and he can't play golf either."

Swimming it was—at the country club where Ryan had membership.

The smell of chlorine hung thick in the air as they entered the pool room.

"Dr. Harper!" a gray-haired gentleman called after Ryan as they started to enter the pool.

"I didn't know you were married—and with four kids too?" The man rubbed a towel over his dripping hair as he dragged his gaze from Destiny to the kids—three of them dove for the water with a splash.

"Mr. Cross." Ryan looked down at her, then to the kids in the pool and back to the gentleman. "Yes...I have kids. This is Destiny." He then pointed at the kids, introducing each of them by name.

"I'm one of the attorneys at Olive Medical." The man shook Destiny's hand.

Ryan didn't say Destiny was his wife or his nanny, which left a slight possibility and assurance that maybe—just maybe—he saw her as something more.

Whether anything would ever come out of their relationship or not, Destiny was glad to be a part of Ryan's family.

RYAN'S CAREER HAD NEVER been as hard as it was now that he was a parent. Weeks that he was on call, between the charity hospital and Olive Medical meant interrupted sleep, missed kid events, and cut-short family dinners.

Despite his busy schedule, Destiny always had a full calendar of outings planned. It made it easier for him to attend one or two when he arrived home in a timely manner. From afternoon hikes, movies in the park, and outdoor park concerts—most of which were free in different cities in the metro area. He loved being around Destiny and the kids and couldn't remember the last time he missed Katie's company.

Though the ache for Bree had slackened to a dull pain, he often found himself wondering what she'd think of him and his parenting skills. Was he a good guardian to the kids?

The last twenty-four-hour shifts felt longer knowing he'd again miss time away from his family. After an entire day at the charity hospital, Ryan drove to Olive Medical for a scheduled eight p.m. surgery. He had enough time to shower in his office bathroom, change into his scrubs, and eat the quinoa avocado salad Destiny had sent him.

The evening started with an emergency endovascular surgery bumping the surgery he had scheduled. A woman who had a ruptured aneurysm. The surgery wasn't successful, and he lost the patient due to severe internal bleeding.

Not exactly how he wanted to start his shift, by walking into the waiting room to anxious family members and delivering news about their loved one. But he'd done so and patted the woman's husband's shoulder as the man sobbed.

Deflated, Ryan sat in his office on the loveseat—death. It was a constant war to stop it, some battles lost, some won. Why did he keep fighting? He could almost hear Destiny's voice telling him to remember all the patients he'd saved.

One of those patients had him jolting upright. The lady he'd operated on two years ago. She had a heart transplant earlier today, and he'd meant to check on her when he arrived. The emergency sidetracked him.

He made his way to the ICU and asked the nurse behind the counter for the patient's room.

She winced. "Unfortunately, she didn't make it through the surgery."

He grabbed the counter to steady himself. "You mean she *died*?"

The air whooshed out of his lungs. He'd been so confident she would survive.

He turned, not wanting to ask what went wrong, afraid he wouldn't endure her explanation. "What a day."

He trudged back to meet his next patient. A man in his late fifties readmitted to the hospital due to major side effects from the brain surgery he'd undergone a year ago.

Ryan was going to go through his recent scans that revealed an aggressive growth they'd missed from the scans before. He intended to discuss a possible procedure and schedule a meeting with the patient and the oncologist.

Since the patient complained of constant dizziness, they'd had to keep him hydrated with IVs. The fact that he was sitting upright on his bed was a good sign. "How are you doing, Scott?"

Ryan pulled the stool closer to the computer so he could open up Scott's chart.

"That will depend on what you found out." Scott rose to his feet. His intense expression brought a shiver into Ryan's spine.

Ryan swallowed at his nearness and closed the screen. "Maybe have a seat, please?"

"I need you to be honest with me," Scott demanded. "I can take it as long as I know the truth. How serious is the cancer?"

Ryan rubbed at his forehead, struggling to relay the results.

Very aggressive. But that was never a response you uttered to a patient, even if you were certain they were dying in less than an hour. "There's a temporary solution at least."

"That's not what I asked." Bloodshot eyes peered into Ryan's. It wasn't uncommon for brain surgery patients to have mood swings, but being honest could earn Ryan a shove to the ground. "I don't need you to sugarcoat it. Tell me, Dr. Harper, did the surgery remove the cancer?" Such fear lurked in those dark-gray eyes. "I need to spend time with my family and not in the hospital in my final days."

"There's no guarantee with a procedure." It didn't cure stage 4 cancer. "But it could slow it from spreading."

Rage flared when the man growled, throwing punches in the air and above Ryan's head until he had to duck. When he attempted to press the call button for backup, a punch struck his eye.

Ouch. He covered his eye with his hand, wincing at the sting, while Scott, busy throwing profanities, didn't notice he'd punched Ryan.

He couldn't hold anything against the patient as he left the room. Scott needed a few minutes to himself, and Ryan wasn't going to send a nurse to a madman. The man would need counseling once he was calm enough to listen.

A patient had never hit Ryan. Occasionally, the psych doctors dealt with similar situations, maybe ICU with acute withdrawal patients.

He felt an oncoming headache as he rummaged through his drawer for an ice pack, not finding one. Pushing through the night with a strained eye, he wouldn't be any help to anybody.

He stopped at reception to push back his appointments for the following day.

"I guess we need to have security on standby in case patients get emotional." Lindsey, a nurse, eyed him.

The man had good reasons, but Ryan rarely faced such a reaction.

Thankfully, two other surgeons were working that night, so calling it a night seemed the most practical thing to do. He gathered up his laptop, and though he should call an Uber, he took the chance and drove up the mountains.

He arrived home just after midnight and welcomed the silence. Assuming everyone, including Destiny, was asleep, he stepped into the hallway. Good! He could ice his eye without answering how he'd landed a black eye.

Except the kitchen light was on. Destiny stayed up if she was expecting him, but tonight, he was supposed to be working another six hours.

As his luck would be, he sighted her in the kitchen. Her back was to him, phone in her cotton shorts pocket, earbuds in her ear, lost in whatever she was listening to while dancing and wiping the counter. There seemed to be a repetition to her movements.

The sight kicked up his blood circulation. Although he was determined to make his escape, his feet stalled for his double take. Plus, he'd feel awkward if she spun and saw him sneaking off.

Memories of her in his arms at the banquet spiraled. The way she'd fit so perfectly in his arms when they danced to a slow song, the way her head rested on his shoulder so naturally... Goodness, he needed to join Scott in getting a psych consult.

He shook his head to shove the memory aside and winced at the motion. He then cleared his voice to announce his presence, but she didn't turn around. He set his computer bag on the counter before sauntering over and tossing the keys in the bowl.

She jumped and yanked out the earbuds when she spun and saw him. Her hands flew to her chest. "Oh, you're home?" she said breathlessly. "I was doing exercises, and I...just..."

Her words were tripping over her tongue, and he stared at her, his mind blank. What was he supposed to say?

The sting in his eye reminded him he was supposed to shield his injury. He lifted a hand to cover it. "You're a great dancer...."

"Thanks." She frowned as her eyes narrowed in on him.

Yanking the phone from her pocket, she set it and the earbuds on the counter. Concern edged her face as she walked to him. "What happened to your eye?"

"Nothing..." He took a step back, not wanting it to be a big deal, because it wasn't.

That should stop anyone else, but not Destiny.

Her wet fingers hit his arm when she lifted it away from his face. "Let's see."

Ryan let her hold his arm, very aware of her closeness.

"Oh my!" She dropped her hand from him, then sped to the freezer and returned with a packet of frozen vegetables. "Sorry we're out of ice packs, but the peas should work."

"I'll take it." Ryan put out his hand for the bag. But Destiny steered him to the island, and he did as asked.

He winced when the frigid cold bag hit his eye until Destiny's sweet scent distracted him. With her standing in front of him—her chest so close he could barely read the font written on it—they were at an even height, which sent his mind into a stir. He closed his eyes, feeling the tingles from her touch, and tried to fight off unholy thoughts. Were her round lips as soft as he imagined? *Gosh, what's wrong with me?* Despite the cool ice on his eye, a sudden rise in body temperature assaulted him.

"Who did this to you?" Her protective tone made him smile, the same tone she used whenever one of the kids talked about a student who said something hurtful. She'd want to know their names and look up their pictures in the yearbook before she considered praying for the troublemakers.

Ryan relayed the story.

"It's sad that he had to get bad news." A sigh shuddered through her chest. "What if he threw you out of the window?"

"But he didn't."

"Good thing God protected you, but they need to have cameras, so when incidents like that happen, you have security ready to back you up."

"They have cameras." But they weren't to spy on patients....

"I'm so sorry this happened to you." She kept pressure on the pack she held to his eye. "Can I get you some water, dinner? I feel I should be doing more than just icing your eye."

A kiss should fix my longing for you. "You should go to bed." He tried to take the bag out of her hand, but she held a firm grip, which only caused their fingers to brush.

"Oh." She stepped back and eyed him. "I'm not doing a good job holding the packet, doctor?"

He chuckled, his heart racing when he glanced at her lips. Then he yanked the bag out of her hand and tossed it over the counter. "You've done a great job." So good that his patience doing nothing was running out.

Her smile vanished, and her gaze flickered down to his lips. But she didn't attempt to leave.

He felt like the cells in his brain were spinning when he took her hand in his.

"If you don't leave, I'm going to..." He swallowed, his voice raspier than the whisper he'd intended.

"To what?" she whispered, leaning forward and nibbling on her bottom lip. He was just as aware of her racing pulse as his own.

He pulled her toward him. "Kiss you." His lips met hers, gentle at first, warm.... And oh, his heart beat painfully at the tenderness of her lips as she kissed him back. Her hand gripped the front of his scrubs shirt, and the other slid up and around his neck as she raked her fingers through his hair.

He deepened the kiss, slipping a hand around her waist, tangling the other in her hair. Their lips fit so perfectly, and it felt as if they'd kissed before—could be that they'd both pre-played the scene several times in their minds.

He could kiss her all night long, and for several seconds, he forgot where they were until Carter's startled cries tore them apart.

There was chest heaving and panting when their eyes met, and they looked at each other—both unbelieving of what just happened. She pressed her hand against her somewhat swollen lips as if checking to see if they were still intact.

"Um..." He wasn't sure what to say, but then Carter's cries increased to screams.

She pointed toward the stairs. "I better go tend to him."

Wow! He sank back onto the stool. That was the kiss of the century. He dragged a hand through his hair, adrenaline coursing through him as if he'd just stepped off a treadmill. Man, he needed to get a grip.

Even if he'd pre-played kissing her, tonight hadn't been that day—not when he was vulnerable after a terrible day and sporting a swollen eye.

He'd imagined their first kiss happening after watching a romantic movie or out on a date in a restaurant or somewhere special.

There was only one problem—he wanted to kiss her again, wanted more of her. Like Lucas said, Destiny was the kind of girl a man would want to marry. Except, there was a ten-year gap between them. She'd eventually want her own kids, besides his niece and nephews. Ryan was too old to entertain the idea of biological kids. Even so, four was plenty.

He should've asked about her plans for the future before he went kissing her. Now that he'd kissed her and spent time in her company, letting her go would be one of the most devastating things to him and the kids.

Destiny was young, though mature in so many ways, and she made him feel young again. Mostly, he liked her so much and enjoyed spending time with her. She also knew how to kiss. Her kiss had ignited and set him on fire, which is why he needed a cold shower.

CHAPTER 20

D estiny handed Josh a Ziploc bag to slide his sandwich into for tomorrow's lunch.

The oil splattered in the pan on the stove as Pete attempted some experiment of cooking oil and water. He wanted to find out if the two could mix if hot. She'd insisted he mostly use water to keep from risking fire.

"Can I add a Twix to my lunch?" Zoe unzipped her lunch box, probably already assuming yes was the answer.

Destiny had bought some treats for the kids when she returned, and she'd told them they could only have one every week. She was trying to balance between Ryan's healthy eating habits and not de-priving the kids. She'd also started a routine of having them help her get their lunches made, and the kids didn't seem to mind.

After putting their lunches in the fridge, she glanced at the floor scattered with darts and then the counter filled with Zoe's paper cutouts and glitter. The oven lit the time at nine thirty. School night, but as long as they made it to bed before ten, they should be okay.

"Before we play Hangman, I need your help cleaning up."

Josh wanted to play the board game as soon as she'd picked him up from basketball practice, but since everyone was hungry, it had to wait.

Pete groaned. "My experiment hasn't changed yet. Oil and water still don't mix."

"Maybe they don't mix at all." Destiny urged him to dump the liquid in the sink. Then, making sure he didn't burn himself with the hot water, she opened the hot water tap to flush it down the drain.

Even if she and Ryan were not oil and water, they had opposite personalities, and she was starting to believe they could never be together. Not after Ryan's silent treatment and absence for the three days since their sizzling kiss.

He was either too busy, or he'd picked up extended work hours. He was gone by the time she woke up at five thirty, and he returned way after they'd gone to bed. He hadn't bothered to communicate his schedule the way he used to before their kiss.

Guess it's for the best. She shoved thoughts of him aside as she played Hangman with the kids, prayed with them, and called it a night.

In her room, she flopped on her bed and pulled up the Bible app. She managed to read Psalms 27.

She tried to focus on, *Teach me your ways, oh Lord...*

It had been almost one year since she'd asked God to forgive her of her sins. *Did I make another mistake God? Kissing my boss?* Not only were things awkward, but also she'd been on this road before. Falling in love with someone who was still attached to his ex.

It seemed evident that Ryan had moved on from Katie—especially in the way he'd kissed her passionately with no reservation whatsoever. She felt a little tingle on her lips at the memory.

Forgive me, Lord. Right, she was supposed to be praying and not having romantic fantasies about her boss.

She turned off the light and slid under her soft comforter. Closing her eyes, she listened for footsteps announcing Ryan's return.

As much as she tried to fight off sleep, her eyes felt heavy, and she gave way, waking up several hours later when Carter's cries sounded through the monitor. From the nature of his cry, he'd probably had a bad dream.

She tapped her hand on the nightstand to grab the phone, wincing at the bright light as she looked at the time. Four thirty.

Taking two stairs at a time, she rubbed her eyes and fought the urge to glance at the opposite side of the hallway—Ryan's room.

By the time she reached Carter's room, his cries had turned to soft moans. With her hand, she rubbed his back in gentle strokes. He stuck his thumb into his mouth when he stopped crying. She stayed until his breathing was steady. Perhaps it was teething and not a bad dream.

If she went back to bed, she'd end up sleeping through the alarm. Praying might be a good idea. She knelt on the rug by her bed. Then, taking advantage of the extra time, she showered—otherwise, the shower would have to wait for when Carter took his one o'clock nap.

By the time she dressed and walked out, Ryan was in the kitchen by the coffee pot, his back to her.

She stilled as her knees buckled, taking a moment to breathe in the scent of coffee and drink him in. A white button-up with the sleeves rolled to his elbows stretched ever so slightly over his back muscles—chest, too, when he spun around and caught her gawking.

Her cheeks aflame, she attempted a couple of steps forward. "Um..." she stuttered. "I...good morning?" Or was it afternoon already? If the sudden kick in body temperature was any indication, then it was.

"You're up early." He opened the top cabinet, pulled out a cup, and then filled it with the coffee from the glass carafe.

He handed her the steaming mug. "Here's some coffee for you."

The soft brush of fingertips as she eased the cup from him caused her hands to shake. She had to rest the cup on the counter so she didn't spill it. "Thanks."

He lifted his cup for a drink before setting it on the counter. Then he leaned against the edge and thrust his hands in his pockets.

"Listen, uh..." He cleared his throat, and his eyes barely met hers. "Sorry I took advantage of you the other day." He trailed off about having been out of his mind after a rough day. "It was very unprofessional of me."

She crossed her arms and kept a steady gaze on him before dragging out a slow breath. "Do I look like someone who can be taken advantage of?"

He dipped his head to one side, lifting his brow. "Huh?"

No doubt he'd heard her. "Are you in the right state of mind today?"

He frowned at her odd question. "Yes?"

In one long stride, she closed the gap between them and stepped on tiptoe. "Let's make it even." Curling her shaky hand around his neck, she brushed her lips to his.

Before she could step back, Ryan pulled her toward him. Bending low, he covered her mouth with his. The kiss was not calm and patient as it had been three nights ago, but more urgent, desperate as his hands raked through her hair.

She made a meowling sound, her hand gripping the front of his shirt. With the other, she tugged at his waist. His kiss ignited flames along her every nerve ending. By the time they tore apart, her hands were trembling, and they were both panting and gasping for air.

"Destiny..." His voice coarse, he rested his forehead against hers. "What are you and Carter doing today?"

It was her turn to be surprised by an odd question. "Nothing much, why?"

She drew back enough to see him, shocked by how wide and vulnerable his eyes were. "Come have lunch with me at the hospital. At one?"

Carter could nap later.

"It's a date." Before her words registered, Ryan eased her in for four more kisses down the side of her neck, his heart pounding against hers. He reluctantly let go when the kids' wake-up alarm rang downstairs.

She went through the first few hours of the morning with anticipation and a thrill of excitement while she took Carter to the library for story time, then to the playground where she fed him his lunch. She stopped by the salad restaurant downtown to buy lunch for Ryan. *No salad for me.* She would nibble on his since the box was big enough for two.

When she texted him, he asked if they could meet in his office. By the time she entered his office on the fourth floor, Carter had fallen asleep in his stroller.

"Somebody played hard today." Ryan crouched before Carter as he brushed the hair from his face.

"Yes, he did." She reached for the salad bag from the stroller basket. "I brought some lunch."

"Yum." He took the bag and set it on his desk, then pulled her into his arms. He stroked a finger along her cheek, making her entire body shiver.

"I hope you can share your salad."

He dipped his chin, more interested in a different topic. "I've been looking forward to doing this all morning."

His lips pressed against hers before she could respond how she'd be disappointed if they parted without sharing a kiss.

When she kissed him back, she felt the growl reverberate deep inside his chest. Her purse clunked to the floor, and her arms wound up around his neck before gliding into his soft silky hair.

They ended up making out like teenagers and skipped lunch. His pager beeped in the pocket of the white doctor's coat he'd worn over his office clothes.

With a sigh, he eased from the kiss and fumbled with the beeper. "Stay and eat before you go."

That kiss was lunch in itself. "I'm not hungry."

"I will see you in a few hours." He planted another kiss on her forehead, then strode out the door.

She practically floated out of the hospital.

RUNNING THE KIDS TO and from school and sports made the days go by fast. In the weeks that followed, Destiny and Carter met Ryan for lunch on days when he didn't have long surgeries or patients to tend to.

Some days, they ate at the hospital cafeteria. Other days, like today, she brought lunch, and Ryan met them at the park close to the hospital.

Leaves crunched under their feet as they strolled toward the playground, following Carter's unsure footsteps as he stopped from time to time to throw the leaves over his head.

They sat Carter in the swing, and Destiny stood beside Ryan as he pushed Carter. A soft breeze ruffled Ryan's hair, slicking it to the side, and he looked even more handsome than when she'd met him.

Dark brown, green, and yellow leaves whisked past Carter's face, and he lifted his hand to grab them.

Destiny chuckled at his curiosity. "It would be neat if Carter had a brother or sister to play with someday." She wanted to see if Ryan's thoughts of having more kids had changed.

"I still think four kids are plenty." He laced his fingers with hers and brought them to his lips. "Plus, I'm almost forty."

"You're not the one who will be carrying the baby."

"Maybe we could have *one* child." He gave Carter's swing a gentle shove. "Do you really need another sibling?"

Carter clapped his hands, smiling with a new set of teeth almost filling the front top.

They'd talked about their future several times—no sex before marriage, Destiny stressed, and Ryan was fine with that.

Keeping their relationship a secret from the kids was easy because Ryan came home late—after the kids went to bed or just an hour before their bedtime, which allowed them to watch the *Mountain Men* show or a movie making-out show of their own.

Destiny still left for Jia's house on Saturday evenings when Ryan didn't have to work. Tonight being a Saturday, she said good night to the kids after having dinner with them.

"Why don't you stay the night?" Josh held the door for her. "We're going to church together anyway."

It didn't make sense to leave Saturday evening only to see them Sunday morning, but maintaining the same schedule was necessary for the kids' sake. "Maybe I'll stay next time."

"Keep an eye on Carter." Ryan urged the kids back inside to escort Destiny to the car. He opened the passenger door and slid into the seat just as she started the engine.

"Josh is right." He dragged a hand through his hair. "You should start staying on Saturday nights."

"I don't want the kids to suspect anything."

He leaned an inch toward her. "I think they'll be glad that their uncle is happy. 'Happy uncle, happy kids'?" He imitated her words when she'd started working for him.

She laughed, the butterflies in her stomach flapping at his nearness. The car felt too tight. She dropped her hands from the steering wheel and rubbed them together to keep them from sweating.

Ryan slid his hand behind her neck and eased her into his arms. When their lips met, she spiraled out of control. She gripped his T-shirt and drew him closer. The console wasn't making it any easier, but his hand tangled in her hair.

At the banging on Destiny's tinted window, they tore apart.

Zoe! Destiny swung open her door.

"Hi, sweetheart," Ryan's voice was hoarse while he gripped the back of his neck. "What's up?"

"Are you going with Destiny?" she said.

Destiny had lost her voice. She could only watch Ryan struggle for an explanation.

"I wanted to double-check a few things with Destiny, but I'll be inside soon."

"We're out of conditioner," Zoe addressed Destiny. "Can you bring some when you go to the store?"

"Uh... Yes, I, uh, c–can...." she stammered.

"All right." Zoe gave a little wave. "'Nite. See you tomorrow."

"Whew!" Ryan let out a sigh when Zoe closed the door and skipped back to the house.

"Do you think she saw us?" Destiny asked.

"Trust me, she would've said something. She's not one to keep revelations to herself."

Destiny remembered the day of the banquet when she'd adjusted Ryan's collar. "Like when you blushed while I took the tag off your shirt?"

"Your lips were an inch from touching my skin." He peered at her with such love. "You can't blame a guy for blushing."

To the kids, everything was the same with Destiny as their nanny. Only Carter knew of their secret kisses shared during Ryan's lunch breaks.

"When should we tell the kids...you know, about us?" It would be more unsettling if they found them kissing in the kitchen or on the couch as they watched a TV show.

"After Thanksgiving." He laced his fingers through hers. "I want to tell my parents when they come."

She hadn't expected that big a step from Ryan yet. Her ex never introduced her to a single friend of his.

Hope surged through her, a smile folding up her lips. "Do you think your parents will be okay...?"

"Mom already likes you."

"She doesn't know we have a thing for each other."

He told her how his mom had always rooted for Ryan to ask Destiny out.

"She doesn't even know me."

"You've talked enough times on the phone for her to know the real you."

That could change after they met. She'd find out in two days when they picked up his parents at the airport.

Despite the steamy heat in her car, she shivered. She'd never had the responsibility of turkey preparations nor had she ever cooked the big bird before. Which meant, she'd have to rely on her possible mother-in-law.

CHAPTER 21

The days that followed, Ryan felt like he'd shot himself with adrenaline.

With his parents visiting for Thanksgiving, commotion and excitement filled the house.

Thoughts of Bree underplayed his every thought—how could they not? She'd always been a part of the holiday excitement and meal planning with his mom whenever their family got together.

Thankfully, Destiny was open-minded and able to connect with people from all backgrounds. Could be from dealing with various family dynamics.

The moment Mom arrived, she'd wanted to see the photo book Destiny made for Ryan's birthday. If Mom hadn't fallen in love with Destiny before, the picture book of family memories had led Mom to conclude she'd gained another daughter.

When Destiny confessed she'd never cooked a Thanksgiving meal, Mom had been thrilled to walk her through the process.

She even let Destiny style hers and Zoe's hair last night in preparation for Thanksgiving Day.

Ryan followed the laughter down the stairs. The savory smell of cinnamon, gravy, and turkey lingered in the air, reminding him of his childhood home, of special moments with Bree.

A ruckus came from the living room where Dad was playing Monopoly Junior with the kids. Ryan had excused himself to take a patient's call and used it as the perfect excuse to withdraw from a game he was terrible at.

Mom and Destiny worked side by side in the kitchen, the setting so natural. The smile on Destiny's face as Mom talked caused him to inch closer.

"What are you two up to?"

They spun around, and he held Destiny's gaze before looking at Mom.

Mom lifted the serving plate toward him. "This last cinnamon roll is yours."

Ryan patted his abs beneath a navy sweater. "Saving my appetite for lunch." He stared at the food and pies lining the counter. "We have enough for the entire community. Are we eating soon?" He reached for a handful of raw almonds from a porcelain bowl, ignoring Mom as he popped the nuts in his mouth.

"In an hour." Destiny poured a glass of eggnog and handed it to him. "This is for you."

Ryan eased the glass from her, looking between two of the three special women in his life. "Are you two plotting to give me a heart attack?"

Mom chuckled and waved a hand. "You grew up eating all this junk, and now you act as if it's foreign to you."

Destiny planted a hand on her hip, her smile questioning and too cute. "Is that so?" Then she nudged Mom with an elbow. "The Ryan I know can only eat junk food if I plead with him."

"I'll tell you everything you need to know about his old eating habits." Mom stuck the plated cinnamon roll in Ryan's hand. The pendant light showcased the gray at the edges of her brown hair. "Like you already know, he loves mint chocolate ice cream."

Oh brother. Ryan looked out the sunroom window. Huge snowflakes hit the ground. "I'm leaving you two...." As he turned to leave, Mom gripped his hand, urging him back to the island.

Destiny covered her mouth with her hand, amusement lurking beneath her fingers while Mom embarrassed him with stories, and he edged the cinnamon roll aside. If Bree were here, she'd be heaping more shame on his head, but that thought only made him ache for his sister more.

"In middle school, he won the hot-dog-eating contest."

Destiny's eyes widened with a glint of laughter. "No way."

Destiny only made it worse when she asked about Ryan's childhood. Mom rested her hands on the counter and started the story from the day Ryan and Bree were born.

He endured it until Carter woke up from his nap, and then Ryan escaped to get the squirt.

Minutes later, they passed several dishes of food around the table. Forks and spoons clanked over porcelain, accompanied by kids talking over each other.

"Mmmm!" Dad addressed Destiny. "You have to try Mel's sweet potatoes. She makes the best...."

Ryan pointed a fork toward Destiny sitting across from him. "The calories in those are more than her cinnamon rolls," he teased, wanting to get Mom's attention.

"It's Thanksgiving, Ryan. We're not talking about calories today," Mom scolded in a tone that should be saying "Do your homework" or "Clean your room."

"A mile or so on the treadmill, and they'll be gone, son," Dad said, untucking his plaid shirt.

Mom traded a loving smile with him. "I know there's a reason I keep you around."

"They love the sweet potatoes," Destiny said, lifting a spoon to Carter's mouth. "Carter just polished his off."

The older kids were sitting at the breakfast nook, but not too far to hold a conversation if they stopped long enough from whatever debate they were having.

"This is good." Ryan stuffed a bite of the sweet potatoes into his mouth. Despite his hesitation for the food choice, Mom scooped a serving on his plate anyway. "I'd forgotten how good your potatoes are." He'd hit the treadmill first thing tomorrow morning.

"This is so delish." Destiny polished off the green bean casserole from her plate. "You're such a great cook, Mrs. Harper."

Mom beamed, obviously pleased at the compliment. "Just call me Mel," she reminded Destiny for the fourth time that week.

Conversing about random topics—everything but Bree's and Gavin's death—they lingered around the table long after they'd eaten. The boys talked Dad into taking them ice fishing the next day while Mom made shopping plans with Destiny and Zoe.

Apparently, both Mom and Destiny loved thrift shopping. They grew animated discussing what stores had the best Black Friday bargains.

"Sorry I have to work," he cut in, wishing he could join Destiny. But, in this case, he'd be hanging around with the boys.

"We'll plan something fun for when you get back home." Her gaze sliced through him, and for a moment, he contemplated how long it had been since he'd been able to kiss her properly. Then he caught Mom and Dad exchanging a glance. He needed to tell them about Destiny, but he hadn't found the right time.

They cleaned up the dishes and stayed up late talking and watching back-to-back Christmas movies with the kids.

The next day when Ryan got home, the scent of pine emanated through the house.

"The boys bought a Christmas tree after their fishing trip," Mom told Ryan as they ate dinner. "Tonight we get to decorate."

He hadn't entertained the idea of Christmas. It was the first tree in his house since he moved in. "Isn't it too early to talk about Christmas?"

"We won't be back for Christmas, son." Dad's fork clanked on the plate when he set it down.

"We need to give our employees a break." Mom slid her empty plate to the side.

The holidays were the busiest for his parents' dried fruit and nut company in Virginia. Taking the time off to come for Thanksgiving was a big deal. "Thank you for coming."

"That's what grandparents do." Dad winked at Zoe.

While Mom and Dad talked about their business, Ryan found himself eavesdropping on the kids' conversation by the nook as they spoke to Destiny.

Zoe was talking about making popcorn for the movie.

Josh plopped his chin in his hands. "How about we watch like three or four movies?"

"I can't wait to decorate the tree." Pete tipped shining eyes to Destiny. "Can we sleep under the tree tonight?"

"Uh..." Destiny turned to the island and caught Ryan's gaze. "Uncle and I need to talk about..."

He shrugged. "That would be fine with me." That's what Bree would want for the kids. "What do you think?"

She glowed as though he'd just played her favorite song. "That will be so fun."

The kids' happy faces and thrills filled any dark recesses in Ryan's heart. Yes, Bree would be happy, too.

They worked together clearing the dishes and wiping down the counter before heading to the living room.

The kids' excited chatter over Christmas music made for the loudest holiday Ryan ever had in his home. Yet he loved every minute of noise. His heart quickened each time he was met with Destiny's heated gaze as they hung the ornaments on the tree.

Most of the ornaments were handmade by the kids over the past years. After Bree and Gavin died, the ornament box made it to Ryan's house.

Destiny, Mom, and the kids had also made ornaments over the last few days leading to Thanksgiving.

An ornament clattered on the tile. Thankfully, it was metal. Keeping ornaments on the tree while Carter kept yanking them off would be challenging.

When Carter went to bed, the older kids brought their sleeping bags to the living room and lay snuggled in to watch *The Grinch* and *The Polar Express*. While Ryan's parents sat on the love seat, he and Destiny sat several inches apart on the sectional.

With Dad and Mom sleeping in Destiny's room, she'd taken temporary residence in his gym downstairs. It felt like she was several miles away from him. Having company had thrown their arrangement off, and Ryan hadn't had a moment alone with her.

Which is why after the kids and his parents went to bed, Ryan snuck downstairs and tapped on her door. The light was still on in her room.

The door swung open, and a loose-fitting pink pajama shirt highlighted the blush on her tawny cheeks—man, she was gorgeous. "Hi," she said breathlessly and peered both ways as if making sure no one else was downstairs.

"What are your parents going to think when they find out that you're down here?" Despite her mild protest, she ushered him inside before closing the door.

"My parents went to bed." He could care less at this moment. Soon his parents would find out. In greeting, he pulled her to him, hooked his arm around her waist, and hoisted her right off her feet. "I've missed you." His lips danced over hers. A whiff of her fragrance played havoc with his insides.

"Me too." Her heart was racing against his, and he set her down, gently backing her into the wall. He admired her flawless face and trailed his fingers on her soft skin. She shivered.

He dipped his head and captured her lips with his, kissing her heedless of his family upstairs. She kissed him back, and her fingers wove into his hair. As he deepened the kiss, wanting every part of her, his arms trailed on her back. His fingers made their way into her hair, threading through the soft curls.

She withdrew from the kiss, both of them gasping for air. "We need to remember where we are."

Ryan glanced at the couch they'd moved from the main room downstairs. To the far side were the treadmill and weights. "We're in the gym?" he said gruffly, aware of what she meant, but preferring to tease her.

A soft rush of laughter slipped from her, her warm breath tickling his neck, and he captured her lips for another kiss.

He rested his forehead on hers and took a deep breath, whispering her name. "I think I'm in love with you."

She chuckled. "You *think*?"

Great. He'd blurted it out way too soon. There was a reason he'd never confessed to Katie that he loved her—to avoid embarrassment. Yet he'd never felt this way with Katie or anyone before. How the words flew off his tongue easily was an explanation in itself.

"I *know*... I'm in love with you," she said.

Thank goodness. Her words warmed his heart. "I'm glad." He threaded his fingers through her soft ones. "Would you like to know when I first fell in love with you?"

She gave a slight nod, her eyes dancing in the light.

"The first night I made the kids' lunches with you—same night you offered to watch the kids so I could do something fun." He'd had a blast on the bike ride with Lucas. "Lucas and I were starving, and the lunch you sent with me hit just the right spot. Even though I didn't know how to, I knew then that I wanted to spend the rest of my life with you."

Her delicate throat worked on something. Then she swallowed. "Wh–why didn't you say something?"

He was still chasing after Katie. "It wasn't the right time."

"Did Jia ever tell you why she got me the *Disney on Ice* ticket?"

"Jia got you the ticket?" He'd wondered, but wasn't sure. "I thought our meeting was coincidental."

She gave a low laugh. "That's what I thought at first, but when you hired me, she told me she indirectly wanted me to meet the family I might be working with."

Ryan shook his head.

She tapped his chin. "I fell for you the day we met at *Disney on Ice*."

She'd done a good job hiding her feelings. "I don't think so."

"When Zoe told me you took care of them, it was the first for me." She ran her free hand through his hair, and he kissed her palm as it passed his face. Laughing, she tugged at his hair. "Then your hair caught my attention too."

Huh? But..."Why were you helping me and Katie go on a date?"

"I wanted to remind myself that you weren't available. Plus, I thought she was the love of your life, so I had to help out."

"Woman of my dreams," he corrected. "You alone are the woman of my dreams and love of my life."

Her eyes dilated. "I think my knees are..."

Ryan laughed. Not ready to say good night, he led her to the couch. "How's your week been?" He pushed her comforter and the teddy bear he'd given her aside. "I know Mom can be overbearing." Based on Katie's comments at least.

Her thigh brushed against his. Despite both of them in long pajama pants, he tried to ignore the rush of blood in his system.

"I like your mom. She's anything but overbearing. Besides, moms are supposed to get a little bit vocal with their kids sometimes." A smile curved the corners of her lips testifying to the fondness in her voice as she spoke. "I loved watching her force-feed you sweet foods."

"Hey!" Ryan kissed the top of her head. "Where's the sympathy? I only ate it because she gave me the guilt trip about using Grandma's recipes."

"I wish I remembered my grandparents. What was your grandma like?"

Conversations with her never seemed to die down. He had no idea how long he stayed downstairs talking to her, but when he kissed her good night, he was confident Destiny was the woman he wanted to spend the rest of his life with.

EVEN THOUGH HE STILL had the ring he'd bought Katie, Ryan had been looking online for a perfect ring for Destiny. It was too late to return Katie's ring since he'd had cold feet the moment he bought it. He now understood why. He and Katie were never meant for each other.

On Sunday, his parents went with them to Destiny's church, and they all went out to lunch afterward. Destiny stayed the night in Denver, planning to return the next day to take his parents to the airport while Ryan worked.

After the kids went to bed, he sat with his parents at the island, listening to them talk about the ups and downs of their business. The scent of coffee filled the kitchen while Dad had his late-night brew before bed. A habit he'd had as long as Ryan could remember.

Ryan rubbed his hands together, waiting for an opportunity to tell his parents about his love life.

Mom touched his shoulder. "Is there something on your mind?"

Not wasting time denying it, Ryan cleared his throat. "What do you think of Destiny?"

"You guys are a great team. I like how you make decisions about the kids together." Mom gave her signature end-of-discussion nod. "She's perfect for you."

Guess I don't need to explain anything after all. "What makes you think that...?"

"You're in love with her?" A grin quirked Mom's mouth.

"You two are not good at hiding it," Dad blurted before bracing his elbows on the island and wrapping both hands around his mug.

"I liked her before we met. I knew it would be a matter of time for you to notice what I sensed of her from our phone conversations," Mom said. "You're so relaxed around each other, just the way a normal couple should be."

"Don't forget to mention those sneaky looks they share across the table."

Ryan grinned, his face heating. "Okay, you got me."

"You love her. The kids adore her." Dad turned his mug in his hands, making sure Best Grandpa faced them, not him—Destiny had helped the kids get it for him. "Why are you not asking for her hand in marriage?"

He wasn't waiting five years to ask Destiny.

The stool scraped the tile when Mom shifted and rose. "I will be right back—don't move." She left for the guest room and returned with a small black box. "Here."

Soft velvet brushed his palms when she handed it to him. Ryan flipped it open. Glints of light sparkled off the diamond ring nestled inside.

"It was your grandma's." Mom stood at his side, one hand on his back. "I think it suits Destiny perfectly."

Totally Destiny—the swirl of diamonds formed a flower. Fun and full of life, the ring seemed ready to dance. It just needed some cleaning and maybe personalizing it to something more fun and spunky. He touched the stones, his mind working at the perfect re-design. "She will love it." Then his gaze met Mom's. "Thank you."

Liquid gleamed in Mom's eyes, even as her smile wobbled. "Mama would've loved for you to have it."

Out of curiosity, Ryan asked, "How come you never gave it to me while I was with Katie?"

"I knew you'd never marry her." She waved a hand, speaking bluntly. "You're smart enough to not marry a woman who doesn't care to know your family."

Guilt cringed through him. He'd ignored all the signs and almost asked Katie to be his wife. "Why didn't you say something?"

A hint of amusement crinkled the edges of her eyes. "Would you have listened?"

Ouch. "Probably not." When he told his mom about the breakup, her tone sounded knowing. "That's not good," she'd said. "But it gives you a chance for a new beginning."

Ryan arched a brow, responding to her knowing smirk, and tried to accuse her. "You never tried hard being nice to her."

A mirthless laugh burst from her. "I thought I was a good host." She raised both her hands in surrender. "I racked up my mind about the weather and whatever—I can't even remember—but she gave me monosyllabic responses and kept typing on her phone."

Ryan had taken Katie home to visit his parents during the summer, and she'd complained about mosquitoes, the uncomfortable bed—you name it. They cut their trip short by two days.

He let out a breath and shifted his gaze to the box. Grandma would want him to have it. But it wasn't his—it was *Destiny's*. He didn't want to hang onto it too long, but he also didn't want to scare Destiny off by rushing things.

First things first, he and Destiny would talk to the kids about their relationship. He hadn't thought how hard it would be telling the kids until the idea settled. Would they be happy, or would they be bothered that their uncle was dating their nanny?

CHAPTER 22

When the servers cleared the dishes and wiped their table down, Destiny remained a silent observer as Ryan explained the status of their relationship. Zoe's face lit up beneath the Christmas lights strung from one corner to another. "Colorado Christmas" played in the background. She'd always associate it with this moment, with all the questions and expectations.

Josh—"Are you getting married?"

Zoe—"I love weddings! Can I be the flower girl?"

Pete—"Do we have to dance in front of everyone?"

The poor boy's face fell—apparently dancing in public was not a thrill.

Ryan's gaze cut through Destiny's across the table before he refocused on the kids. "We haven't talked about wedding plans, but when we do, you can help us plan the wedding."

"Can you get married tomorrow?" Zoe bounced in her seat, jostling her water glass as she clapped.

Destiny could only smile, letting Ryan do the hard work—after all, he was their uncle.

"Maybe tomorrow or sometime soon."

"That's lit!" Josh smiled at Destiny. Then to Ryan, he gave a soft nod of approval. "Either day is fine with me."

The chair scraped the tile, and Zoe shifted, almost knocking over the vibrant autumn-colored roses and daisy poms, sunflowers, and orange lilies gracing their table. After a glance from the maître d', Zoe slowed her pace and walked—yes, *walked*—around her chair to Destiny.

When the girl threw her arms around her, Destiny engulfed her in a warm embrace, and Zoe whispered in her ear. "I'm so happy you get to be with us forever."

Her chest constricting and heat burning behind her eyes, Destiny hugged the precious girl tight. "Thank you, sweetheart."

"Can I invite all my friends to the wedding?" Josh narrowed his gaze. "You will have lots of food, right?"

"Yum...yum!" Carter bubbled, screaming and pointing from his high chair as the server wheeled a fancy cake to the far side of the room.

"Can we eat cake now?" Pete ogled it as the server left.

"You ate all your dinner, so you get to have cake." She still had no idea why Ryan, who always complained about the kids eating sugar, had ordered an entire cake for their family.

His phone rang for the third time that evening. He gave it a cursory glance before uttering his response. "We will get to the cake, in just a few."

He had reserved one of the restaurant's private rooms. In celebration of letting the kids know about their relationship, he wanted to go to a fancy restaurant. Destiny had worried the kids wouldn't like the food, but they'd loved the cocktail shrimp and the pasta dinner. Except for Josh, who said he preferred Destiny's pasta.

The door burst open, and two guys emerged. A tall one with blond hair falling over his shoulders. The other with a pierced nose. Both had guitars slung on their shoulders. Without talking, they strummed the chords and burst out singing "All of Me" by John Legend. She and Ryan had danced to the same song during the banquet.

Ryan sure knew how to celebrate. Destiny enjoyed watching the kids' fascination with the music. Carter clapped and garbled some noise as if he were singing.

When she looked at Ryan, as the song nearly ended, his smile vanished, eyes intent on her as if he were remembering the night they'd entwined in each other's arms, dancing to this song.

Her body heated when he pushed back his chair, and in a second, he was down on his knee. There'd been no sign or hint. Was this what a proposal seemed like?

He plucked a small black velvet box from his dress coat. Nestled tight inside, a sparkly diamond? Not just any diamond ring dancing in the light when he flipped open the box. She blinked twice to make sure that her eyes were not blurred. A canary yellow diamond. Her hands flew to her heart as his lips parted to speak.

"Destiny... That night when I first made the kids' lunches with you, you told me 'happy uncle, happy kids.' You're the kindest and most selfless person I've ever met. And yes, you've made my life so happy that I find myself a better parent for the kids." He looked at the kids. The boys were wide-eyed and grinning. Zoe was inaudibly clapping, her always big eyes aglow above her smile.

"Before I met you, I was anxious and stressed, but then you came along with your adventurous spirit to our family."

Her heart was racing so hard, she couldn't contain it even if she wanted to. As his chest expanded and his voice cracked, she could sense his words were full of passion.

"I look forward to coming home and spending time with you and the kids. You've become my best friend, and I want to spend every single day for the rest of my life with you."

Tears formed in her eyes. Her throat felt tight. Ryan was her best friend. Hearing him say the same released a flood of tears streaming down her cheeks.

"Will you marry me?" Then he gestured to the kids, and a tear dripped down his cheek. "Marry us, technically."

"Say yes!" Zoe sang out.

Destiny wiped her palms across her face. Her vision blurred, and her throat felt like her vocal cords had been cut out. It might have been ten seconds that felt like minutes before she could gasp her words. "Are you kidding me?" She reached out and squeezed Pete's, then Josh's hands, before holding her hands out to Ryan. His moist eyes flooded her with happiness. "Yes...I will marry you."

Her hands shook as he slid the princess cut ring on her finger. The swirl of diamonds formed a flower around the canary diamond. The ring fit perfectly, with enough wiggle room for her finger. Even more meaningful when Ryan said it belonged to his grandma—Destiny had nothing left from her family.

They shared a G-rated kiss suitable for their audience. It was surreal, and she couldn't comprehend her emotions. Shock, excitement, and love blurring into something too big for one heart to contain—good thing they had six. The musicians resumed playing. "Marry You" by Bruno Mars.

Ryan's phone rang again as soon as the song ended.

When he answered it, Mel was loud enough for Destiny and the kids to hear, even though she wasn't on speakerphone. "What did she say?"

Ryan's grin resembled the one stretching out Destiny's mouth so wide it hurt. He sat there smiling from ear to ear while the kids shouted, "She said yes!"

Having enjoyed hanging out with Mel during their Thanksgiving visit, Destiny was warmed by Mel's compliment when she dropped them at the airport and whispered that she felt like she'd gained another daughter.

Destiny had been motherless for so long. Had she finally gained a mom? A tear slipped down her cheek. "Thank You, God," she whispered so low even Ryan wouldn't hear her.

While the kids gobbled the cake, Ryan took her hand in his. Blue eyes gazed into hers with a tenderness that stole her breath.

If she'd had any doubts about Ryan's love for her before, they would have vanished in that instant.

It was an exciting moment, to start the next step in her relationship with the one she loved.

DECEMBER STARTED ALMOST mild. Colorado winters were often mild, with a mix of snow and sunshine. The kids didn't have school due to teacher planning. Destiny took them to the park in Denver since it was 40 degrees and sunny, much warmer than the foothills where they lived.

She and Ryan had a date planned that evening to celebrate their engagement. So Destiny felt it necessary to give the kids enough attention to keep them content in Holly's care.

The kids walked beside Destiny, careful not to step in goose poop on the concrete loop snaking around the park.

The geese scattered throughout the golden grassy area. Pete scampered toward the lake, squinting at the sign.

"Come on, Pete," Destiny called from the sidewalk.

"That lake looks fun for skating." Pete loped back. "But the sign says thin ice. How come the geese aren't sinking?"

Destiny explained what Pete already knew about the weight difference between humans and geese.

He sidestepped the stroller to reach her other side. "What happens if I try to skate?"

"You drown." Josh cuffed him.

Pete scowled. "But I can swim."

"Not in the frozen lake." Zoe shivered.

Pete's interest was always piqued when things had a caution.

"Let's just go to the playground," Destiny suggested as the bright-colored play equipment came into view.

Josh opted for the exercise equipment to use the bars and the elliptical.

Destiny pushed Carter in the swing a few inches away from the exercise equipment. Pete and Zoe went down the slide. When her phone rang, Destiny fished it from the basket of Carter's stroller and smiled at Jenny's ringtone.

She'd become friends with Destiny two summers ago when they'd met at a Zumba training camp and talked Destiny into teaching evening classes at her studio.

"Gosh," her friend gushed. "it's been hard to hear from you ever since you got engaged."

It had only been a week, but long enough to not have returned her friend's text. "I'm sorry I didn't get back to you."

"I take it you will stand in for me?"

When Jenny sent her three consecutive messages asking her to fill in for the lead dancer at a charity event, Destiny intended to pray about it and get back to her, but she'd forgotten. She now felt obligated to say yes. Perhaps if she used an excuse, Jenny would think of something else.

"I don't have time to practice."

Jenny chuckled. "You don't need to practice. You already know the moves. Remember, you're the one who suggested them to Hannah?"

Carter whined when the swing stopped moving, and Destiny gave him a shove as she thought of a solution. Hannah was the lead dancer, but with her sudden leg surgery, she wouldn't be recovered for another six weeks. "I'll teach *you*."

"Cut me a break here." Jenny huffed. "You know how I stink at salsa dancing."

Truly, Jenny should cancel the salsa dancing and stick to belly dancing or cha-cha.

"Destiny!"

She jerked at Josh's panicked voice. "I'll do it. I gotta go!"

"Pete..." Josh bounded for the lake.

Destiny's stomach dropped when she caught a glimpse of Pete's head submerging under the surface. *Oh no!*

She should have seen this coming. As usual, Pete's curiosity led him to wander where he shouldn't.

She held back a scream when she looked around. They were the only ones at the playground. Her limbs shook. She tossed her cell phone to Josh. "Call 9-1-1 and Holly!" she shouted, adrenaline kicking in as she sprinted to the lake. She had no idea how she was going to save Pete, but she needed to do something while they waited for 9-1-1 to show. "Oh, Lord, please..." Her lips shook as she mumbled a prayer. "Help me get to him before he drowns."

Without a thought to possible implications, Destiny charged to the hole broken in the ice where Pete fell. She forced herself down the water sinking beneath the weight of her tennis shoes and sweatshirt.

Frigid water, cooler than a freezer, struck her, stealing her breath, her focus, her thoughts. In the darkness, she outstretched her arms and feet to try to feel for something. Ice stung her cheeks, cold slipped through her fingertips—then... *Thank God!* She felt something. Pete.

Frantically grasping the child, she drew him closer. Pete's small hand clutched her sleeve as she struggled back to the surface. While still in the water, she shoved him toward the ice. A distant siren whirred. *Thank You, Lord.* They'd made it safe.

Her body shivered. With a shaky hand, she gripped the ice to leap out of the water, but her hand slipped, and she tumbled backward.

Her body weight cracked the ice beneath her, and her head hit something hard. Then it was dark.

CHAPTER 23

Despite the air conditioner, the Operating Room felt warm, just the way it did after standing for hours around the operating table. Another successful seizure procedure.

Beneath the mask, he smiled at the victory. He needed to keep his happy elation throughout the day and into the evening when he and Destiny would go on their first date without the kids.

Several doctors and nurses stood around as usual during the operation. He glanced up at the clapping from those watching through the gallery. Then he asked his surgical assistant to close the wound as he pulled off his gown and gloves before exiting the Operating Room.

In the prep room, Ryan turned on the faucet and dipped his hands, letting the warm water rinse the suds from his skin. He needed a shower, but it would have to wait until after his clinic rounds.

Excitement coursed through him when Destiny came to mind. He felt an eerie sense of calm since he'd asked her to marry him. Each time he looked into her vital green-blue eyes, he anticipated a splendid future. *What's she doing with the kids today?* He intended to find out when he called her before his rounds.

The door swung open, and Lucas peeked his head in. His presence at the surgical suite was alarming, since a different anesthesiologist had worked on this case.

"It's Destiny and Pete."

Lucas's sullen face stole the air out of Ryan's lungs. He blinked, his hands dripping with water when he crossed the threshold and grasped Lucas's shoulders. "What about them?" he nearly screamed.

"Destiny's unconscious and unresponsive in the ER. Pete's okay. He's being treated for hypothermia."

Ryan started sprinting for the ER while Lucas fell in step with him.

"She dove in the lake after Pete and..."

Lucas's words bounced off Ryan's back as he took three steps at a time. The elevators would take forever.

Code blue and doctors being paged on the intercom kicked up Ryan's heart rate—any of those doctors could be called to Destiny's room.

Please, God, not another death. Almost a year ago, Bree and Gavin died. *Destiny has to make it, God.*

In the hallway, he shouted at anybody in his path, ordering them out of his way, and by the time he reached the ER's front desk, his heart was pounding so hard it seemed to be trying to rip out of his chest.

"Where's she?!" He uttered Destiny's name to the nurse behind the customer service desk computer.

"Only family members are..."

"I'm family!" Ryan shouted. Destiny had him and Timon as her main contacts, thank goodness.

"They got the pulse and..."

Even if family members were not allowed in the ER while doctors were attempting to resuscitate a patient, Ryan demanded the nurse point him to Destiny.

"Harper..." Lucas called, catching up just as Ryan stormed through the automatic double doors. "She's going to be okay."

He could only hope. "We don't know that."

He had to see her.

When he stormed into the room, his blood ran cold at the sight of Destiny's pale face, the tubes and IVs hooked to her face, the doctor shouting orders. A nurse eased Ryan out of the way while they wheeled her to the ICU.

A hint of hope surged through him when a nurse told him, they'd found a pulse, although she was still incoherent. Not taking his eyes off her, Ryan swallowed. A lump tightened in his throat. As he walked alongside the nurses, he clasped Destiny's hand in his. "Don't you die on me!" he gasped, his heart breaking as he forced the words out. "You have to make it." The last words emerged in a plea.

He needed her. The kids...needed her. Where were the kids? He dragged a hand through his hair. They were probably at the firehouse or something.

In the ICU, the nurses continued to work at upping her body temperature while the doctor relayed the information from the paramedics.

"She was underwater for almost ten minutes." The doctor relayed the medication they'd given her to resuscitate her.

Thinking she'd had no pulse when she got to the hospital took Ryan to a dark place. A world without Destiny? Without her when he got home after a long day at work? Her warm smile becoming a memory? No way. He dragged a hand through his hair.

"We're keeping up oxygen intake and treating hypothermia right now." The doctor's words brought him back. "As soon as she stabilizes, we'll take her to Radiology for a CT scan."

"Do you think she had a head injury?"

The doctor shook his head, eyeing Ryan's badge over his scrubs. "We both know we can't come to conclusions without running tests—just like we know the consequences of being without oxygen for longer than five minutes. The only reason there's a chance she's not brain dead is the water's extreme cold temperature."

Yes, Destiny had such a low body mass. She'd have gone almost into suspended animation. He'd heard the saying among rescue crews—"You're not really dead until you're *warm* and dead."

After getting further answers to his questions, Ryan walked over to Destiny. He couldn't bear to look at her pale face. It was a good sign that her body was shivering. He pulled a chair close and squeezed her cold hand. "Please be okay..."

His chest hurt. He stayed there watching as nurses walked in to check on her, keeping up with her IV and oxygen intake.

"She's a fighter." Ryan spun at Lucas's voice as he stood beside Ryan. "She will be up and chasing the kids in no time."

Kids? Yes, Ryan stood. "Do you know where they put Pete?"

Even though Lucas assured him Pete was fine, Ryan needed to check on him. Destiny's condition had almost paralyzed his brain, or he'd have checked sooner.

"They moved him out of the ICU thirty minutes ago." Lucas told him he'd received Josh's call and Holly was taking care of the kids.

Josh must have called Lucas when he couldn't get a hold of Ryan.

Ryan asked his friend to stay by Destiny's side while he made his way to the pediatric department and asked for Pete's room.

"That woman saved his life." The nurse pocketed her hands in pink scrubs. "His lungs are in great condition...." She continued to relay Pete's condition, each word easing another burden off Ryan's chest.

When he entered Pete's room, the boy's face lit up. "Uncle."

"Hey, bud."

"How many cups of Jell-O can I have?" Pete set an empty container on the tray.

Ryan let the pent-up breath out of his lungs. Pete was feeling better. "As much as you want." Ryan ran a hand over Pete's slightly pale face. Because of Destiny's protective instincts and selflessness, his nephew was alive once more. Always putting everyone's needs before hers.

"Is Destiny going to be okay?"

Ryan swallowed, composing himself as he thought of a less threatening response. "She will be—the doctors are taking care of her."

"Can we pray for her?"

Having no idea what to say, Ryan closed his eyes, intending to make it a silent prayer, but Pete prayed aloud. "God, Destiny is so nice. Help her to feel better. I promise not to step on an icy lake again."

Ryan's eyes tingled. Pete's prayers motivated Ryan to pray. When he left Pete's room, he went straight to the empty hospital chapel and sank to the back bench.

As he closed his eyes, the words flew out of his mouth, without scrambling.

"God, if You bring her back to us, I promise to believe in You and all the things Destiny told me about You." Was that something to tell God even? Why would God listen to him? "That is, if You care about me and the kids."

God doesn't help us because of our promises. He will help us because we ask Him as His children and if He thinks it's what's best for us. Destiny's words stirred in his mind.

He left the chapel, assuming it was God's will for the orphaned kids to have a mother in their lives. What could he do for the kids when his job demanded so much of his time? He walked back to his office to call Holly and update the kids.

"We're praying for her and Pete," Holly said. "We will watch your kids tonight if you need to stay in the hospital."

He needed to be around when Destiny woke. The kids would have to miss school tomorrow. "I'll be glad to pay you."

"It'll not be necessary." Such concern filled Holly's tone. No wonder Destiny trusted her with their kids.

After talking to Holly and calling his mom and making arrangements for another physician to take his place for the afternoon rounds, Ryan stepped out of his office. He went to reception to push back all his appointments for the next two weeks. This was an emergency, and treating patients while he was emotionally unstable wasn't even ethical.

On the way back to the ER, he ran into Katie. "Oh!" She stopped him. "I've been looking everywhere for you. I heard about your nephew."

Her concern softened some of his tension. "Yeah, he's okay. Thanks."

"Your nanny is something else. How is she?"

"Destiny," Ryan said her name, tasting it and needing her, as the realization hit that her life was hanging in the balance. His chest rose and fell with the weight of it, heart thrashing against his ribs. He wasn't going to cry in front of his ex. "She's..."

As the word choked his throat, Katie wrapped her arms around him. "I hope she's okay."

He stepped out of her embrace. "I need to be there when she wakes up."

She peered at him, her brow crinkling.

He never talked much about his family life to his colleagues, except a few friends. Katie was a colleague lately, but she deserved to know. "She and I are engaged."

"Oh..." Katie blinked, opened her mouth, then closed it.

With no time to explain there wouldn't be a wedding unless Destiny survived, he gave a curt nod and headed to Destiny's room.

It was more than looks with Destiny. Katie was intelligent and beautiful—but he and Destiny clicked. She was street smart, and she loved his kids. They shared undeniable chemistry, and she made him feel alive again. She made him look forward to an unknown future.

Ryan stayed by her bedside all afternoon. Timon stopped by and brought her flowers. He left Timon by Destiny's bedside as he went to check on Pete. He prayed with him before he fell asleep.

Ryan went back to Destiny's room after Timon left. He scooted the chair near her bed and prayed, unsure if he was saying the right words. He whispered to her all the memories they'd shared and what she meant to him. He talked throughout the night.

When she squeezed his hand during the wee hours of the morning, Ryan kissed her hand, jumped up, and leaned over her bed.

"Destiny," he called, his eyes intent on her as she blinked.

Joy surged through him. Moisture pooled in his eyes, and one tear trickled down his cheek.

"You don't look so good." The oxygen mask muffled her voice. She lifted her frail fingers, dragging them along his jaw before wiping at his lone tear.

"You scared me," he whispered, his hand stuck in her now-tangled hair. "I told God I'd believe in Him if He brought you back to me."

A smile curved her lips. "Be careful of what you promise God." Her words slurred, but he understood clearly. "Having regrets?"

"No." God truly had saved her! God had heard *him!* All these years, he'd thought God a myth. Something a logical doctor couldn't believe in. But... God was real.

"Believing in God is an extra gift alongside the blessing of having you in my life." He brought her hand to his lips. "But I'll need your help to learn more about Him."

Her eyes shone, a promise in their depths. "I still haven't figured everything out yet, but we can learn together.... Is Pete okay?"

"Yes. The doctor said he could go home that afternoon."

"Can Pete have a dog?"

He chuckled at her sudden request.

"Yes." He'd give her the world if it meant he could see her smile every single day for the rest of his life.

"Josh wants a phone. Can we get him one for Christmas?"

"Taking advantage of a vulnerable man, aren't you?"

Her eyes rolled as if ready to sleep again.

"How about Zoe?" He might as well ask—he wanted to hear her voice anyway, believe she was alive and he wasn't hallucinating.

"Lots of slime."

He should let her rest, but he was selfish, wanting her awake, afraid that, if she fell asleep, she might not wake up again.

"Can I go home?"

They needed to run more tests. He could ask her the questions himself to see if she had a brain injury, but she didn't seem strong enough to hold a two-minute questionnaire.

"I will see to it that I take you home soon." What good was being a doctor if he couldn't take care of her from the comfort of their home?

CHAPTER 24

A week later, Destiny lifted her head when a hint of light glinted through the blinds in the big window. With one eyelid cracked open, she glanced around the light gray walls. In the far corner was a familiar face—Ryan. Sitting in a recliner, eyes shut, he leaned his head against the wall. The Bible in his hand was almost slipping off his lap. He'd been reading her one chapter each night before she fell asleep.

He was coming to accept more than God's existence but also God's giving them His Son and Jesus' sacrifice. Even if Destiny had reminded him several times that Bree and Gavin's death had nothing to do with him, he still felt responsible. In understanding his need for forgiveness from sins, Ryan had confessed his greatest sin: babysitting for Bree that night, stopping God from keeping her and Gavin home. It would take more time to heal him of that burden he'd wrongfully taken upon himself this year, but the healing was slowly taking its course.

The sweet guy was exhausted from taking care of her. He looked handsome, even with his thick brown hair tousled.

Although his mom had flown in to help with the kids, Ryan had taken two weeks off work. Holly and Timon had brought cooked meals daily, which helped Destiny feel at peace in her helplessness.

She studied Ryan's chiseled jaw, covered in a few days' worth of growth. How did she ever get so lucky to have him in her life? He was the most handsome man she'd ever met. His tender heart only served to kick up her love for him.

He blinked as he opened his eyes and stretched his hand to yawn. The width of his shoulders filled the gray T-shirt as he dragged a hand through his hair. His lips curved into a soft smile when he realized she was looking at him. "I dozed off."

"Glad you did."

He gathered the Bible on his lap and set it on the nightstand. The wide bouquet and the handwritten cards the kids had made for Destiny took up most of the nightstand.

A haze formed around the red digits on the alarm clock—5:03. Too early for him to start his day if he wasn't going to work. The air mattress he'd been sleeping on in his room must have deprived him of sleep.

She scooted to the king-size bed's far end and patted the warm space she'd vacated, urging him to join her. The kids would be up in one hour, but his mom helped get them to school.

Ryan raised the corner of the blanket and slid under the covers. Her heart skipped at the feel of his arm wrapping around her waist.

Images moved through her mind as memories unfolded. The panicked tears that streamed down his cheeks while he sat by her in the hospital—the fear and love in his eyes when he said "I love you" more times than she could remember. She ached for him even more.

"How did you sleep?" he asked.

Although still weak, with the way he and his mom pampered her, she was regaining her energy. Conscious about her morning breath, she pulled her hand from Ryan's waist and covered her mouth before responding. "I need to brush my teeth first."

Ryan yanked her hand away. "Morning breath is the least of my worries." He brushed his lips over hers. "You almost died."

"I'm here now." She squeezed his hand. "I'm also ready to go back to my room." She'd come home too ill to argue when he carried her straight to his room. He'd insisted it made it easier for her to get to the bathroom and was more convenient for him to keep an eye on her.

"You can't go back to your room until Mom leaves." He rubbed her shoulder, reminding her Mel was staying in Destiny's room. She'd helped Destiny get to the bathtub, although Ryan had helped her most with getting to the bathroom.

For a moment, they were silent while they looked at each other, drinking each other in. He trailed his warm fingers along her jaw. She shivered at his touch—a good sign that she was mending.

"I love you so much." His words were evident through his eyes. "You scared me."

It didn't help that Bree had died this month one year ago. Although Destiny wasn't afraid of dying, thinking of Ryan having to endure her loss was what bothered her. She wasn't ready to be separated from him, from the kids. Her eyes were suddenly moist, and tears slipped through their corners. "I love you too.... I'm sorry I scared you."

Trying to steer away from the memories, she talked about the kids' Christmas gifts instead. "When are we getting Pete's dog?"

His jaw dropped. "I thought you were dreaming in the hospital."

She smiled at his light tone. "In my dream, you said yes."

He stayed silent for a while. "As for Josh, I like the phone idea. It could be handy when he does after-school sports."

"Why do I sense hesitation?"

"What if he browses through the internet and comes across X-rated images?"

Holly had given her some suggestions for that before Destiny brought it up with Ryan. "We can set some filters."

"Good." He traced her jaw again. His finger then tapped her lips. "Can I get you something to eat before you take your medicine?"

"Your coffee would be great."

A clatter of pots and pans sounded from downstairs. "I'll go and blend you a smoothie before Mom takes over the kitchen."

With each passing day, Destiny continued to regain her appetite and strength. Before Mel left for Virginia, they all went to the cemetery and put poinsettias on Bree's and Gavin's graves.

Ryan and Destiny spent the following afternoon shopping online for Josh's phone and Zoe's art supplies, slime, and gymnastics mats for her cartwheels.

Before Ryan returned to work, after dropping off the kids to school one morning, they'd gone to the pet shop and bought a German shepherd for Pete, intending to pick it up on Christmas Eve.

To dull the memory of the loss of Bree and Gavin, Destiny researched several Christmas activities for the family. It was the last week of school before the kids' Christmas break, and she took them from one event to another each night.

They'd made cookies the night before and shared them with the neighbors. Last night, Ryan came home before nine and drove them to see Christmas lights in Downtown Denver. They then drove to different homes on the Parade of Lights.

Destiny had scored bargain tickets to a Philharmonic Christmas show from one of the church members who played the violin in the concert. Thursday was a big night for the kids, but they were thrilled to go to the concert Downtown. Destiny wished Ryan didn't have to work, so he'd be with them that night.

Pete was more excited about the free hot chocolate in the lobby. He tossed marshmallows into his steaming cup. "Can we drink as many cups as we want?"

"Yes, but just drink one for now."

Josh drank water and ate two mini-marshmallows.

Zoe and Carter were eager to have candy canes instead. After sipping the hot chocolate in the crowded lobby, Destiny hoisted Carter on her hip as she plunged with the kids through a sea of bodies to the auditorium.

Being first come, first served, they sat in the sectioned-off area to the far left. Close enough to the front, but secluded from the general seating. Perfect to manage the kids in one area.

The chatter died down in the room and the chandelier lights dimmed, leaving only the stage light. When the conductor moved his stick in a pattern, the violinists started playing a Christmas melody.

Carter was content with his candy cane. His sticky hands left a smudge on Destiny's tan dress. She should've worn red to camouflage the candy stain.

Besides the Hallelujah chorus, the kids hummed "Somewhere in My Memory" as the band played the song from *Home Alone*. Carter clapped—apparently even he remembered the movie they'd watched two weeks ago.

At intermission, she took the kids to the bathroom.

Josh and Pete went to the men's room while Zoe and Carter stayed by Destiny in the long line to the women's restroom. She and Zoe took turns going after Carter, since he wasn't interested in waiting around while there were several doors to explore.

They met the boys back in the lobby. The space was warm with the scent of cinnamon.

"Can we have more hot cocoa?" Pete asked.

Long lines snaked through the chaotic lobby as people waited at different beverage booths. Excited voices and laughter added to the festive spirit.

Carter wiggled out of her arms, and Destiny set him down. Understanding his eagerness to walk, she kept a tight grip on his little fingers, afraid she'd lose him in the overflowing crowd.

"My hot cocoa is too hot." Zoe puckered up her lips after a sip.

With no line at the water dispenser, Destiny took Zoe's steaming cup to add cool water to it. In an attempt to lift the water handle, she let go of Carter's hand.

That's what it took to turn a perfect evening into a nightmare.

Carter was gone. She spun around, breaking into a sweat. Then she asked Josh, who was already getting taller than her, if he'd seen or could see Carter.

Josh paused from his drink, widening his eyes. "He was there with you."

"Can you stay here with your siblings?" Trusting him to keep them calm and together, she pushed through the crowd. Each step tightened the knots in her stomach, fear cinching them in place as she burrowed through the tangle of arms and legs, scanning low for any little body. Her voice cracked when she yelled, "I lost my child!"

Soon, concerned people started looking, and someone called for security. A man's deep voice crackled through the walkie-talkie, asking staff members to search and lock all the exits. "No one enters or leaves the building."

"What does your child look like?" a tall police officer prepared to take down a description.

Destiny was sobbing as she shook. She couldn't think of Carter's description. "He's a...happy...little."

"Where was the last place you saw him?"

"Lobby..." She couldn't breathe. Her mind replayed all the possible places he could be in the old building.

Ryan needed to know. She fumbled for her phone from her small shoulder purse, but could scarcely push the call icon with her hands shaking.

"You're okay?" Ryan's voice was already alarmed.

She sniffled. "It's Carter...lost."

"What do you mean *lost*?" His voice was a shaky growl.

Her sobs grew louder, and she spoke in gasps, assuring him they were searching everywhere.

"I'll be right there."

She resumed the search, joining the others from one level to another. The three-story building had way too many rooms, but each one they walked out of with no Carter in sight sent her heart into a dark place.

"Maybe he exited the building before lockdown." A woman's voice, sounding through the crackling walkie-talkie, deflated Destiny as she sped down the stairs three at a time.

She tumbled down the last two steps on the second flight, thudding at the bottom. With no time to dwell on the pain, she rose and kicked off the ankle boots hindering her progression to the lobby. With people back in the auditorium for the second part of the concert, it was less crowded now.

"Did you find him?" three kids asked at the same time.

Destiny threw her arms on her head and gulped a response, but with her chest so tight, she couldn't speak, except to shake her head.

Just as she turned to the hallway where she'd started the search, movement caught the corner of her eye. She peered into the wide-open door. In front of a massive Christmas tree glistening with lights and colorful ornaments was... "Carter!"

She darted to the empty room, relief flooding her. They'd looked in every room in the building, except the one closest to the lobby.

Most of the sparkly angels within Carter's reach were scattered on the floor. He burbled happily as he pulled an ornament off the tree, unaware he'd scared her to death. She scooped him up, kissed his head, his cheek, and sank to the floor, not trusting her shaky hands to hold him.

"You scared me."

He fussed when she carried him out to the lobby. She told one of the men who were helping with the search. "He was fascinated by the Christmas tree."

The man made an announcement canceling the Code Adam.

The kids were hunched, leaning against the wall where she left them. Their sad faces lit up when they saw Carter.

"Where did you find him?" Josh asked.

She relayed the story, handed Carter to Josh, and reached for her phone. "I better call your uncle."

"Did they find him?" Ryan asked as soon as he answered.

"Yes." She glanced through the glass doors and saw him emerging, in blue fitting scrubs with his badge clipped to his shirt. His tousled hair was an indication of how he'd run his hand in it out of frustration. She waved him over, and his stiff shoulders relaxed when he saw them.

"Let's go home." He scooped Carter out of Josh's arms. "Where was he?"

His sharp tone bespoke the fear he'd endured.

"Playing with ornaments," Zoe said, and Josh relayed the story Destiny had told them.

Destiny grabbed her shoes and went back inside to retrieve their coats, then joined them in the lobby.

"Did you drive here?" she asked, sliding her arm into her wool coat.

"Uber."

"Would you like us to drop you off at work?"

"I took the rest of the night off. I'll go after my car tomorrow." His responses were edgy, and he wouldn't look at her.

She bit her lip. His edgy responses unnerved her. Why wouldn't he look at her? "Would you like to drive?"

"No."

Was he mad at her? Or scared? Could he imagine how *she* felt? Her hands shook on the steering wheel, and the tension emanating from him beside her made it hard for her to concentrate on her driving. With her grinding her teeth and him brooding, the drive was quiet except for the tapping of his hand on his bouncing knee.

"That was too close." He exhaled, his voice gruff. "I can't be at work and worry to death about when the next tragic call is going to happen."

"I know." They'd had several of those lately.

"I hired you to keep an eye on the kids." He sounded like the boss he should be, not her boyfriend. "You take far too many risks. Do you have to hit every adventure there is?"

She did it for the kids, but she wouldn't say it in front of them. Her shoulders inching up toward her ears, she gripped the steering wheel tighter, trying to ignore Ryan's escalating tone and keep a steady gaze on the road.

"You're reckless, and you put the kids in vulnerable situations to get hurt or lost." He flailed his hands in the air. "I can't do this anymore."

Can't do what? The words lodged in her throat. If she asked, she'd burst into tears.

It was Saturday—her day off anyway. When she pulled into the driveway, Destiny cleared her throat and forced herself to say good night to the kids.

"Are you going to pray with us first?" Zoe asked, and Destiny told her that their Uncle would pray with them.

Her chest was burning with too much hurt to mask through prayer time. They were supposed to be partners—equals. Not employee and employer. *Reckless! Is that what he thinks? That I don't even try to keep an eye on the kids?*

Nannying was supposed to be a temporary job for her. Why had she thought she was qualified for such a complex position?

She burst into tears as she fired the engine to her Bug. Resting her head on the leather steering wheel, she gave in to memories of Ryan when he'd sat in the passenger seat. The passionate kiss they'd shared before Zoe almost walked in on them.

If only she'd let Zoe get water for herself, Carter wouldn't have gotten lost, and their night would be normal. She blew out a shuddered breath as she reached for a napkin from the console to blow her nose.

It had been great to dream about a future with Ryan—while it lasted. By now, she should know that nothing stays the same. She'd tried to ignore any fears about losing everything without warning, but again, that was the story of her life.

She couldn't remember the many foster homes she'd been part of, the families she'd hoped could become hers. Except, Ryan's family wasn't a foster—it *was* her family. Her chest hurt over what life was going to be like without them.

She shook her head as if to erase any memories. It was high time she resumed her spontaneous jobs, like teaching dance for less pay—any jobs that didn't hold her accountable for another's life.

She'd start practicing for Jenny's charity dance three days away. She hadn't planned to go for the dress rehearsal on Monday, but she had nothing but time on her hands now.

She drove into the forming fog. She didn't put much thought into her future with Ryan and his family. The fog was just a clear reminder that, as much as she wanted them in her life, this night might be the last she'd ever see them.

CHAPTER 25

"We didn't pray," Zoe reminded Ryan when he told them to get to bed.

"Not tonight."

"But Destiny told us you'd pray with us."

"Destiny's words, not mine."

"Can you tuck me in?"

No doubt Zoe sensed the edge in his tone, the more reason she was testing him. Unfortunately, he had no patience, not tonight when his emotions were jumbled up. "You're already nine. It's high time you learn to cover yourself."

She knew how to cover herself, of course. The whole tuck-in thing was a comfort for her. Something Bree did for her. Something Destiny did for her.

Zoe's lips quivered, which didn't help ease his already tight chest. She darted down the stairs, her loud sobs rising up. *Great!*

He'd messed up, big time. Destiny's departure was a farewell. He sensed it. He'd hurt her with his unfiltered words.

The least he could do was not turn into the Grinch. After putting Carter to bed, Ryan took a sharp inhale of breath to calm his tense nerves before going downstairs.

Zoe's door was wide open, and the lights were on. Whispers died down when he walked into the room where she sat between her brothers on the bed.

Their fear-stricken faces pierced through his heart. Even so, it was sweet how they comforted their sister.

"I'm sorry." He ran a hand over his face, feeling awful for his outburst. "I just..."

270

They cut him off all at once:

Zoe—"Are you mad at Destiny?"

Pete—"Did you fire her?"

Josh—"Why did you?"

Ryan sensed accusations in their tones.

"No, I didn't." Unless she quit. To answer Zoe's question, he crouched before her. "I wasn't mad at Destiny, I was scared." And overreacted.

"Destiny was so scared," Josh said.

"I've never seen her cry before," Zoe said.

Josh relayed the story from their intermission to getting hot chocolate and Carter's disappearance.

"It was my fault." Zoe shuddered. "She was helping me cool my hot chocolate, and she let Carter's hand go."

"Mine, too," Pete said. "I wanted more hot chocolate, and we—"

"No one's in trouble." Ryan was responsible for the kids' sudden fears.

He prayed with the kids and spent several minutes answering their questions and assuring them things between him and Destiny would be okay. He could only hope so.

In his room, after checking Carter once more, he stripped off his clothes and stepped into the shower, lathering himself. He added side jets to the overhead waterfall. Closing his eyes, he tried to relax as the stream soothed his numb bones. Images of Destiny flashed in his mind. The eerie sense of calm he'd felt prior to proposing. Being with her felt like eternity. It was such a beautiful moment when he'd knelt on one knee and shed tears of joy. They belonged together.

Shutting off the tap, he stepped out and dressed. When he lay down, the evening's events erased all happy thoughts.

He'd seen Destiny's swollen eyes, reddened from tears spent, and he'd ignored her pain.

Like a jerk, he'd acted impulsively over his panic. He'd treated her like a servant—someone paid to do what he wanted. He moaned and yanked the pillow from beneath his head and put it over his face. *Reckless.* Had he really called her reckless? She was anything but.

Then the rest of his words assailed him. How sharp he'd sounded! She'd needed comfort, and he'd been thoughtless, cruel.

He punched the pillow. "What was I thinking?" Impossible not to think of her when his bedsheets smelled like her. She'd slept in his bed for an entire week—remembering her there contributed to his raging emotions. He slid out of bed and reached for his phone. He needed to make things right—for his sake and the kids'.

His heart jolted when he saw a text from Destiny. The thrill deflated when he read it.

Destiny: I'm not a professional nanny, as you already know. Sorry to leave you hanging, but I hope that your other nanny is still available to start on Monday.

He'd recommended Valeria to one of the psychiatrists, but even if she was available, he didn't want any other woman in his house, but Destiny.

He started typing his response, deleting and retyping several times before tossing the phone back to the nightstand.

Apologizing by text wouldn't cut it. He needed to see her in person but would have to wait until church tomorrow.

Several minutes later, his phone rang, and he leaped for it.

"I've been worried about you guys."

"Mom?"

Certain it was Destiny, he hadn't bothered checking.

"It's almost midnight, Mom." Surely, she knew they were usually in bed by then. Plus, it was even later in Virginia.

"I couldn't get ahold of Destiny all afternoon, and earlier in the night, she always calls me back...."

"People have other things to do besides waiting around for your call."

"Oh, boy, what did you do to her?"

Feeling like growling at his mom, he ended the call and set it on vibrate mode. He tried to ignore the vibration, but Mom wouldn't stop. Unless he wanted her to call Destiny, he'd better answer.

"Let me guess. You two had your first fight?"

Ryan blew out a deflating breath before relaying the night's events. She'd understand why he got upset. She always sided with him.

"For someone without experience, Destiny does a lot for the kids, more than I did for you guys." So much for siding with him. "She plays with them, takes them all over...."

"I know."

Mom reminded him of the time she'd lost him at the grocery store, then forgot Bree at the playground after Ryan's baseball game. "It doesn't take a reckless nanny to lose a child. Kids are just adventurous. Besides, she's your *fiancée*. You shouldn't be treating her like a *nanny*."

Mom's words stung like acid to his wound.

"I'm not coming to rescue you. If you make things right, she'll be back to you and the kids by Monday."

The night dragged on as he tossed and turned. A world without Destiny—without her giving nature—all but terrified him. Mom was right. He could fix things tomorrow.

He looked at the lit alarm clock several times. When it was almost five, his eyes felt heavy, and he fell asleep, waking up at almost nine.

Of all days, the kids slept in that morning, and he didn't make it to church.

With the kids out of school, Ryan had less than ten hours to figure out daycare plans for Monday. He could plead with Destiny, but then she might assume he only wanted her because of her help with the kids.

He contemplated calling the drop-in daycare, but they wouldn't take kids older than ten. He called Holly's husband instead.

After Destiny recovered, she'd encouraged him to talk to Jake if he needed a godly man to talk to and pray with. He'd called several times asking about what it was like to be a godly father and expressing many other questions.

"How have you been?" Jake asked when he answered.

"Good." Ryan tried to stick to the point. "Do you think Holly would be available to watch the kids for me tomorrow?" Surely, homeschoolers took Christmas break too.

"Hold on. Let me check with her." The phone went silent. Then Jake returned. "She says she can watch them."

Whew! One problem solved. Plus, Jake didn't ask anything about Destiny. He and Holly had probably heard everything at church.

Ryan called Destiny that night, but she didn't respond. He couldn't blame her for needing a break. He left her alone as he worked Monday and Tuesday.

Holly watched the kids both days. On Wednesday evening, as planned by Destiny two weeks ago, Holly babysat the kids. Ryan took the day off in preparation for the charity hospital event. He bought two restaurant gift cards as a thank you for Holly and her family. Jake argued that he didn't have to do that. The guy had no idea how much they'd rescued him.

Still, Ryan missed Destiny, and so did the kids.

He hoped to stop by her house on his way back from the charity event.

CHRISTMAS INSTRUMENTALS muted soft conversations as Ryan, along with several other people, perused the auction items displayed on cocktail tables in the back of the room. As he and Lucas walked back to their table, he tried to ignore Lucas's accusations. "You think you can survive another week without her?"

"I've got to give her the space she needs."

Lucas's eyebrows shot up as he dropped into a chair. "And that's what you think is best for the kids? For *Destiny?*"

He'd waited almost four days. A few more hours wouldn't hurt. Ryan shrugged. "I don't have a choice."

Waiters passed shrimp cocktails, fancy appetizers, and fluted champagne glasses. Lucas took a glass, and Ryan declined, afraid he might drink too much and show up at her house reeking with alcohol. Plus, he had to drive the kids home.

"Ryan? Lucas?" A man paused by their chairs.

"Brady Sharp?" Lucas slapped the table, then pulled out a chair. "Sit down, man!"

"I thought I recognized you back there." Brady gave them each a nod and sat down. "You two are still causing trouble together, huh?"

Brady had grown up next door to Ryan, and they went to the same schools. Although Lucas had been Ryan's best friend, he'd hung out with Brady quite often. He was always that kid hitting every garage sale in the neighborhood and reselling the items for profit.

"What brings you here from Manhattan?"

Brady straightened his navy suit and motioned his head to the front table. "Here to support my mentor, Eric."

Lucas's eyes widened. "You hang out with billionaires now?"

"I'm a businessman," Brady said. His brown hair was combed back and vibrant underneath the recessed lighting. A typical businessman. "With Eric Stone's help, I'm not far from that status."

Despite his wealth, Eric Stone was the most generous and humble man Ryan had ever met. He supported several charities. "Seventy percent of the hospital's support comes from him."

Lucas nodded. "He's the most Christian soul you will ever meet."

"He adopted six more teenagers to top his four kids." Brady braced his elbows on the tabletop. "I have a feeling he's going to build a school for more kids on his property someday."

Dinner was served, and Eric Stone took the podium. He acknowledged financial donors and volunteer doctors including Ryan. Then introduced the live auction. With the auctioneer chanting in a rhythmic monotone, it was hard to keep up with the bidding war.

Ryan got caught up in bidding for a Fiji vacation package for two. He thought of Destiny when he started his bid at 8,000 dollars, and in the end, he was the highest bidder of $20,000. Whether he took Destiny there or not, the money went to a great cause.

"She must be special." Brady peered at Ryan.

Hot after the bid-now-or-lose-it war, Ryan loosened his tie. "Yeah." Very special. But would she be back in his life or not? Lucas was right—he wouldn't make it an entire week without her. He wanted to bolt before the event ended.

As the entertainers came on stage, the banquet hall lights dimmed, a single strobe focused on the stage, revealing the dancers—Destiny!

His jaw dropped. He could barely hear what she spoke into the microphone, but he got the vague idea she introduced the three kinds of dances.

Not until they started dancing, did he remember asking her to come with him to the charity event. She'd said she had to dance—a favor for her friend.

They started with the dance she called the African Kukuwa. Full of movement, the dance seemed a physical expression of joy—so suited to Destiny. As she moved it was as if her body were her voice. He kept his gaze on her, hoping her eyes would find his in the crowd.

Then they danced to two other songs, a Latin dance and something else he couldn't remember, mainly because he could focus on nothing more than her—her vibrant movement, her rich skin, and luscious hair, her body swaying in rhythm to any beat. He slid off his coat.

When Destiny wished the crowd a great evening, her eyes found his and held them for a beat before she handed the microphone to the announcer. His breath caught, and his heart found a wild rhythm.

"Was that Destiny?" Lucas asked. With her costume, it may have been hard for him to recognize her, but not Ryan.

"Yeah," he barely whispered as he pushed back his chair and stood. "That's...my Destiny." He walked toward the back, determined to follow the dancers wherever they headed. They exited the door and down the hall, vanishing into a room.

The door was left wide open, but he wouldn't dare step inside. Loud chatter and laughter rumbled inside. He hovered at the edge and scanned the room for her, spotting her in the far corner as she laughed with two ladies in her circle.

When she glanced at the door and her gaze sliced through him, Ryan's heart pounded. His palms broke out in sweat until he was pretty sure he was having a panic attack.

He forced his cheeks to lift into some mockery of a smile and nodded toward the hallway, giving her an unspoken request to follow him.

What a relief when she made her way toward him. "Ryan?" She walked past him down the hall, then turned to another hall away from prying eyes.

She stopped and spun around. Her warm eyes seared into him, and he was tempted to shove unruly wisps of hair from her face and tuck them into her ponytail, just an excuse to touch her soft skin.

Her chin jutted up, and she crossed her arms. "How did you know I was going to be here?"

Was she upset he came? "This is the event I had asked you to accompany me to—the charity hospital I work at."

"Oh."

"You're an amazing dancer." Couldn't he ease this tension he'd created between them?

She shrugged and gave half a smile. "How are the kids?"

Ryan cleared his throat. "They miss you. I miss you the most." Not wasting any time, he said, "I'm sorry for what I said. I overreacted—"

"It's okay." She waved a hand. "It was good to know where our relationship stands. You and I are so..."

"Different," he finished for her. "Yet we complement each other."

"But..."

"No, Destiny." He tried to shove the words he'd used against her to the back of his mind. *I hired you to take care of the kids.*

He rubbed his hand back and forth across his forehead. Was he sick or having a psychotic breakdown? He broke the gap between them. "As far as nannies go, I couldn't ask for a better one. But you're more than a nanny. You're practically the mother of my kids—definitely the love of my life."

Her eyes glistened as they filled with tears and he took her hands in his. "I'm sorry for being a bit careless. I guess nobody ever taught me about boundaries and limitations. I'll try to do—"

"The last few days without you have been a nightmare," he interrupted her apology, eager to mend things. At least she still had the ring on her finger. "I can't promise to always keep my words in check, but I want you to know you make me laugh and I'll never think of you as an employee or treat you as less than an equal again. You're my best friend." He had to remind her in case she forgot. "I love you so much. I can't picture a future without you."

"Oh, Ryan." Gorgeous eyes, offset by her darker skin, glowed with so much love and desire. "I–I missed you so much."

Her hands slid out of his, and she flung them around his neck. He dipped his chin to kiss her. She kissed him back, their tension melting like lava as he yanked the hair tie and tangled his hands into her dampened hair.

"I love you, too." She spoke over his lips after their kiss.

"Come home to us."

"Do you want me to come tomorrow?"

She'd add excitement to the two days before Christmas. "Tonight if possible. We have a puppy to pick up in two days."

"I first need to go to my house and change."

"I'll pick you up after I get the kids."

He didn't want to wait another day without her. He'd never understand how his life turned out the way it did, but he knew one thing—Destiny had always been part of God's plan for his future, even if Ryan took several detours to get there.

EPILOGUE

Almost two years later...

What a perfect September Sunday afternoon! Destiny stretched out her legs, sitting on the grass beside her husband in their new spacious backyard. Happy squeals rang from the trampoline as the older kids took turns showing off their flips.

Choosing to sell their house last year had been hard, but Ryan was worried Carter would want to venture on the boulders. One afternoon as they took a stroll, a lone house listed for sale on the lane drew them closer, and Ryan felt God's prompting to move.

They'd married the weekend before the kids' spring break. Ryan's parents took care of the kids for two weeks while they honeymooned in Fiji. They stayed in a romantic luxury safari tent with breathtaking views from the deck. At night, lapping water lulled them to sleep. The relaxation could only explain why she'd gotten pregnant with James during their honeymoon.

While their nine-month-old crawled over the grass and picked up twigs, sticking them in his eager mouth, Carter chortled when he tossed a stick to Pete's dog, Chase, who brought it back to him.

As they watched their kids' explorations, Ryan took her hand in his and kissed it. "I can't believe we have five kids."

"Six, in seven months." She'd found out last night after taking the pregnancy test.

He gawked at her. His dark-blue button-down deepened his eyes to cobalt as a smile crinkled their edges. "Is that why you've been wearing thick sweaters in the seventy-degree weather?"

She'd been cold lately, mostly in the mornings and afternoons. She hadn't had morning sickness like she'd had with James. "Might explain it."

He draped an arm over her shoulders, warming her. Then he bent and pressed his words to her hair. "I hope the baby has your eyes."

James had Ryan's blue eyes. "I hope she or he has your gorgeous hair." She then patted her hand on her white sweater as she rubbed her tummy. "You think we can handle it?"

"'Course we can." Ryan grinned, pulling her to him and kissing her forehead. "I'll show you how well we can handle it." He waggled his brows. "We can let Josh watch the kids while we go back to the house and, you know...?"

Her pulse raced at his flirtations. She playfully elbowed him. "You're so naughty."

"That's what happens when you have a hot wife."

"Ditto." She was even crazier about him now than in their first year of marriage. With Ryan's demanding job and their growing family, they had more responsibility and less alone time for each other.

Her shoulders drooped a little. "I'm starting to think the dance studio was a terrible mistake."

"Train a manager and other dancers to run it for you." He squeezed her hand, encouraging her the way he always had. "You used to be a manager. That should make it easy for you to find the right person."

Their first Christmas together, he had leased a studio for two years as her Christmas present. Becoming a business owner on the spot caught her off guard. Thankfully, he'd already hired a graphic designer for the website and put people in place to promote the studio on social media.

They used their kids as the website models since she'd started with after-school kids' dance. The mountain community was excited to have its first dance studio. Clients who came had heard of the studio by word of mouth.

With the high demand for adult lessons, she offered morning Zumba classes and even hired a childcare worker so parents with preschoolers and younger kids could enjoy the classes. She took Carter and James to work with her and paid a nanny to watch them during the two-hour period. Besides that, Ryan insisted a nanny come to their house once a week so Destiny could have a break from tending to everyone. Though not too crazy about the idea, Destiny soon felt more refreshed and had more energy to offer her family after having a few hours to herself.

"Being a business owner is tough."

"But you're hardcore." He winked. "You can do it."

She could do anything with his support. She leaned in and planted a soft kiss on his lips. "How did I get so blessed?"

"Destiny, watch this!" Josh showcased a flip he'd been trying on the trampoline for the last two days.

"You were worried he's still mad at you."

"Maybe I'll give his phone back."

Ryan arched a brow. "No. You said one week. You have to follow through."

She'd confiscated his phone when he'd tackled his sister against her will. "I hate giving consequences."

"Welcome to parenthood."

Parenthood... Destiny smiled as Ryan's words registered. God had put the pieces in place for her. Once a homeless orphan, now a parent with a family, married to the man she adored—a man whose passion was to nurture people back to health. Contentment warmed her and mingled with the realization that they'd have more challenges along the way, challenges they'd overcome together because they'd become partners and equals in all things.

A NOTE FROM THE AUTHOR

Thank you for reading *The Doctor's Nanny*. It's always a blessing to meet new readers. And to those who have read all my stories, thanks for giving me another chance and for your reviews and notes of encouragement.

My husband and my kids were an inspiration behind this story. I can never forget to thank God who enables me to create these stories. Thank you Lord!

You can connect with Rose on Facebook or email her at rjfresquez@gmail.com

ABOUT THE AUTHOR

Rose Fresquez is the author of the Buchanan -Firefighter series, The Eron Outsiders-Romance, The caregiver series, two short stories and two family devotionals.

She's married and is the proud mother of four amazing kids. She loves to sing praises to God. When she's not busy taking care of her family, she's writing.

13857311R00178